THE
CREEPER

By the same author

CUTTERS END
STONE TOWN
BROKEN BAY

MARGARET HICKEY

THE CREEPER

BANTAM
SYDNEY AUCKLAND TORONTO NEW YORK LONDON

BANTAM

UK | USA | Canada | Ireland | Australia
India | New Zealand | South Africa | China

Bantam is part of the Penguin Random House group of companies
whose addresses can be found at global.penguinrandomhouse.com

Penguin
Random House
Australia

First published by Bantam in 2024

Cover photography by Getty Images/Abstract Aerial Art
Cover design by Christabella Designs © Penguin Random House Australia Pty Ltd
Author photograph © Charlotte Guest
Typeset in 12.5/17.5 pt Adobe Garamond Pro by Midland Typesetters, Australia

Printed and bound in Australia by Griffin Press, an accredited
ISO AS/NZS 14001 Environmental Management Systems printer

A catalogue record for this
book is available from the
National Library of Australia

NATIONAL
LIBRARY
OF AUSTRALIA

ISBN 978 1 76134 202 8

penguin.com.au

MIX
Paper | Supporting
responsible forestry
FSC® C018684

We at Penguin Random House Australia acknowledge that Aboriginal and Torres Strait Islander
peoples are the Traditional Custodians and the first storytellers of the lands on which we live and
work. We honour Aboriginal and Torres Strait Islander peoples' continuous connection to Country,
waters, skies and communities. We celebrate Aboriginal and Torres Strait Islander stories, traditions
and living cultures; and we pay our respects to Elders past and present.

To my bushwalking friends

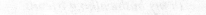

PROLOGUE

'Tom, are we lost?'

No answer.

'Tom!'

He was looking at the map again, head close to it, a thin line of sweat running down the back of his neck.

Laura took her pack off and slumped to the ground. Immediately, ants converged, and with a heavy sigh she got up and stumbled to a fallen log. *Let spiders come and bite me*, she thought, sitting down. *I don't give a rat's.* She had a drink of water, then felt about in her pack for a muesli bar.

The sun was fast losing its warmth. Through the steep valleys and ridges of Mount Razor, shadows crept closer.

'I'm getting a blister,' Laura moaned. She took her boot off and inspected her heel. 'Have you got a Band-Aid?'

He still didn't answer, and when she looked up at him again, she saw he had the compass out. For the first time in two days, Laura felt a prickle of alarm.

'Tom. *Are we lost?*'

Her boyfriend put down the map and stared at her. 'I think we missed the turn-off to the campsite. Remember the sign we passed about an hour ago? We should have gone left rather than right.'

'Bloody hell!' she exploded. 'You said you knew where we were going!'

Tom began folding the map back up. 'We'd better get moving, it's getting dark.'

Laura shook her head and rubbed her foot again. Honestly, she might break up with him after this. What was the point of having a boyfriend who said he loved the outdoors when every time he was outside, he got fucking lost? She shook her sock out and put it back on.

He'd been pretty annoying this whole hiking trip, actually. Going on about how she shouldn't have worn new boots for the walk, and how noisy her sleeping mat was. *I mean, shoot me*, she thought. *So I want to be comfortable.* And that English accent she'd found so charming at first was now just plain irritating.

As she pulled her boot on, she felt a shadow pass over, casting everything one shade darker. It wouldn't be long before they needed headtorches. And, just to make matters worse, she felt a cold drop of rain on her face. Zipping up her backpack, she stood.

'Hurry, Laura,' Tom said. 'And don't forget your water bottle.'

Hurry, Laura, she mimicked to herself, but as she leaned over to pick it up, the bottle rolled a short distance down the hill before stopping at a large rock shelf.

'Leave it,' Tom said, 'we've got to get moving.'

'Are you kidding?' Laura was already sliding carefully down the slope. 'Those drink bottles are, like, twenty bucks. And it's just here.'

Something in the corner of her eye made her start: a dark figure, kneeling beside the rock. For a few beats she stood stock still, until the realisation hit that it was a wallaby.

'Oh god!' she called out to Tom. 'I just got the fright of my life!'

Tom muttered something in reply.

'What's that?' she answered, as she retrieved her bottle.

'Be *quiet*.' Tom's voice was sharp.

Laura edged up the slope.

'Can you hear something?' He helped her back onto the rocky path.

'No.'

His face was taut with concentration. 'I thought I heard something – further up the path.'

Laura felt a twist in her gut. It really was getting dark now. 'It's nothing. Come on.'

They started walking.

'There it is again.' Tom turned abruptly. 'Listen.'

Laura stopped. Silence. Then, on the ridge behind them, maybe five hundred metres away: a movement. Something making its way towards them. She narrowed her eyes along the ridge path. Yes – she could make out a definite shape.

'A kangaroo?' she said after a pause.

Tom hesitated, gave a short nod, and then began walking back the way they'd come. She followed, faster now. Yes, it had most definitely been a kangaroo.

Her foot began rubbing again. 'Tom, I seriously need a Band-Aid.'

'Really?' he said. 'Can't it wait?'

'No, it—'

A scream sliced through the air.

Tom and Laura stared at one another, then looked behind them.

The dark shape was now taking human form, running – or limping – towards them through the snow gums on the winding path. Three hundred metres away.

Tom dropped his backpack and began rummaging through it. 'Binoculars,' he said, and handed them to Laura. 'You can see better than me.'

Laura held them up to her eyes, adjusted the setting. The sky was a deep velvet, merging into black. It was difficult to see. But yes, she was sure it was a person. She magnified her view.

A young woman was running, mouth open, glancing behind her, and at the same time pushing forward in their direction. Was that blood across her face?

Laura lowered the binoculars. 'I think she's injured, but I'm not sure.'

'What's she running from?' Tom asked.

Another scream, and this time the words rang through the night, echoing up and down the deep valleys and jagged plains.

Help!

He's coming!

They're all dead.

CHAPTER 1

'For weeks, Australia was fixated by the image: a beautiful woman, running screaming through the bush at night. What occurred in the remote mountainous region of North-East Victoria dominated every TV news program, every magazine and newspaper. What police found shocked the nation . . .'

The reporter on the screen was walking through dry bushland, hair perfect, face solemn. He looked like a Ken doll. Sally sniggered at his tight suit pants and jacket, so unsuitable for the environment. *This reporting is crap*, she thought. *I should switch it off. I really should.*

She turned up the volume.

'One body, lying mangled in the bush, hacked to death. Four more fatally shot. The Parks Victoria officer, local James Brear . . .'

'Jim!' Sally called. 'Get in here, you're on the telly!'

'. . . who was first on the scene, reported a fox already sniffing at the site.'

Sally sat back. The mention of the fox was a bit too much, bordering on the macabre. Yet she knew viewers would love the grisly detail. Plus, it was true: Jim had told her about the animal on one of the rare occasions he spoke about that day. *The fox,* he kept saying, *it didn't leave, even when I tried to shoo it away. It just stared at me.*

The television screen was now filled with images of the people who had died that night, and then a map of the bush terrain in which they'd been found.

Sally stood up, did a couple of lunges, stretched her calves. It was important to stay fit: one demand of her job she liked. Outside, thick gum trees, closely set, dripped with last night's rain. The air was heavy with it, even indoors. And to the back of the bush, Mount Razor rose like a god, its peak invisible in the cloudy morning air. Water would be cascading down its gigantic boulders; lacy ferns would droop like ballerina hands; and creatures would take cover in logs, burrows and caves. Everything bowed towards the mountain around here, the people most of all.

Sally called out to Jim again before dropping down to a plank position. She was trying to plank each morning for five minutes; it was excellent for the core. The report turned to early footage once more; this time, the police commissioner and a family member were being interviewed.

Barely kilometres from where she was planking right now, Sally thought, as her gut tightened and her breathing became laboured. A massacre just up the road.

'And now, ten years on, the sole survivor, Laura Wynter, has finally agreed to talk about what happened that night. Her story, her words. Catch our exclusive on the Mountain Murders on—'

'Why are you even watching this?'

Sally started, she hadn't heard Jim come in. Her plank wobbled.

'It was just on.' She gave up the position and lay on her side. 'I thought you'd be interested.'

'I am not one bit interested.' He was staring at the screen.

'Well, like it or not, it's about to blow up.' Sally glanced at her boyfriend. 'Ten-year anniversary.'

Jim made a *humph* sound, walked to the fridge, and took a long look inside. 'I hate the way they're going to rake it up. You weren't here when it happened, Sal. You don't know what it was like for everyone.'

Sally went quiet. The reason she didn't know was because he barely talked about what he'd seen that day.

Jim rustled about in the fridge and selected a large apple. 'I wonder why she's talking now,' he said to the piece of fruit. He was referring to the beautiful woman whose face was plastered across the screen. *Sole survivor.*

Ten years ago, in the dark of night, Jim had carried Laura Wynter to safety, fifteen kilometres through rough terrain on the Razor. *What does that do to a person?* Sally wondered, not for the first time.

'I'd say a million dollars is why she's talking now.' Sally didn't like the peevish tone that had crept into her voice. 'Wouldn't you?'

Jim nodded and walked past her, touching her absentmindedly on the shoulder. 'Probably,' he said.

As he headed outside to his Parks Victoria ute, she knocked on the kitchen window and he turned around. She gave him a heart sign with her hands. He gave it back. They did it jokingly, of course, but it made her feel better.

Sally's eyes turned back to the screen, where the reporter was now kneeling by a small marker, touching it reverently, closing his eyes. She knew that marker, had read it a dozen times when she'd been walking along the Razor track.

In memory of the five hikers who tragically lost their lives on this trail
24th February 2014
Brooke Arruda
Kate Barone
Tom Evans
Lyn Howlett
Russell Walker

Five hikers. The sign didn't include the local deer hunter, who was charged with murder-suicide. He didn't rate a mention. Bill Durant: known as Deer Man to some; The Creeper to others. It was only recently, now the anniversary loomed, that Sally was beginning to hear his real name spoken.

Senior Constable Sally White picked up her keys and, after locking the house, climbed into her work-issued Toyota and drove the short distance to the police station. She passed one car on the way, gave the driver a toot: it was Don from up the road. Sally liked Don. He brought her tomatoes from his garden and gave her advice on the best walking tracks. Two months ago, she and Don had pushed a barrow full of zucchinis all the way up the Razor for charity. The man was nearing eighty, but he could walk like nobody's business.

She drove over the Garrong River bridge, noting the rising swell of water beneath. Among other things to do today, she'd have to check the weather reports – road closures over Clearcut Creek might be necessary. For now, the sun shone through the clouds. A good song was playing on the radio: 'Lazy Eye' by Silversun Pickups. She turned up the volume and sang the tune out loud, beating her hands against the wheel as she made a sharp left down a dirt road and then a sharp right into the main street of Edenville.

Sally killed the engine, but not the song; she sat in the police car singing along. It was Thursday morning, all quiet in town. Stone gutters gushed with leaves and water; footpaths glistened; trees bent low. Despite the summer month, everything was lush and green. Six months into her work here, and Sally still marvelled at her luck: a posting in a mountain town, a hot boyfriend, good people and valleys and rivers and waterholes and country pubs. It was a world away from her Adelaide upbringing, then boarding school in Melbourne, flitting between the cities like a migrating bird.

People always talked about the death of small country towns, but it wasn't the case here – no siree, it was not. The whole town glistened with newfound wealth. New businesses were setting up in the main street: a wholefood store, a wine bar scheduled to open in weeks. Old weatherboards lining the river were being torn down and rebuilt in handsome wood and steel; enormous windows with views of the mountains and the sky. House prices were edging past a million; rents were soaring. It was pricy here in Edenville, but ah, what wealth could do! She looked with pride at the maple-lined streets and evergreen poplars. For the tourists, tree-changers and grey nomads, Edenville was a shiny Christmas present under the tree.

The song ended with a steady beat then a high thrum. Sally pulled her long blonde hair into a ponytail, briefly checked the mirror and stepped out of the car, ripping up a few weeds as she walked into Edenville police station. It was a pretty building, like something from a children's book: white weatherboard, roses and geraniums. Add that to the list of good things about her life: a picturesque police station all to herself. Her friends in the city worked in offices where they were crammed two to a desk; it was like dodgem cars, they said. You bumped shoulders every time

9

you reached for your half soy. And that reminded her: Corina and Jac, two friends from school, were coming up tomorrow night. She whistled a bright tune. Fun times ahead.

Inside, the phone was ringing. Sally picked it up, put on her good voice.

'Senior Constable Sally White speaking, Edenville Police.'

'Seen the news?'

'Is that you, Lex?' Sally's heart sank. The gravelly voice was that of Lex Durant, younger brother of the deceased deer hunter accused of the Mountain Murders.

'Need to speak with you today.'

'Can you come into the station, Lex?'

'Can't. Foot got caught in a rabbit trap. Can't do nothing for a week.'

Rabbit traps were illegal. She'd told him that before.

'Have you been to the clinic about it?'

'Yeah, nurse give me some tablets. Done nothing.'

A young mother walked past the station door, two little children in tow. They looked like something from a 1950s poster, till one of the kids kicked the other hard up the bum. The younger one wailed.

'So, can you come here?' Lex repeated.

The mother handed the screaming child a ball, and the noise stopped instantly.

'No, Lex. You'll need to come to the station.'

There was a pause.

'I'll put the dogs on a chain.'

During her first week in Edenville, she'd been called out to a disturbance on the Durant property. Illegal burning. As soon as she'd climbed out of the police vehicle, three dogs had rushed her, scaring her to death.

Lex's property was down a dirt road on the outskirts of town, situated at the foot of the Razor. The mountain's shadow often covered it in a dark shroud, as if the house was in mourning, and kneeling before a giant. In the near darkness, the old weather-board structure had had a definite *Wolf Creek* vibe.

Lex cleared his throat down the line. 'Got something to tell you. About my brother.'

A twinge of interest. Sally stretched her calves as she stood. 'Yeah?'

'You should come around.'

Lex had something to say about Bill Durant, did he? The whole country wanted to know about The Creeper right now. Sally looked at her day's schedule. It was relatively free. She made a show of shuffling papers and muttering about work.

'Okay, Lex, I can fit it in. I'll be there just after one.'

The weak ray of sunlight beaming on her desk strengthened, then faded. Maybe it was a sign, Sally thought, before hanging up and turning to her work. Her friend Amelia paid a lot of attention to 'signs'; and not just the run-of-the-mill, black-cat-crossing-your-path kind of stuff. Amelia thought that if someone offered you an orchid at a party, you would die before midnight. But Amelia smoked a lot of weed. So.

Sally looked up the growing list of road closures and made some calls. A woman came in, asking her to sign passport photos. Someone else dropped an eighteenth birthday party invitation on the desk, suggesting she check it out this Saturday night, because it could get wild. Sally noted it all down, then headed off to investigate the state of the roads. *What's a wild eighteenth look like these days?* she wondered. At hers, she'd played beer pong with her mates, then hit the clubs. She'd kissed someone from Ballarat before stumbling back to her share house, her hangover hours away, the sun rising over the bay, and her high heels clicking in her hands.

At the Garrong bridge leading out of town, a Vic Roads worker was already setting up detour signs. The river wasn't yet at flood status, he informed her, but if there was more heavy rain, they'd be closing the road altogether. The worker and Sally both raised their faces to the overcast sky.

'Hang on, won't that cut the town off?' Sally felt a sudden pang of alarm. What about her friends coming from Melbourne?

'Don't worry, town'll be safe as houses,' the worker said, chewing gum loudly.

Sally took out her phone, noted it down. If the town was closed off, she'd have to let the school know, call the larger station in Wexton, check what the full procedure was.

But now, a different emotion – a slight excitement – bubbled up. The town cut off, and her in *actual charge*?

CHAPTER 2

Once back at the station, Sally phoned her boss in Wexton, Senior Sergeant Patrick Kennedy. Tall and nearing forty, Pat could be dismissive and gave off a distinctly private-school vibe; the man *whiffed* of old money. And yet, despite his tendency to wear white linen, he was somehow universally liked. The first time Sally met him, he'd told her to call him Pat (rather than the usual 'boss' or 'sir') and invited her to a barbecue at his house. There, his wife Gina had plied her with wine, while his three energetic daughters had braided her hair so tight she had a headache for four hours straight.

Now, Sally gave Pat an update on the closures, and then listened as he ran through the procedures: who to call, what to monitor, what her role was in the event of the town becoming isolated. Sally put him on speaker and typed dot points into her phone. That was the arrangement they had: as a relatively new senior constable in a small one-person station, Sally had a daily call with her boss in the nearby larger station, plus regular visits. The everyday duties of running a station she could perform on her own, but if there were any arrests to be made, or tricky home calls to be carried out, or a scene of crime to establish, she had to wait for a senior officer to accompany her.

So far, her time in Edenville had been relatively quiet. She had pulled people over and booked them for speeding; she'd issued fines for drunk and disorderly behaviour and had attended two car accidents with serious injuries, but no deaths. Just the one suicide, thank goodness: an old farmer named Harry Pickett. That had been hard. She'd sat in the kitchen with his crying wife while Pat and the other officer cut the body down from the roof of the shed. Trudy Pickett had known what was in there, she'd told Sally. A note on the roll-up door said, *Trude, don't come in. Call the police.*

No one else called her Trude, his wife had told Sally. They'd known each other since school.

Remembering now Pat's ashen face and Trudy's quiet sobs, Sally was reminded that the town's newfound wealth wasn't shared by all. There were smaller landowners being hedged in by solar, out-farmed by large corporations. There were the dysfunctional and the disengaged. 'For Sale' signs didn't always promise a boat and a Queensland holiday. There were the family violence calls, intervention orders ignored, the cycle happening again and again. Usual stuff for a young copper. Never a murder. Not yet.

When Pat had finished going through the instructions, Sally mentioned her first phone call of the day, Lex Durant insisting he had something to say about his brother Bill. 'He reckons he's got something new to add.'

Pat Kennedy swore down the line. 'More like he'll be whining about his neighbours, threatening restraining orders, or complaining about the dozen he's already got listed against him.'

'Lex doesn't have any intervention orders against him.'

'His older brother then, Neil. That one does. Half the region has one out on him, and a good thing too. I've a mind to take one out on him myself, save some of the hassle.'

'Lex hasn't been much trouble since I've been here.' And he hadn't. Apart from a warning about illegal burning and advice on traps, Sally didn't have an issue with the man.

'There's a Durant family in every town,' her boss continued. 'The family that takes up all your time with their accusations and dodgy claims. Lex might have been lying low, but my guess is you're in for a spate of complaints.'

'It's kind of weird that he's popped up again now. You know it's been ten years since the Mountain Murders? Anniversary of the killings is next weekend. News reports are all over it.'

Her boss was quiet for a moment. 'Saw that on the news this morning. I meant to say, I'm sending someone over to help you deal with it all next week. The usual cranks will be calling in.'

Sally knew who he meant: the true crime podcast nutters; the ones who spent their days gazing into crystal balls; the people who liked to centre themselves in drama.

'I should be okay, Pat. It's nothing I can't handle.'

'You weren't here when it happened,' Pat said, in an echo of Jim earlier, reminding her again of her outsider status. 'First cops on the scene were traumatised. It was huge. The families of the deceased demanding answers, Homicide up to their necks, locals making a killing with the extra business but hating the gawkers: it wasn't pretty.'

'At least the perp was dead.' Bill Durant had shot himself after killing the hikers.

'Deer Man, yeah.'

There were various monikers provided by the media to describe Bill Durant: Bad Bill, The Creeper, Camp Killer and Deer Man.

While Deer Man became the most commonly used in the press, it was The Creeper that Sally found the most disturbing. They called him that because of his propensity to sneak up on people he claimed had trespassed on his property. And when the police found his body, his camera was filled with images of the campers he'd shot.

'He was a different breed altogether,' Pat continued. 'A mean bastard, and half mad from living by himself most of his adult life. A gifted hunter, that's for sure – but always hunted on his own. He was born in that house Lex lives in now. Bill used to spook campers up on the Razor, shining his torch on their tents in the middle of the night, firing shotguns near walkers.'

'Taking photos,' Sally added.

'Yep. His father was a lowlife too – shot at police one time after they visited on a family violence call. Injuries sustained, cop had to leave the force. That was years ago and before my time, but we don't forget.'

No, we don't, she thought. Cops had a long memory for such things: her stepfather, Assistant Commissioner Angelo Conti, knew the name of every officer shot dead over the last decade; knew their circumstances, the events leading up to the tragedies. When he gave speeches and marched on Blue Ribbon Day, Angelo would talk about the dead as if they were family members. When Sally once asked if he also remembered the names of the people who did the killing, her stepfather gave her a pointed look. 'Remember them? There's zero chance I'll ever forget.'

Sally looked down at Lex's address on her notepad. 'Well, this interview should be fun. Last time, I had a blast.'

'If it wasn't for me having to drive out to Hatfield today, I'd come with you. Keep your phone close by, and don't go in if you don't want to.'

'I'm not worried about Lex,' Sally said.

'Maybe take that big hulking boyfriend of yours with you,' Pat suggested. 'Just to sit in the car, make you feel better. Lex isn't violent per se, but if he's anything like his big brother, *may he rest in peace*, he could be intimidating. Especially now his brother's name is being dredged up again.'

'I'll see.' Sally glanced at her watch and sniffed. How should she react to Pat's suggestion that she take Jim? He wanted her to feel protected, sure – but there was also the insinuation she couldn't handle herself. Such comments from Pat were rare, but they bit.

'Although,' her boss went on, 'visiting Lex at this time is a good look. If the press asks, we can say we're always interested in investigating new evidence, listening to the victims' families. Good line to keep them off our case. Never mind the man who did it is already six feet under, the media loves to beat up cops.'

'I know, I know, will do.'

'Also,' Pat added before hanging up, 'I heard your father speak to the new recruits on Tuesday.'

Stepfather.

'He mentioned you, said how proud he was to have a daughter in the force.'

Sally gritted her teeth. 'Nice of him.' And she heard a chuckle down the line as she hung up.

Out the window, a light rain had started up again; faint taps on the glass, like fingertips rapping on a board. *Bloody Angelo*, she thought. *Barely speaks to me since I've started this job, and now he's crowing fatherly pride?* In his new job, her stepfather was bound to be distracted, but surely he could find the time to pick up the phone? An old niggling anxiety – that he'd forget her once he'd split with her mum – bubbled up, and she quashed it with moderate success. It had been over five years since the separation, and Angelo hadn't wiped her. Not yet.

Two men decked out head to toe in Kathmandu entered, asking for directions to the Browers hiking trail – a challenging walk rarely taken, which ran almost straight to the top of the Razor. Sally got out her map, showed them where to start, told them how long it would take and what equipment they'd need. As with most of the tracks on the mountain, she'd walked the Browers a number of times. It was part of her duty to be aware of all the routes along the Razor. People got lost up there all the time.

The men left with their map and Sally documented their visit, along with all of her other duties for the day, in her work diary. She then filed a report from a man about a stolen mountain bike and listened as a well-dressed woman asked if a bright blue raincoat had been handed in. It was her favourite; she might have left it on her walk, or maybe it dropped out of her bag when she was taking it to the car. 'I really loved that raincoat,' the woman said as she left. 'I hope you find it for me.'

Sally widened her eyes, looked at her notes. 'I'll do my very best.'

The phone rang: a possible break-in at the gun club, nothing taken. Sally told the owner, a man known as Soupy, she'd pop by later.

Next, she texted Jim, asking if he'd come with her to visit Lex. It was still a joy to text him. Knowing his number off by heart. Not proprietorial, but something close. She had a boyfriend whom she could casually ask these things. When she started texting his name, it filled out magically in predicted text: *Jim*. James Brear. Jim Bear. Her bear. Her him.

I'll be free at one, he said, and then signed off with the love-heart emoji.

Sally smiled at the little red heart for a few seconds. It was kind of stupid, how much joy the sight of it gave her.

Out of interest, she sent a text to her friend Marni, the only one of their school friends who was married. **Do you add a love-heart emoji to Carl when you send him texts?**

An answer came back: **Never.**

After a visit to the local school to talk about road safety, followed by tea and a toasted cheese sandwich, Sally was ready for her meeting with Lex Durant. She drove to the Parks Victoria office and wound down the window as Jim walked to her car.

Tall and thin, with broad shoulders, Jim was like something from a catalogue for hot firemen. And in fact, he was literally a fireman. In the summer months, he spent long days on call, responding to blazes and helping property owners to enact their bushfire survival plans.

Jim climbed into her police car, moving the seat back so he could fit.

'Had a good morning?' Sally pulled out onto the road.

'Yeah. Been out to the Cradle Ponds. Deer have been stomping all over them. Have to think about a serious cull soon.'

'You can ask Lex about it,' Sally said. 'His family were all deer shooters.'

He looked sideways at her. 'I don't plan on talking to Lex any more than I have to. I'm just here as your minder.'

'Do you know him, or any of the Durants?'

Jim gazed out the window, drumming his fingers on his knees. 'Everyone knows the Durants. One time there was a whole batch of them – brothers and sisters, half siblings, step-siblings, whatever. Five or six kids, all living on the same property Lex is on now. My dad was the same age as some of them, said they hardly ever went to school, spent their time working on their guns and cars and stealing from people.'

'Sounds sad.'

'It was sad. I think a few of them got taken by Human Services. A couple of others ran away. But they were mean too. It's hard to be kind to people when they're doing burnouts in your front yard and tearing off your windscreen wipers. Everyone was glad when they left.'

'Bill stayed.'

'Yeah. He stayed. Still caused trouble now and then – fights, scaring people by appearing out of the blue at campsites in the bush, that sort of stuff. Then, after he shot those people and killed himself, his brother Lex returned to the family home. But Lex pretty much keeps to himself. I never see him around.'

They turned down a dirt road, all potholes and soft edges. Sally drove carefully, noting the thick trees and the lack of neighbouring houses. The rain had eased, black clouds hung low in the sky. Three fox skins were strung up along a rusting fence. For all her resentment at Pat's suggestion, she was glad that Jim had come along.

The beaten weatherboard house sat close to the road, rotting posts piled high in the front yard and to the side, a rusty old swing set. Sally considered it for a moment, shuddering. In Melbourne, someone would call the Durant residence a renovator's delight; here, they called it a dump.

Dogs barked as they entered the yard, vicious creatures with mean features, teeth bared; no cuteness, none at all.

'The dogs are chained up,' Sally reassured Jim, who was eyeing them nervously.

'I'll stay out here,' he said. 'Give us a shout if you need me.'

'I won't, but thanks.'

A black cat slunk under the porch and turned to watch her, its eyes shiny in the dark afternoon. *Amelia would have a fit*, Sally thought, as she negotiated her way up the rickety wooden steps.

Lex met her at the door and gestured for her to follow him into a dank front room. Sally detected no signs of a limp as she walked behind him, but noted his greasy grey hair and dirt-encrusted neck. With his tall, thin frame decked in grubby jeans and a brown flannelette shirt with rolled-up sleeves, Lex seemed older than his fifty-seven years. He had the look of that character in *Oliver!* who coerced kids into crime. Sally had seen the musical in London. She mostly hated musicals, but that one was surprisingly okay.

In the room that Lex had led her to, grimy lace curtains hung over window panes covered in dust. A table was piled high with old power drills, nuts and bolts. Only in the corner of the room, on a pine mantelpiece, was there some hint of a family home. Half a dozen framed photos were crammed on top of it; faded people peering through dirty glass, not much smiling going on. One showed a woman in a dress and sneakers standing next to a crowded clothesline and three small children. In it, the sheets on the line partly covered the woman's body, pressed into her as if she was being engulfed. There was a photo of a young girl in communion dress, and in a frame to the side was a photograph of the man himself, Bill Durant, smirking and holding a gun to his side. Sally gave an inward shudder: this was the same image the press had used after the murders. The Creeper.

'I mean, *why* would he kill them?' Lex followed her gaze and nodded his head towards the image. 'What reason would he possibly have to shoot five unarmed strangers?'

'Is that what you had to tell me, Lex?' Sally kept her eyes on the photo.

'Part of it, yeah. I've been thinking.'

'Your brother regularly threatened to shoot people, especially those who wandered onto his land. It's all in the files.' Sally tore her gaze from the picture to the man in front of her, just as tall as his older brother, but thinner and less confident.

'But where they were found, it was National Park. It wasn't our land, was it?'

'It was near enough, you know that. The National Park backs onto this property.'

The Durant property was two hundred acres, mostly bush. A small portion of it was used for old cars and a couple of goats, but the majority was thick with mountain ash. The family used it for hunting and camping. She'd been told that in the early days, there'd been rumours of a dope plantation, but police drone footage showed that that was long gone.

Lex picked up a rusted bolt, really studied it.

'Police take threats to kill seriously, Lex,' Sally continued. 'We wouldn't be doing our job if we didn't.'

The man put down the bolt. 'But that's the thing. Bill threatened to shoot people *all the time* – he said he'd kill half our family at one point or another. But he never did. He was full of bullshit like that. Unless you were a deer, you'd be more or less safe around him. Scared maybe, but safe.'

Sally paused before speaking. 'Lex, your brother was found alongside the weapon that killed the victims.' She didn't like remembering it, but she'd seen the photo of Bill, half his head shot off, lying in the bush with the gun in his hand. She felt a knot in her stomach, recalling the blood and bone.

'A 30-30!' Lex exploded. 'Bill never used a 30-30! He was a 30-06 man his whole life.'

'That night, he had a 30-30.'

'Bill was a deer hunter, not a bloody fox shooter.'

Sally suddenly felt tired. She was explaining things to Lex that he already knew, that everyone knew. It was all in the papers at the time. She'd read the reports. What was she even doing here? Through the window, she could just make out Jim, leaning against her car, staring into the trees.

'The 30-30 was registered in your father's name.'

But Lex persisted. 'I can't remember him ever using it.'

'It wasn't only about the guns, Lex. Where the hikers were killed, up at the Precipice campsite, it's not that far from the top corner of your boundary. Everyone knew Bill didn't like people wandering around there.'

'Cos he didn't like people trespassing!'

'Bill took photos of people, he spied on them.'

It had been a game to him, locals said. Spying on campers, then suddenly startling them, or more chillingly creeping around their tents, his shadow slowly moving across them, tent pegs undone one by one . . .

'The photos were to prove the trespassing, and the rest wasn't true.' A vein bulged in Lex's scrawny neck.

'Hours before he killed them, he took photos of his victims on their walk. They weren't on your land, Lex.'

The old man glowered.

'And' – Sally added the most damning point of all – 'there was the DNA found on one of the victims that matched your brother.'

She fell quiet as Lex glared at her for a moment longer, then shook his head. There was a dripping sound; water from the roof leaked down the wall. The smell of damp clothes and fetid air . . . She fought the urge to leave.

'No one ever believes us,' the man said, quietly. 'Town like this, people will never change their minds.'

'It's not about changing minds, Lex, it's about the law.'

Lex took out a box of tobacco and began rolling a smoke. 'The law's a dog.'

She could see Jim talking on the phone now, walking back and forth across the muddy ground.

'And,' the old man kept rolling, 'I'm not talking a good dog, like a blue heeler. I'm talking a crappy dog, like a fucken poodle or some shit thing like that.'

'Like a shih tzu,' Sally offered, and the man nodded gravely.

'Yeah, like that.'

Sally looked at her watch, said if that was all he wanted to tell her, she had to go.

Lex scratched at his dry neck again, and flakes of skin scattered. In the weak sunlight filtering into the dank room, they drifted like a flurry of snow. It could be beautiful, Sally thought, if only it wasn't so gross.

'Just letting you know, copper.' Lex's tone was harsher now. 'Got a call from a reporter. Wants to interview me about the murders.'

Sally groaned. 'Oh Lex, think carefully about whether that's what you want to do.'

'Could get the word out – that it wasn't Bill that killed those people.'

'Lex, all the evidence . . .'

The man took a puff of his smoke. 'Plus, it's a chance to let the papers know exactly how the police have treated my family for decades.' Sally watched as Lex's face twisted with bitterness. 'Everyone knows it. Dad shot that fucken cop, forty or so years ago. He didn't mean to – he could be a stupid old bugger. But the police went mad for the family afterwards. This house was ransacked. False arrests, beatings, family split apart. Faith, the youngest, she was only five. It all started up again after Bill was accused. Fucken nightmare.'

'Okay, well, I didn't know that.' Sally frowned, momentarily distracted. 'But even so, I wouldn't talk to the press, Lex. It could jeopardise things if the case is ever reopened.'

Lex glanced at her. 'Really? You think it could be reopened?'

'Well, no. I—'

'Thought so.'

The man's desolate face, wrinkled like a dried-out date in some dusty pantry, released something in her, and she felt a pang of compassion twist in her chest. Sally wished she could hide this part of herself more easily, the soft part which didn't suit the job she was in, the part she tried to cover up with jokes and a false bravado that didn't quite work.

'Look, I'll have a talk to my boss in Wexton. See what he thinks.'

The man gave a dismissive snort but nodded all the same. There was another flurry of skin-snow, and this time Sally noticed the red-raw patches on Lex's wrist and forearm.

'Are you okay, Lex? That looks sore.'

'Eczema,' he mumbled. 'Gets worse in the cold.'

'You got something for it?'

'Something, yeah.' Lex looked down at his arm for a moment, before pulling himself up and turning to her. 'Got lots I can tell that reporter about how Bill's not the guilty man. You cops didn't do your due diligence. I've been doing some digging of my own.'

'No need to, Lex, the police are on it. This isn't your job.'

'Like hell it isn't. This is my brother we're talking about. Time things got shaken up around here. Really fucken shaken up, like a fucken category ten earthquake.'

'That's massive.'

'A category six then, or seven. Whatever the fuck it is' – Lex looked at her directly – 'things need to fucken change.'

'Are you okay?' Jim put his hand on the back of Sally's neck and gave her a rub. He'd volunteered to drive them home.

She didn't reply. All she could think about was Lex's red-raw arm and faked foot injury. She wasn't cross that he'd lied about it. People like Lex didn't enjoy coming into town, and even less so to visit a police station.

He's lonely, she thought. When she was a kid, Sally used to worry about people and things being forsaken. Her bike, resting against the shed, all alone on a dark night; orphans in books; a doll with no other toys to sit beside. And Lex, there in that depressing home with photos of his killer brother and sad siblings. It got to her.

'He's a rough old bloke, I know.' Jim returned his hand to the steering wheel.

'He's all right,' she said, looking at the dark trees rushing by. Two feet in and you wouldn't be able to see a thing. 'Did you know his father shot a cop? Injured them?'

'Didn't know that. But can't say I'm surprised. That family is capable of anything.'

He turned up the radio, a cheesy eighties song. Jim wouldn't know much about dysfunctional families. He had a solid one: decent parents and a brother he spoke to regularly. When she'd once asked if there'd been many fights growing up, Jim told her a story about a big argument over who'd stolen a Toblerone that his mum was saving to put on the Christmas trifle. 'The row went on for *years*,' he said, shaking his head. 'We really got fired up.'

Sometimes, Jim could be a real dork.

Eighteen months now, since she'd met him at a pub in Fish Creek, after a hike in Wilsons Prom. A whole year and a half. Sally still marvelled that someone like her had managed to snag a boyfriend as handsome and wholesome as Jim Brear.

Now, she googled 'Durant family, Edenville', and got an old newspaper report from 1983 about Robert Durant shooting at officers who had responded to a call to his home. *One officer remains in hospital in a serious but stable condition*, the report read. *Mr Robert Durant, father of five, has been arrested for aggravated assault and a string of other charges.*

Sally sat back in her seat. Lex would only have been a teenager then, sixteen or seventeen. She imagined him as a kid in the school yard, standing separate from everyone else, scratching his arm. Lex was lonely, but he was angry too.

'Do you think Lex has any friends?' Sally asked. 'Anyone who likes him in town?'

Jim frowned. 'I doubt it. Who would want to be friends with him?'

CHAPTER 3

That night, Sally lay quietly as Jim read in bed beside her. She turned her phone to silent and scrolled TikTok for silly videos; they always cheered her up. She stifled a laugh at a woman mimicking young Australians who came back from overseas with an accent. Sally had a friend like that, one who kept saying 'all right?' like a Londoner, even though she was from Swan Hill and had only been in England for two weeks.

Jim turned the pages and muttered something under his breath. It was probably something really smart. Sally turned off her phone. She respected readers but had never been one. She usually found herself falling asleep after one page. But people like Jim who read books by Tim Winton and Margaret Atwood – Sally thought highly of them. They must be very serious. Once, she'd tried to read a classic, but the woman in it was useless, just wandering around the moors crying all the time, getting rained on. Why didn't she get a job, or move, or *go inside*?

'Listen to this.' Jim gave a chuckle. He read out a passage about someone who thought someone else had an evil face 'smoothed by hypocrisy, but her manners were excellent'. It didn't sound overly funny to Sally, but still she snuggled into Jim's warm body.

'What's the book?'

'*Jekyll and Hyde*. It's a bit boring.' He placed the book on the bedside table. 'Strange reading it.'

'Why?' She nudged further into him.

Jim stared at the ceiling. 'Because after the murders, when I was carrying Laura Wynter back to the hut, she kept raving about this book.'

Sally stiffened. Suddenly, her bedroom with the little origami swans, her netball trophy, her police certificate and the photos of her school friends looked childish and cheap. She took a moment, aimed for a light tone. 'Why would you bring that up now?'

Jim clasped his hands above his head, his eyes still fixed on the ceiling. 'I don't know,' he said. 'You visiting Lex, the stuff on TV this morning. It's got me thinking.'

I bet it has.

'Ten years ago' – Jim turned to her – 'you would have been what, fifteen?'

'Almost.'

'Just a baby,' he teased in an annoying way. Jim, as she knew full well from the various websites and newspaper articles she'd devoured in the early days of their relationship, had been nineteen years old. The photos of him were always gorgeous; his puzzled features, the way he kept running his hand through his hair, that interview where his cracking voice relayed what he'd seen – all of it was heartbreaking.

'You're old.' She aimed for playful. 'Soon you'll be complaining about your dodgy knees.'

Jim carried on speaking as if Sally hadn't said anything. 'She kept going on and on about some book she was studying. I really think this is the one.'

'Well' – Sally sat up and turned on her bedside light – 'she was traumatised, poor thing.'

Jim nodded. 'I can't believe she's doing an interview – why would she want to remember that night? She's never spoken about it before.'

'You mean in an interview, or . . .' Whenever Laura's name was mentioned, Sally's pulse quickened and her throat felt tight.

'We text a couple of times every year,' Jim said, only half listening. 'I follow her on Instagram. She's set up a production company, wants to get into making films.' He rubbed his eyes and yawned. 'Now she's talking to a journalist?'

Maybe she's 'smoothed by hypocrisy', Sally thought, and, without speaking, got up from the warm bed and left the room.

In the low light of the kitchen, Sally switched the kettle on and opened her laptop, typing 'Mountain Murders' into the search engine. There were many websites dedicated to the case: 'Razor Horror', 'Brutal Slaying on Popular Hiking Track' and 'The Five: We Remember'.

The massacre had occurred along a rarely used track named Jagged Ridge. The campsite there was mainly used by people wanting to climb a rocky outcrop known as the Precipice.

Kettle boiled, Sally made herself a tea and sat down at the table. Outside, the dark night was still, but she knew that if she opened a window and waited, she'd soon hear the noises of the bush: owls, possums, a feral cat. It unnerved her sometimes, the sighing and groaning of the land, although she was getting used to it. Sort of.

'You coming to bed or what?' Jim called.

'I'm working.' She was only half lying. 'Go to sleep.'

They were at the stage where Jim slept most nights at her place. Even so, it was still a joy to wake up beside him, see him lying there next to her. Right now, if he urged her to come back and join him, she would go, she would.

She waited a minute. Nothing.

With a sigh that turned into a yawn, she clicked on the police file of the murders, the one she'd read before, when she first joined the Edenville station.

First up was the photo of Bill Durant, dead, gun by his side, pale in the grey-green of the bush. With a jolt, she realised what had bothered her back at Lex's house. It was the photo of Bill holding a 30-06 rifle. In the image of his corpse, the murder weapon lay by his right hand – but in the photo on Lex's mantelpiece, she was sure Bill held his gun proudly in his left. Maybe something to check on? She made a mental note.

Next, there were the images found on Bill Durant's phone, which police had copied for the files during the investigation. She gazed at the photos of the hikers who'd died in such dreadful circumstances a decade ago. The media had beat it up, of course; there was no victim hacked to death – but one had been bludgeoned with a rifle and the others shot in their tents, or as they tried in vain to flee. And the detail that especially horrified the public: The Creeper had taken photos of each of his victims, on the afternoon before the murders.

It was eerie looking at people in their last hours of life, the ordinariness of it all: Brooke Arruda by a stream checking her foot, Russell Walker lying under a tree, Kate Barone lighting the

Trangia stove. The fact that the photos were taken at the Plunge Pools – an idyllic spot on the Razor where the river looped, then fell into a series of deep swimming holes – somehow made the whole thing seem so much more awful.

How unsettling to think that the hikers didn't know Bill was watching the entire time, from just there, among the trees. Disturbed, Sally flicked through all thirty images. Russell stretching his back, Lyn sipping her tea, Kate leaning on a log, Brooke pulling at her hair. Kate taping Brooke's foot.

The Creeper – it was a good name for someone who could move quietly through the bush without being observed. Stalking was the hunting term, the following of prey leading up to a kill.

At the sound of scraping in the roof, Sally paused. Bloody possums. Their cuteness was growing stale.

Tucked under the printouts of the photos was a simple list of the murder victims. She scanned it slowly:

Kate Barone, local guide, 35
Lyn Howlett, 55
Russell Walker, 52
Brooke Arruda, 23
Tom Evans, 22 (not part of hiking group above)
Laura Wynter, 22 – SOLE SURVIVOR (with Tom at the time)

What happened out there? She scrolled back to the faces. *What happened to you all?*

32

CHAPTER 4

Ten years earlier

Clear sky, cool breeze, a mountain free of crowds – perfect conditions for bushwalking. Kate Barone rubbed sun cream onto the back of her neck. If everything went to plan, she thought, she'd be home by Wednesday lunchtime. She ran through the hike again: Day 1, across the Saddle of the Razor to the Viking campsite; Day 2, up Devil's Head, then down to the Plunge Pools, up to the ridge and across it, camp at the Hangar. Day 3, walk across the plains to Dargie camp. Day 4, short walk to Alpine Road and a lift back to town. Thirty-two kilometres in total, not counting the optional Devil's Head. A fine walk for the moderately fit.

Kate gazed over at her group, busily tending to their packs, taking things out, putting things back in. 'Leave that!' she called to a young woman who was looking at a hairbrush. Hadn't they read the equipment list she'd forwarded?

There were three in this group: Lyn Howlett, Brooke Arruda and Russell Walker. Kate tightened her boot laces, did a few stretches. She wished, not for the first time, that she'd been able to vet, or at least question, the participants' level of fitness before the hike. Despite his family name, Russell did not look like someone who ever moved beyond a couch. Brooke's gear was completely new and Lyn – was Lyn seriously butting out a cigarette?

'Okay, everyone.' She cleared her throat. 'Let's get going! Today will be pretty easy, and we'll have plenty of rests. This is the last chance you'll get to use your phones, so take a minute to send a text or give a quick call. Next time we'll have a signal will be Wednesday.'

It was amusing, watching the group dive for their mobiles. Lyn and Russell texted purposefully, while Brooke took a few steps away and made a discreet call. Kate grabbed the opportunity to quickly check the satellite phone, make sure it was working. On the last walk she'd guided, the sat phone had had a flat battery the entire time. She didn't tell anyone that.

She then scanned her client notes again: Lyn used to be a hiker many years ago; Russell was once a runner – although looking at his beachball gut, that was hard to believe. And lastly Brooke, the attractive twenty-something, was a regular gymgoer.

At the sound of a raised voice, Kate looked up to see the young woman speaking intently into the phone, her hand clasping her ponytail, mouth pulled back. 'Please!' she said. 'For once!'

Kate turned away.

A final pack check: sat phone, medical kit, tent, sleeping bag, sleeping mat, socks, camp shoes, waterproof jacket, merino thermals, headtorch and food. She'd already given the others their tents and a share of the provisions to carry, although her pack was undoubtably the heaviest. She didn't mind. At thirty-five, Kate was as strong as she'd ever been. Burdensome loads? Ha! They were her bread and butter.

Minutes later, Kate was relieved to see that Brooke had collected herself.

'Everything all right?' Kate studied the younger woman as she walked towards her. 'Didn't mean to, but I caught a bit of your call.'

Brooke clutched at her ponytail again. 'No, but it will be.'

'Well, this walk will do you good,' Kate offered, sounding older than she was.

Brooke gave a pinched smile. 'That's what my mum says.'

'Mums know best.' *Do they?* Kate wondered how many other clichés she could come up with. What was next – *There's plenty of fish in the sea?* In any case, Kate thought with a pang, that one definitely wasn't true. There was only one fish in the sea for her, just one.

Russell and Lyn were taking photos of each other by the signpost that marked the beginning of the trek. Brooke and Kate looked on as they then took a selfie on Lyn's phone, Russell making rabbit's ears behind the woman's head.

'I imagined the group would be different to this,' Brooke said, flatly.

Same, Kate thought. You could never pick who would come on these hikes, especially ones that were arranged online. Still, money was money, and that appointment with the bank beckoned.

'Everyone ready?' Kate hoisted her pack onto a bended knee and then her back, before tying up her hip and chest straps. The others did the same.

'All righty,' she said, cringing. Why *all righty*? She never said *all righty*. 'Let's go!'

Day 1: twelve kilometres of grassland, and then exposed ridge walking along the Razor's saddle, around Bald Hill on a rocky but easy-to-navigate path. Small clutches of woodland further ahead, snow gums bending and graceful along the path. The Viking campsite was in a cleared area, sheltered by tough trees and shrubs. No fires allowed, but a basic toilet, drinking water and plenty of sites for tents. The path ahead was narrow but clear. Clouds to the far south gathered like gossips at a party, but for the most part, the sky was blue, blue, blue.

The group began walking over the open grassland; Lyn at the front, then Russell, then Brooke and Kate at the rear. She should be at her regular day job at the plant nursery, she thought. But despite the pang of guilt she felt, the sheer enjoyment of being on the Razor overrode it.

And after this walk, she'd be so close. She closed her eyes. *So close.*

CHAPTER 5

Jim was already gone by the time Sally woke up the next morning. He'd left her a note on his pillow: *See you tomorrow; dinner at the pub.* She rubbed her eyes, smiling at the punctuation. It looked like a little wink. Yawning, she took a few bleary seconds to remember: it was Jim's turn to check the huts along the Razor walk. He usually spent a night in one of them before returning the next day. She'd accompanied him on a couple of these trips when they'd got together after that first meeting in Gippsland. It was one of the reasons she'd applied for the Edenville posting when a chance vacancy arose: the mountains; the windswept meadows; the thin, clear air; and, below it all, the bustling rural town. In those huts up on the Razor – boiling water for their pasta dinners, drinking wine from plastic glasses and admiring the view – she'd had a glimpse of what sort of life she could have with Jim, far away from the clubs of the city.

Normally, she'd miss her boyfriend's company on a Friday night, but this afternoon, her two friends were driving up from Melbourne, and they'd be having drinks and going out.

Sally liked drinks and going out; she liked it very much. Her stepfather Angelo used to say she was a 'rager', which was Generation X's way of saying she liked to have drinks and go out.

Sally lay back and gazed out of her bedroom window. The sun shone through the trees; the tip of the mountain was just visible between the clouds. The night before, poring over details of the Mountain Murders, seemed long ago now, the details muted in the crisp morning light.

She wished she could lie here all day, but when her alarm went off, she rummaged under her bed for her runners, found one shoe, and then spent a good fifteen minutes looking for the other. There it was, under a pile of washing. It was only 7.20 am. Time for a quick run before she had to leave for the station.

Programming her watch for forty-five minutes, she set out at a good pace along the dirt road at the front of her house. To the left were more houses, to the right was bush, then paddocks, then bush, and then the mountain veered up majestically. She decided to go left and ran on the squidgy road till she reached the bitumen, and then the footpaths of the town. Grand avenues of oak and maple lined the main street. It was a joy to run alongside the old trees, to feel their strength and resilience. They'd withstood all the elements: droughts and bushfires and heatwaves. And above them, all around, if you gazed upwards, was the mountain, covered as far as the eye could see in thick bushland, grey and green.

For now, Sally concentrated on the footpath and the shops beside it. The bridge, the neat park and picnic tables, the museum, the bakery and the post office. She waved to Kirsty in the pharmacy and was overtaken by two men on bikes riding without helmets. Should she tell them off? Not today, not now.

Picking up her pace, she ran past the caravan park and the old dredge, where a couple of early morning swimmers were braving the icy water, their capped heads bobbing like seals in a dark sea. Sally jogged on the spot for a moment, admiring them. The dredge was cold, but higher up on the mountain were the Plunge Pools, or the Ladies Baths as locals called them – where the river cascaded over boulders into natural swimming holes, perfect for jumping off rocks and escaping the heat.

Sally circled back, taking care to avoid the slippery gutters. What a weird summer. Barely a day over thirty, and rain every third day. Hard to predict what the upcoming snow season would be like with the climate going nuts. *Probably a tsunami at this rate.*

A bloke in a ute beeped at her; she waved, not knowing who it was. People knew the local cop, heard stories about them before they arrived. She was well aware there were townsfolk who muttered about her youth and inexperience. She tried not to let it bother her. *Stuff them*, she thought bravely. *Who can't handle a few missing mountain bikes and a possible road closure?* She lengthened her stride, picked up the pace again, just as the small voice in her head chirped: *What about a mass murder? Could you handle that? Or even the anniversary of one?* She gave a grunt. Clearly Pat didn't think she could handle any sort of crisis, if he was sending someone over to help her next week.

It was just before 8 am when she spotted Lex Durant's old ute parked up alongside the cafe. She slowed, wondering what to do. The small pharmacy she'd passed had looked almost open; there had been a light on. Checking her watch again, Sally ran back in the direction she'd come and tapped on the window.

'Hi, Kirsty!' she called, and then, in a minor panic, wondered if the woman's name was in fact Kristy.

'Is everything okay?' the woman asked, eyes wide.

'I just need to buy something? Something small?'

Kirsty or Kristy looked at her watch and gave a deep sigh. 'All right,' she said. 'Just for you.'

Grateful, Sally entered the store, and after a brief scan along the aisles, found what she wanted. She thanked the pharmacist before jogging to where Lex's ute was waiting.

'Eh?' The man seemed confused rather than startled when she knocked on the passenger-side window. Sally made the gesture for him to wind it down.

'What the fuck now?' Lex barked, looking around. 'I'm allowed to park here.'

'I know, I just wanted to see how you are.' The sore patches on Lex's arm were still red raw.

'I'm all right.' The man sat up straighter.

'Nice day.' Sally did a couple of hamstring stretches. 'How's all this rain?'

Lex stared down into his takeaway coffee cup.

'You buy that from the cafe? Any good?'

'Yeah,' he said, 'every morning. Can't do nothing without it.'

There was an awkward pause.

'Here.' Sally passed through the window the small tube she'd just bought. 'It's a cream, helps with eczema.'

Lex hesitated for a second before taking it and looking at it closely, reading the label.

'One of my stepsisters gets eczema,' Sally explained. 'She uses this to soothe it. The cream won't fix it, but it might help with the soreness.'

Still Lex studied the little tube.

Sally waited for a moment, then: 'Well, I've got to go. See you, Lex.'

'Didn't used to get eczema when I lived by the sea,' he said.

'Yeah? You used to live by the ocean? Nice.'

Lex sniffed. 'More dogs than seagulls.'

Sally laughed. She knew what he was talking about; the seaside towns where a summer stroll was a constant game of elastics, trying to negotiate the leads.

Lex glanced at her quickly, then out of the windscreen. 'Used to think that if a volcano erupted like in Pompeii, all they'd find in a thousand years would be people with their hands outstretched, holding leads with a dog on the end.'

'I can see it now.' Sally grinned and waved a hand in the air. 'Pompoodle.'

'Eh?'

'As in Pompeii.'

'Oh.'

'Why'd you move back here then?' she asked after another awkward pause. 'Even if you didn't like the beach, it would have been good to avoid the eczema.'

'Family. Our home's here.'

Sally examined the man's gaunt face. How much family loyalty must he have to move back to that depressing, rundown shack on the edge of town?

'I've got to go,' she said again. 'But I'll need to chat with you soon, Lex.'

'Yeah,' he nodded. 'Thought so.'

'Hey, Lex, was Bill left- or right-handed?'

The man frowned. 'Left,' he said. 'Like our mother. Bill could use his right hand just as good, but he mainly used his left. I think.' Lex looked down at his own hands then, as if the correct answer lay there.

'Use the cream,' Sally advised as she moved off, but the man didn't respond.

On the final stretch of her run, Sally saw Don in his front yard, staring deep into a lawnmower.

'Bit wet for mowing, isn't it, Don?'

'Yeah, but my daughter thinks I can sell it on the Facebook. There's a market on it, can you believe? A market on the web! This is John Deere.'

That's how Don spoke: in short sentences, to the point. Jim once said that Hemingway would have liked Don. She had no idea what he meant. Whatever, Sally liked Don. She leaned over her neighbour's fence, feeling the first warm rays of sunshine on her face.

'Hello, John Deere.' She smiled at the mower.

Don made one of the mower parts say 'Hello, Sally' back, and they both laughed.

'Don, did you know Bill Durant?'

The old man moved back to his mower, paused by it. 'Yes. As far as you could, a bloke like that.'

'I've been chatting with Lex, his brother.'

'Ahh, one of the younger siblings, or was he a stepbrother? Half? I don't know. Could never tell with that lot.'

Sally waited while Don ran through names on his hand, listing them. 'Neil – he was the eldest – then Bill, then Lex, then Annie – and there was another one – a girl. I can't remember them all. One or two are dead. From what I know, Lex wasn't as bad as Bill or Neil, but . . . he's a Durant.'

'What was Bill like?'

'Loner. He was in the same class as me. Only came to school when he felt like it. Got in trouble with the police. Had a mean stare. We steered clear.'

'And all this stuff about him stalking people, being called The Creeper, did you know about that?'

'Oh yeah.' Don pulled the mower apart, set the pieces neatly on an old sheet on the lawn. 'There were always stories about that. One time, I met this young couple, Danish or Dutch. They'd hurried down the mountain, pale as a pair of wedding boots. They said that they'd found this nice place to camp by the creek. At night, they'd woken to see the shadow of a man standing by their fire.'

'Bloody hell!'

'Yep. They called out. The Dutch bloke poked his head out of the tent. But the figure was gone. A few minutes later, when they were wondering what to do, they see the shadow again. This time circling the tent.' Don made big O shapes with a spanner as he spoke and Sally followed them, eyes wide open. 'Next, they smell something – and then they see that there's a ring of fire all about them.'

'What?'

'Yeah, Bill had put a line of metho around the tent and then lit it. Poor kids were out of their minds. Picked up their bags and ran the two kilometres down the mountain into town. I saw them in the main street, trying to find out when the next bus out was.'

'Cops get involved?'

'Yeah, but what could they prove? The tourists didn't see him clearly, and he would have denied it. Everyone knew it was Bill though.'

Sally nodded, thought about the things everyone knew to be true in a small town. How they were often true, but sometimes they weren't.

'And what about how Bill's father shot a policeman! Did you know that?'

'Oh yeah – big news at the time. The old man was crazy. He went to jail for it, I know that. The officer didn't die. The shooting just made the town hate them all the more. Durant Senior died in jail, six months before he was due to be released. Lung cancer.'

'What happened to the mum?'

'She died a few years before her husband went to jail. Car accident on the way to Wexton. They got her to a hospital, but nothing could be done.'

'Geez, what a family,' Sally said. 'No wonder the kids were all messed up.'

Don considered the mower parts. 'Not an excuse to go about murdering people though, is it?'

'No. Definitely not.' Sally rolled her neck from side to side, soaking up the sun's rays as Don left the mowing parts and picked up a pair of secateurs, began clipping the hedge. They chatted about the weather. Don snip-snipped, a clean, pleasant sound. Sally was just thinking she should get ready for work when, in her peripheral vision, she saw a light-coloured stick move on the path beside them and, before she could properly register it, a snake had slithered up Don's fence post and into the hedge.

'Snake!' she called, stepping back. 'It went right in there — move away, Don!'

'In here?' Don parted the hedge, poked his face right into it, swivelled his head left and right deep into the foliage. 'Nothing,' he called back.

'Jesus, get out, Don. It was a tiger snake, not a tennis ball.'

The man emerged from the hedge, a couple of twigs poking out of his hair. Sally felt a deep affection for her neighbour. He'd been a resident of Edenville for all his life, yet unlike some old-timers, he never made her feel like an outsider.

'I couldn't see it,' he said. 'Tiger?'

'I think so.'

Don whistled for Rollo, his Jack Russell. 'Stand back,' he said, banging the side of the hedge with his clippers. 'This could go any way.'

Later that morning, at the station, Sally called her boss and told him about Lex's assertion that while his brother used to threaten people, he never actually hurt anyone.

'That's what Lex *told* you, Sally.' Pat sounded weary. 'Lex didn't live the whole time at the house like Bill did.'

'Well, what about the fact that he was left-handed? I saw a photo of him holding a gun in his left; the crime photos have him holding it in his right. Even his brother told me that Bill was left-handed.'

'You don't think we looked into that? Come on, where's your faith?' Pat scoffed. 'Thing is, Bill was such a good shooter, he could fire left- *or* right-handed. He was known for it around town. Ha! Did you think you'd found the smoking gun, Sally?' Pat chuckled. '"It was his left hand, not his right!" That's for movies, not real life. Ahh, Sal, you're a classic.'

'Okay.' Sally frowned into the phone, not liking his tone. 'But what was Bill's natural hand, like, if he was just going to pick up a glass of wine, would he use his left or right?'

'You think Bill Durant ever picked up a glass of wine?' There was still laughter in Pat's voice. Maybe he'd tell the other cops the story after he got off the phone. That'd be a hoot for them all. Sally felt her cheeks burn at the thought.

'I don't know,' she replied, cross. 'But you get what I mean, don't you?'

'Yeah, I do.' Pat sighed. 'Believe me, Sally, we investigated the murders properly. The whole nation was looking at us then;

we couldn't afford stuff-ups. And that's not to mention the locals involved. Kate Barone was from around here, remember? It was tense – we needed to get it right. And what we concluded – after the gun, the precision of the gunshot wounds, the photos, the history, *the DNA* – was that Bill Durant was our man. No one raised any objections then.'

'Not his family?'

'Maybe a couple of the brothers, but come on – name me a murderer who didn't have some sort of family back-up. Ivan Milat's mother was shouting his innocence till the day she died.'

Sally didn't say anything.

'I've had a call from the media,' Pat continued. 'You're right, they are sniffing around. They're going to speak to Lex, so keep on top of it, eh? Check the records, show them that we've done our job.'

'Lex mentioned that the cops went hard on the family after the murders. He came back to live in the house shortly after it happened. Would that be right, Pat? Did the police give him a hard time?'

She heard her boss cough down the line. 'Well, after what they'd seen up there. Everyone was pretty het up.'

'What's "het up" mean?' She had a few guesses.

'It means what you think it means,' Pat said. 'It's cop drive-bys, it's additional searches, it's stopping them in the street and outside their workplaces. Not proud of it, not at all – but that sort of thing happened. Doesn't now.'

'And what about that other incident, years ago – when Bill's father shot a cop? Lex says that's when the harassment started.'

'Eh?' Pat said, distracted. 'What did he say?'

'Forty years ago the police harassment started, and Lex says that it went on again after the Mountain Murders. That's some serious grudge against the family.'

'I told you the Durants were trouble: Bill and the others being as they were, lot to do with their upbringing. Surely you're not surprised that a family like that has a bad relationship with the law.'

Sally thought of Lex talking about his family being split up, and her boyfriend mentioning the social services. 'Lex said that after his dad shot that officer, the family got split up, and Jim mentioned that some of the kids were taken away. Could that have been part of it? Manufacturing lies to get the younger Durant kids removed?'

'No,' Pat said, firm. 'That's hearsay. Those kids were neglected years before Durant Senior fired any shots, and well before Bill went and killed the hikers. Everyone knows that. If they were removed, it was because of their own family.'

On her notepad, Sally drew hills and trees, added in leaves and shrubs as she thought. 'I'll look into it a bit more,' she said finally. 'Go into the records, as you say.'

'No need to take up too much of your time, but yes – if you look at it again, it might help to keep any complaints at bay.'

'Lex is serious about going to the media. He's also doing his own research on the murders.'

There was a snort. 'He'll want compo at some stage.'

'Maybe.'

Her boss paused on the other end of the line. Sally could hear the tapping of a pen. 'Okay then, take some time, placate the Durants. No need to pretend we're interested in anyone else but Bill for the murders; but show Lex that we really did all we could to get the right evidence. It may stop him from becoming all aggrieved about these harassment allegations if you pay him some attention. We do not want to spend time reinvestigating a case that is already tightly closed.'

'I'll get onto it. Thanks, Pat.' Sally ended the call before her boss could change his mind.

CHAPTER 6

Ten years earlier

A magpie swooped past the hikers, its melodious carol a welcome introduction to the walk. Kate Barone watched it ride a gentle wind down the mountain.

As a side hustle, guiding hikes was not too bad at all. She could do it standing on her head, and lately it gave her a chance to clear her mind. She looked about. Alpine herb fields gave off a minty, woody smell, and carpets of snow daisies and yellow billy buttons stretched across and down the ridge.

'Beautiful!' Brooke called out to the elements, her arms flung wide like Julie Andrews in *The Sound of Music*.

Kate had been hiking and skiing in this area since she was a kid; she'd grown up nearby, on a five-acre plot north of Wexton. Her husband, a local farmer, knew the mountain too. She remembered hiking here with him on school camps. They'd met in Year Ten.

The group walked with first-morning energy at a good pace. Lyn was in front, her small wiry body engulfed by the pack on her back.

Russell was slower, but steady. Behind him, Brooke kept stopping to take photos on her phone.

Almost two hours later, they came to a copse of wildflowers and low moss-covered rock. Kate, noting the group beginning to fade, suggested a rest.

'Morning tea,' she called out, stopping under a shelter of bending snow gums. 'Let's have a breather.'

'It used to be called "smoko",' Lyn said wistfully.

Taking her pack off and resting it on a fallen log, Kate set the Trangia stove on the ground as the others watched. 'Have a seat.' She waved her hands to the grassy surrounds. 'But watch out for ants.'

From a steel bottle, Kate poured cold water into the Trangia's aluminium bowl. She then set up the little dish, pouring metho mixture into it, before lighting it and sitting the water pan on top.

'It's like magic,' Brooke said. 'A tiny oven for the bush.'

Christ on a bike, Kate thought, but she smiled.

Russell was looking gloomily at his pack. 'It's so heavy,' he said. 'It's like I'm carrying bricks.'

'You're carrying a tent on your own,' Kate said. *Same as me*, she might have added. 'It adds an extra kilo or so.'

Russell flicked an ant off his arm. 'I thought people were going to be carrying our bags.'

'What, like Sherpas?' Kate was amused. 'This isn't Nepal.' She rummaged around in her pack and retrieved a packet of biscuits. 'You've earned these,' she said, passing the biscuits around.

Brooke gave a cheer.

'I'm finding the pack heavy too.' Lyn reached over for a biscuit and ate it while she did a slow 360 turn. 'But my god, this is worth it. I'm so grateful we've been given this opportunity.' She stared across the mountains.

It was funny, Kate thought, how different people reacted on hikes. There were those who trekked across them, eyes on the finish line, ticking boxes, looking at their pedometers every second. There were the ones who stopped to examine every plant, study each bird. And then there were those who felt that the walk was more of a pilgrimage, a chance to self-reflect and heal. Lyn's use of the word 'grateful' smacked of the healing-out-loud sort. The #blessed #mylife #natureissoulfood type. But Lyn didn't look like that. Instead, the older woman appeared as if she'd already climbed a mountain, was now descending from it, and breathing clearly for the first time.

The water boiled. Kate put tea bags in mugs, and Brooke helped to steady them while she poured hot water in each one. For the rest of the trip, they'd make do with powdered milk, but for the first morning tea, Kate always liked to bring along a little carton of long-life milk. She passed it around for everyone to tip into their own mugs.

'I'm loving this.' Brooke picked off a snow gum leaf and sniffed at it. 'I can't believe I've never hiked up here before.'

'It's terrific,' Lyn said nodding, handing on the milk to Russell, who said nothing.

'Like, I knew this area *existed*, but seriously, I'm blown away.' Brooke shook her head in mock disbelief. 'What have I been doing my whole life?'

'Good wineries here too.' Russell had already finished his biscuit. 'Except they're at the bottom of the mountain.'

'And like, I know it's called the High Country,' Brooke continued, 'but we are *seriously high* right now.'

'We're at around 1900 metres,' Kate said. 'Not high by international standards, but for Australia, absolutely.'

The group fell silent, sipping their tea and taking in the surroundings: the rounded peaks, the eucalypt forests unimpeded through the valleys and slopes, giving way to alpine grasses and snow gums and silver daisy and white herb bush.

'I wish I could stay here forever!' Brooke lay back on her shiny GORE-TEX jacket, hands outstretched. 'Never go back to Melbourne ever again!'

'What's so bad about Melbourne?' Russell frowned. 'I like Melbourne.'

'All the hassles about work, and the bustle and the rubbish and the crowded trams and the men asking you to . . . always getting you to . . .'

'To what?' Lyn's voice had a sharpness to it.

Brooke sat up and brushed down her jacket. 'Oh, nothing really, and anyway, I shouldn't say "men", I should say "man".'

'Asking you to what?' Kate probed.

Brooke took a sip of her tea. 'Cave,' she said finally.

'If it feels like pressure, then don't do it,' Lyn said.

'Amen to that,' Russell added.

Kate, who loved her husband very much, said nothing.

Brooke shrugged, turning away.

'Oh, look!' Kate stood, pointing to a bird flying low over the next peak. 'It's a wedgie!'

'A what?' Lyn held a hand up to shield her eyes from the sun and searched the sky.

'A wedge-tailed eagle!' Kate said. 'They're the largest raptor in Australia. What luck to see one up here!'

The three novice hikers stood to admire the bird soaring above the crest of the mountain. 'Their eyes are like binoculars,' Kate explained, still looking at the bird. 'They can pinpoint their prey from incredibly long distances – and then suddenly they dive down, down, down and kill it.'

CHAPTER 7

Sally pondered whether or not to turn on the police station's air conditioner. The crazy weather – rain and then bursts of hot sun – made the air muggy, but the last time she'd turned it on, there was a horrible clunking sound and then a lingering smell of eggs.

Opening a window instead, Sally flicked through the notes she'd printed out from the files. So many newspaper articles, police notes and photographs, it was difficult to know where to begin.

'Placate the Durants' was the mission, and the best way to do that was surely to show them that the police were taking Lex seriously. Lex had questioned why his brother would commit such a crime, implying that despite the threats Bill made – the spying, the stalking of campers – he'd never actually done anything besides scare the shit out of people.

Sally found a couple of news reports that focused on the man before the shootings:

Alpine Times, 24 April 2012

An Edenville man has been questioned by police over allegations of stalking and intimidating behaviour. A number of tourists to the High Country have reportedly complained about the man frightening them by taking photos of their campsite without permission, calling them abusive names and following them. In one instance, a woman claimed that the man had taken down her tent while she was sleeping, and persisted in shining a light into her face even after repeated pleas to stop. Police also allege the man has been instrumental in harassing a local family by throwing rocks into their yard and scaring their children.

Wexton Chronicle, 22 November 2012

Police attended an Edenville home on Saturday evening after reports of a disturbance. A fight broke out when neighbours claimed that the residents of the home in question had been involved in vandalism of their property, and threats to kill.

One man was taken into the station for questioning.

Alpine Hunting and Fishing Magazine, September 2010

Edenville resident Bill Durant once again claims the biggest deer kill in the High Country for this year's hunting season. Durant killed a mature male sambar after stalking it for a number of days in country up to 1500 metres. Durant declined to be interviewed, but we can confirm he used a 30-06 to get the kill. Durant is a study in how patience pays off: Hats off to the hunters who play the long game!

Accompanying the article was the same photograph Sally had seen in Lex's house – the unsmiling man, hat on head, rifle in left hand. She considered it for a moment with a twist of embarrassment. A tiny part of her *had* felt like she'd come across something momentous when she'd realised that Bill was left-handed, and a tinier part had imagined being congratulated by senior police, her stepfather even, on the discovery. But of course the police had already established the shooter's profile. In a profession that valued experience, Sally was once again reminded of her youth. She could feel her cheeks warming.

She continued reading, this time on the first reports of the Mountain Murders:

The Melbourne Herald, 25 February 2014

Six adults, including the killer, have been shot dead in a remote camping spot in Victoria's High Country in what is among the worst mass shootings in the state.

VIC Police Commissioner Renae Dawson said the five victims were all unknown to one another and appeared to have been camping at the Precipice campsite along the Jagged Ridge trail. At least four of them are thought to have been in the same hiking group.

Police at the scene confirmed that the next-of-kin have been notified, but they are yet to publicly release the identities of the victims.

Commissioner Dawson said officers were called to the Jagged Ridge trail last night. A Parks Victoria officer had assisted a survivor and was present to help guide police to the scene.

Sally paused. That Parks Victoria officer had been Jim. What must it have been like for him, to hear a panicked scream, find the two bodies and then the cowering girl? Because that was what had happened: he'd found the only survivor and carried her along the trail to safety. It was February, but the weather had turned: the wind would have been icy cold whipping through the gums, a hint of snow in them despite the summer month.

When would Jim tell her about it in real detail? His mother said that apart from his first press interview, when her son was still dazed and confused, he'd barely said a thing about that day.

The article continued:

It appears that a male person known locally has shot himself after killing the five individuals. Locals and police confirm that this individual has been involved in altercations on the mountain before. At this stage, there are no other suspects.

Sally put the paper down and stared out of the window. The police hadn't considered anyone else but Bill for the murders. Sure, there was the DNA, the gun beside him and his reputation – but, but ... Sally rubbed her face: maybe Lex Durant had a point. Shouldn't the authorities at least have checked out other potential suspects?

Edenville Chronicle, 21 June 2014

Complaints have been made to police by the Durant family regarding harassment and intimidation from local enforcement after the murder of five hikers by their brother, Bill Durant, who killed himself at the scene. Neil Durant filed the complaints, which at this stage are confidential pending investigation.

Sally yawned. She walked to the kitchen, made herself a tea and, as an afterthought, helped herself to a biscuit from a tin with the Queen on the lid. She'd found it at the back of the cupboard, never noticed it before. Bonus. Time for a pick-me-up snack.

The biscuit was stale. Gross, it had probably been there for years. She spat it into her hand and threw it in the bin. What would the old Queen have felt about *that*? Biscuits – particularly stale ones – reminded Sally of her Nonna Conti in Adelaide, who was constantly baking inedible things. But Nonna was always kind to Sally and treated her just the same as the other grandchildren, even though Sally was technically a step.

*Step*child. For Sally the word conjured up a lurching, sickening dread. Angelo could call her one of his own as much as he liked, but to his other kids – the ones he had with his first ex-wife – Sally was the step. The last stair. Lucia and Isabelle were in Adelaide, and she was here in Edenville. Out of all of them, Sally had been the only one to enter the force, like Angelo. You'd think he would have shown a little more interest in her new job. Fair enough that he'd split from her mum – but come on! They'd lived as a family for almost ten years. Absentmindedly, she took another biscuit and crumbled it into the bin. Maybe it would be just her and her mum from now on, she thought, glumly. *What are families even for?*

A beep on her phone; two beeps. Her friends were on their way, driving up from Melbourne. Would they have to swim over flooded roads to get to her? No, Sally explained. The rivers were high, but there would be no swimming needed: the heavy rain had held off. Her friends said they wanted to meet strapping country lads, drink Bundy, do doughies in a paddock. Sally chuckled. Corina and Jac were in for a surprise. The larrikin country folk they imagined were largely a thing of the past. At the local pub, they'd see pokies and racing on huge screens. If there was a singer or a folk band, some Outdoor Education types might emerge in their beanies, smelling of weed and BO. Her friends would be more likely to pick up an earnest bushwalker from Melbourne Uni than a handsome farmer with a ute. She sent them back a message – **Can't wait**, with the dancing girl emoji – and reminded herself to clear the second bedroom for them to sleep in. It was currently stacked high with clothes she was meaning to give to the op-shop, and she needed to make space for when Jim was moving in, at the end of the month.

Sipping her tea, Sally made her way back to the front office and sat down to read through more of the police files. A duty officer had taken notes of the complaint by Neil Durant, made a few months after the massacre.

Statement by Neil Durant. 20 June 2014

Transcript:
A few days after the murders, when everyone was saying Bill was responsible for the killings, I came home from where I was living in Shepparton. While I was with family members, we were visited by three members of the police. They barged into the house, telling us they would make our lives hell for what our brother did. They ransacked the place and said they were going to plant drugs inside, so we'd all go to jail. They lined up cans of beer on the back fence and made my sister and me shoot them with one of our guns while they stood about laughing. When my sister shot every single one, they said they'd shoot us and say she was responsible. Then I lined up the cans and shot them all, one after the other. The officers cheered. They were drunk, and cooked themselves roast dinner and made us clean up afterwards. They threatened to burn a hut we owned. Another time, they tied me up and hoisted me from the roof, leaving me there for two days before returning. They stole $5000 from my bedroom and shot through all the tyres in my car. There were three officers in black suits, all wearing dark sunglasses.

Sally pushed her seat away from the desk. Ludicrous! The whole report was laughable. Hoisted him from the roof *for two days*? Police in black suits and sunglasses? Hanging from the roof? And that ridiculous detail on the roast dinner – no wonder the police didn't take it seriously. She looked at it again, screwing up her face. Besides, the Durant siblings would have been at least in their forties, if not their fifties, when the Mountain Murders occurred. *Made my sister and me shoot cans?* The statement was surely a mish-mash of the two periods of harassment – after Durant Senior shot the policeman, and then after Bill Durant murdered the hikers. Clearly Neil Durant was not a good witness. Nonetheless, she should check it out. Maybe speak to him about it. 'Placate the Durants', smooth things over so that Lex didn't go to the media. She rang Lex, left a message for him to call her back on the whereabouts of his brother, Neil.

One thing she couldn't ignore was the total lack of interest from police about other suspects. Lex was doing his own research – maybe she'd do some too.

Sally sculled down the rest of her tea and scanned the reports she'd already read on the murdered hikers – something stood out. She located the words again: *the five victims were all unknown to one another*, and then, *At least four of them are thought to have been in the same hiking group.*

There had been some confusion about this, Sally remembered vaguely. Three of the victims had been members of a walking group, and the fourth was the guide. The fifth was Tom, a separate hiker. Local woman Kate Barone had advertised herself as a walking guide on Facebook, specialising in cheap hikes across the Razor, and the three inexperienced hikers had presumably seen the ad and signed up individually.

Facebook was full of people asking about hikes, suggesting hikes, advertising for people to share petrol money, or to join walking groups. When she'd been walking in Wilsons Prom, on the same weekend she'd met Jim, Sally had got talking to a woman from Wales who'd shared a car journey and accommodation with other backpackers she'd met on Facebook only two days before.

Taking her phone out now, she opened up Facebook and typed 'hikes in high country' into the search bar. Ten links popped up, groups all seeking people to 'share experiences' with. Tragically, after all this time, Kate Barone's group still appeared in the results. It had been called 'High Country Adventures – walk with a local guide and experience the thrill of the mountains'. There was a rather formal picture of Kate: solid and pleasant, the sort of face you'd want to lead you on your first ever hike. She googled Kate's name, noted the scores of heartfelt obituaries. There was one from her 'Loving husband, Riccardo Barone'. It didn't take long for Sally to locate another detail, this time from the Wexton Rovers Football Club, stating that a dinner for the widower had been held to say goodbye and honour his years of service as a player and assistant coach at the club.

The bell at the station door dinged, and Sally looked up to see that the Grade Six primary school teacher had entered. Some people called the popular teacher 'Gandhi' because of his round glasses, but she never did.

'Hi, Glen.'

'You reading your star sign?' He nodded at the notes in front of her.

'Yeah: "You will have a visit from a teacher."'

'That's pretty boring. Sure it's not, "The man of your dreams will walk through the door at 11 am?"'

There was a beat, overlaid with slight embarrassment, then relieved laughter. Sally cleared her throat.

'Hey, Glen, did you ever play for the Wexton Rovers?'

'One game, when they needed numbers. They never asked me back. Said they needed more talls, not smalls.'

Sally, who'd been called a pocket rocket since she was a kid, sympathised.

'When I was twelve years old, I played ruck,' the man continued. 'Three years later I was rover, and benched most of the time. Now, I pretty much skip around the packs in the seconds.' Glen made his fingers into little dancing figures, skipping them in the air.

'Did you ever know Riccardo Barone?'

'The husband of the woman who was shot?' The dancing fingers vanished. 'Yeah, I knew of him. He was much older than me. Good man, from what I've heard. Left Wexton soon after the murders. Couldn't handle it. Sold up and moved to Brisbane. Poor bugger.'

'You got a number for him?'

'Nah, no point.' Glen shrugged. 'Ric died just months after his wife. He'd been really ill.'

'That's awful.'

'Yeah, everyone knew he had it – there was this expensive drug from America that they were buying – but after Kate was killed, he left for Queensland and died not long after.'

'Did you know her, Kate?'

'Not really, maybe to say hello to. She was from near Wexton. Used to work at the nursery on Alpine Road.'

Sally knew it: Native Gardens Nursery and Outdoor Furniture. There had been three wheelbarrows stolen from there a few months before, located upside down in the river not long after.

'It was really sad.' Glen kept talking. 'Funeral was huge.'

Sally fell silent. What a tragedy. Kate Barone shot dead on the mountain, then her husband dies soon after.

'We had a fundraiser at the club for him.' Glen narrowed his eyes in thought. 'Some Richmond footballer donated a jumper – we raised a shitload.'

The phone rang; Sally looked at it, then at Glen. 'I've got to get this, sorry.'

The teacher pointed to a piece of paper he was holding. He placed it on the front desk, scribbled something on it, then backed out the door, signalling that she should read it.

She held the phone to her ear and nodded back at him. 'Edenville Police, how can I help?' She was using her good voice again.

'Rob Gains from *The Weekender*, wanting to know how you are feeling about the ten-year anniversary of the Mountain Murders and if there's any statement you'd like to make on behalf of Victoria's finest.'

'No comment.' Sally had enjoyed her media relations training course. It was good to finally be able to put it into practice. Say *No comment* like a school ma'am.

'The Durants still live in Edenville, don't they? Some of them are making complaints about the behaviour of police towards their family. Maintaining their brother was innocent and it was a stitch-up. Big miscarriage of justice. I've just spoken to one of his brothers, Lex.'

'No comment.' Sally sniffed, pious.

'And how do you feel, officer, about the sole survivor, Laura Wynter, travelling to your town next weekend to film a documentary?'

'*What?*' Media relations training gone to the dogs.

'Ha! Got you there.' The journo was smug. 'Didn't you know?'

'I have to go.' *Laura Wynter?* Briefly, Sally wondered if Jim knew she was coming.

She walked over and shut the window, jiggling the flyscreen into place. Why did the mention of that woman always make her so agitated?

Her eyes rested on the piece of paper that Glen had left for her. The school fete, next Saturday, from 10 am till 1 pm.

Clever of him, she thought, looking at the poster advertising cakes and show bags and a jumping castle, to make the date of the school fete the same weekend as the murder anniversary. He'd have to have known that more people would be in town – media among them. The poster showed a coffee van and a pop-up takeaway truck.

Come, it'll be fun! Glen had written on the side of the poster, and Sally, looking at the smiley face beside the words, felt the beginnings of a blush. Did Glen like her – like, *like* her? She thought about his frequent visits to the station, his friendliness and vague questions about what she was up to on the weekends, the comment about the man of her dreams walking through the door. She shuffled things around her desk, dismissing the idea. He knew she had a boyfriend.

It was the issue of the alleged police harassment of the Durant family that she needed to focus on. Especially now that the media had definitely cottoned on.

She called Lex again; no answer. Next, she googled Neil Durant. Two news reports: another short article on his allegations of police harassment, and the second, a brief report in the sports section of the local newspaper from 2008, which stated that Neil Durant had won a shooting competition in Albury, beating his two brothers Lex and Bill in the process.

So, Bill wasn't the only talented shooter in the family, not that that really meant anything. Edenville was full of talented shooters, men and women who'd been brought up knowing their .22s from their .243s, their Lee–Enfields from their Rugers. She'd seen a sticker on the back of a ute the other day: *Fight Crime: Shoot Back*. At the time, she'd scoffed.

Now, she didn't.

CHAPTER 8

Ten years earlier

After morning tea, the group kept walking, slower now, along the ridge. Another band of walkers passed them, red-faced but cheerful. They'd seen the wedge-tailed eagle too.

The sun speared down, making the rocky track shimmer and shift. The track thinned as the ridge narrowed out. The drops either side wouldn't kill, but it would be difficult to see how you'd climb back up without the help of ropes. Far down in the valley, the thin line of the Garrong River wound itself snakelike around the mountains. A cool wind whipped up, then died.

They stopped for a lunch of Ryvita, salami and cheese. Brooke and Lyn still looked energetic, Russell less so.

'How heavy are these packs anyway?' he asked once they'd got going again.

'Yours is about fifteen kilos – it'll go down as we use up the food,' Kate said. 'Mine is about seventeen. I've got the satellite phone, medical equipment, some extra food.'

'I didn't think it would be this difficult. It's been a long time since I've done any exercise,' Russell admitted. 'And a lot more since I've spent this much time outdoors.'

Kate didn't mention Devil's Head. Maybe, she considered, Russell could stay behind with the packs while the rest of them climbed it.

'Well, what made you come on the walk then?'

'Let's just say I was strongly encouraged,' Russell said with a wry smile.

'What about you, Brooke?' Kate asked, making her voice louder for the woman in front. 'What made you come along?'

Brooke half turned around. 'A friend gave me a voucher for this hike as a gift. She knew I needed to get away.'

Kate vaguely remembered receiving a voucher request, and then hurriedly making one up on the computer at work. It was the first one she'd ever had to do. 'The vouchers are really popular,' she fibbed. 'Great idea for anyone who loves the outdoors.'

'I should buy one for my friend Kevin,' Lyn said. 'He loves the mountains.'

They kept walking, slower now. Kate looked at her watch and then studied the track ahead. She calculated less than an hour to go.

Brooke took another photo. 'I'm loving the trees up here! They're like little gymnasts, all strong and bendy.'

Kate thought it was a good comparison for the hardy gums. 'They're snow gums,' she said. 'Also known as White Sallys.'

'How come?'

Kate shrugged. 'I'm not sure, maybe because of the white flowers – they blossom in the summer.' She ran her hands over a smooth, twisted bark. 'I read somewhere that they're planting them in Scandinavia now, they're so versatile.' It wasn't difficult to see how the trees would thrive in such countries. Just like eucalypts thrived in Israel. Australian natives were tough, and none more so than the White Sally. They could bend to almost horizontal in the snow to avoid snapping, and unlike other eucalypt species, they were bred to bear ice and fierce storms.

'Impressive,' Brooke said, looking at them.

'Yep.'

'How long to go?' Lyn turned around from her place in front, sounding weary for the first time.

'Thirty-five to forty minutes,' Kate said, matter of fact. 'We'll be there in good time for sunset.'

In fact, they'd been slower than she'd hoped. Brooke's continual photos, the lengthy morning tea, the stops to marvel at a view, Russell's glacial pace – they needed to move along. Kate was about to ask Brooke to put her phone away, when a piercing shot rang through the thin air.

'God!' Lyn said, stopping short. 'Was that a *gun*?'

Kate looked around. 'Yes.'

'Nearly gave me a heart attack,' Russell said, and Kate thought, *No, please not that – not out here.*

'Probably a hunter,' she reassured them.

Brooke frowned. 'Bit dangerous, isn't it? Hunters and walkers in the same area?'

'They're all regulated,' Kate replied, urging them on – but privately she thought, *Yes, it is dangerous.* Despite her outward calm, the shot had rattled her nerves. 'It's the tail end of the hunting season, so no need to worry,' she lied.

Maybe Parks Victoria? Rogue shooters?

Lyn cocked her head, listening for further shots. 'Sounds like a rifle for big game: deer maybe, or brumbies.'

'You can tell that from the sound?' Brooke asked.

Lyn shrugged. 'My husband liked to hunt.'

'He hunts brumbies?' Brooke looked offended.

'Hunted,' Lyn said. 'He's dead.'

'You didn't shoot him, did you?' Russell asked.

'I did not. Although there were times I would have liked to.'

With Kate hurrying them along, the group kept walking till a clearing in the distance gave them reason to cheer: the Viking campground. A little sign warned them to treat the tank water and to sleep in the wooden hut only in the case of bad weather. The campsite was empty apart from one sole camper, a man in his sixties hiking on his own. Kate's group selected sites close to each other and Kate moved around them, helping set up the tents, secure the guy ropes. Russell was considerably happier as he threaded the poles through the roof of the tent and fastened the loops. 'I'll sleep well tonight,' he announced. 'And then only two more nights to go.'

Kate looked up at the darkening sky, where stars were beginning to poke through the purple glaze. To the south, a coven of black clouds gathered, like witches at a wake. The weather was holding. *Yes, two more nights after this one*, she thought, crossing her arms against her chest and hugging herself. Three nights in total and then she'd be home.

CHAPTER 9

Pres were the most fun part of any night – that hadn't changed since Sally and her friends were at boarding school, drinking in their rooms before sneaking out to go clubbing. Now, with Corina and Jac in her lounge listening to Dua Lipa up loud, Sally relaxed into her vodka and lime.

The three of them had been friends since school, had back-packed together, lived in a share house, knew each other's families. None of them smoked or took too many drugs, or had serious eating issues. They'd never had a major fight; they weren't jealous of one another; they never stole each other's boyfriends. So many books and TV shows depicted female friendships as battlegrounds, women in close proximity who fought about men. Sally couldn't understand the appeal. She hated that show *Girls*. The main character was a pain in the arse.

She rubbed her eyes now, closed them for a moment, before opening them again. Her new lenses were not the best. She was trying bright green ones; they made her feel daring with their glinty emerald spark. And green eyes were the rarest in the world. It was nice, Sally thought, to feel unique once in a while.

People often said that she reminded them of someone they knew, that she looked familiar. She was always being mistaken for a former school friend or someone's cousin – and everyone was someone's cousin, weren't they? She was someone and everyone. The green contacts, though, they gave her an edge. But, she was forced to accept, it was her thick black-rimmed glasses which were the most comfortable. She took her lenses out and put her clunky specs on.

With her feet curled up beside her, Sally cracked open another UDL and watched as her friends bickered about the facts of a story they were reminiscing over. She snacked on some chips and then called for the others to get ready. It was almost nine thirty and the pub usually shut at midnight. Vanity getting the better of her, she popped her emerald lenses back in, gave her lashes some serious mascara action, and sprayed dry shampoo into her blonde mane, roughing it up seventies-style.

'I haven't washed my hair for two weeks,' Corina said blithely, looking gorgeous. 'I don't even care.'

Twenty minutes later, they were stumbling to the pub, avoiding muddy potholes and scaring each other about the dark. 'God, I hate the bush,' Corina said, peering into the night. 'What's it even for?'

'Can we get an Uber home?' Jac asked. 'I don't want to be walking back here at serial killer o'clock.'

'No Ubers here.' The light on Sally's phone made jagged beams through the bush. She swung it around and across the road. The shapes of trees and shrubs jumped out at them.

'Don't!' Corina cried. 'It's like a werewolf movie.'

In the jarring light, the bush did resemble a horror show – a girl running, looking behind her; the sound of breathing, the darkness hemming her in. Sally steadied her phone.

At the Snow Lights pub, a fire was roaring, and a man with a guitar was doing a good rendition of a Gang of Youths track. The bar was crowded: tourists, loggers, greenies, bikies, a group of older women on the way out. Sally swayed on her feet, looking at them all fondly: *My town*, she thought. *My little patch*.

'Drink?' Corina was shouting in her ear. 'Jac doesn't need one – she's plastered – but I'd like another. You?'

Sally wrinkled her nose. 'Nah, I'll wait a bit.'

Jac was sitting on a chair near a table, eating from a bowl of cold chips someone had left or forgotten about.

'That's gross,' Sally said.

'It's just one. We didn't eat at your place.'

There was a slight note of accusation in Jac's voice, although her expression was pleasant enough. If they'd been at Corina's house, they'd probably have had some sort of platter, with grapes and different cheeses and dried fruit arranged artistically. Sally had offered Cheezels. Twenty-four was too young for platters: leave that to couples in their thirties.

Now, Sally looked longingly at the chips.

'Have one.' A guy about her age, with neat blond hair and a slightly chubby face, sat down on the stool next to her and pointed to his own bowl. 'I can't eat the rest.'

Sally took one; Jac took three.

'You girls hungry?' he said, grinning.

'She didn't feed us.' Jac pointed to Sally.

'You'll live.' Sally rolled her eyes.

'You're the cop here, aren't you?' he asked. 'Sally White?'

She peered at him. The stupid cloudy green lenses and the vodka made her brain foggy. He looked a bit like a baby at a wedding, with his round cheeks and groomed hair.

Finally, she nodded. 'You work at the Wexton station with Pat, don't you? I met you there when I had my induction.'

'Yeah, I was running the paperwork,' the man said with a grin. 'Probably the most exciting thing I've done since I've been in the job.'

Sally blinked, trying to remember his name. *Kyle? Lyle? Noel?*

'How old are you?' She wouldn't have asked it if she wasn't pissed, but she wanted to know.

'Twenty-five.' Kyle or Lyle or Noel looked amused. 'You?'

'Twenty-four.' She tried not to feel smug about being younger than him but more experienced in the job. It was so rare to find anyone more junior than her.

The pub was warm. She took off her jacket and looked around. Corina was still at the bar; Jac was nodding to the soulful musician. 'I'm going to do a request!' Jac shouted in Sally's ear, before making her way through the crowd.

'God, I hope she doesn't ask for Celine Dion,' Sally muttered. Jac was notorious for singing that song from *Titanic*.

Her colleague from the Wexton police station chuckled. 'My name's Kyle,' he said. 'You've got a busy week coming up, with the Mountain Murders anniversary and everything.' He sipped his beer. 'Pat's sending me to your station for a few days, in case things get out of hand.'

Sally rolled her eyes once more. 'What could get out of hand?'

'That family, the Durants – they're trouble. I'm born and bred Edenville: I know all about them, believe me.'

'I don't need any help.' Sally looked petulantly into the bowl of chips.

If he heard the resentment in her voice, he didn't show it. 'Your friend is smashed,' Kyle said, pointing. Jac was standing next to the singer, holding a fake microphone and swaying on her feet.

'No, she's not.' Sally was defensive. 'She's only had—'

'Sally!' Jac shouted out over the crowd into her fake mike, pointing to the musician beside her. 'Check out this guy!'

'Yeah, okay,' Sally said out of the side of her mouth. 'She's smashed.'

Corina joined Jac, and then Sally did too, and they danced around each other, doing a bit of disco, a bit of the bus stop. No one cared; everyone was dancing. Sally bought another drink, had a chat to Steve, the owner of the pub. Steve had a monobrow he was proud of, and honestly, you had to respect a man like that. Glen, the school teacher, was beside her, and she danced with him and then with someone else. She got another drink. Kyle raised his eyebrows at her as she made her way back from the bar, nodding at her full glass. Sally shrugged; it wasn't often she had her two best friends up for the night. She slugged the rest of the glass down. Someone called out to her, and she was pleased to see it was a girl from her netball team, dancing with one of the footy players. They hugged each other, and Sally felt full of love for her teammate, whose name she couldn't remember and who was probably nice because she played Wing Defence.

'Hey, it's Sally, the cop!' the footballer beamed, and Sally nodded in time to the music. 'Is it true you can do that Russian dance?'

'She can!' Wing Defence yelled in his ear. 'She did it at Zara's party!'

Ah yes . . . Zara's party . . . Only three weeks into her new job and she'd said yes to the invitation. In her excitement, she'd drunk way too many premixed margaritas. Her biggest regret afterwards wasn't her version of the Cossack dance, which always went down a treat, but the fact that she'd briefly kissed a footballer named Disco. Disco wasn't bad, but she had a boyfriend in Jim, and the kiss lingered guiltily in her mind like a bad seventies beat.

'Let's see it!' the footballer yelled, and the next minute there was that tune on and she was doing her Cossack dance, and this time it seemed like a very good idea. She could see Corina and Jac's smiling flushed faces, netball friends were clapping, others were trying to do the dance alongside her, a little circle had formed, and she was kicking higher and higher and even adding in the wide arm flourishes at the end of each kick into the air. Soulful Outdoor Edders gazed gently at her through red eyes, the locals cheered, and an older couple waltzed obliviously on the side.

When she finished, everyone was cheering. 'That was amazing!' someone yelled into her ear.

Then two men, one of them teacher Glen, started doing parallel worms along the squelchy carpet and, impressive as it was, the sight was making her nauseous. 'I think I'm going to spew,' she said, aloud or to herself.

She spied a door, stumbled to it, and stepped outside into a grimy alleyway.

Sudden quiet. Relief.

Leaning for a moment on the side wall, she closed her eyes, felt herself dipping and swaying. She opened them, took a big gulp of air and then another. It was slightly better now, with the cold breeze on her face. Already, though, she was beginning the process of self-recrimination: she was a cop here; she was an adult; she'd done the dance in front of everyone? She was an idiot. When would she ever, ever be serious and grow up?

She was twenty-four! Groaning, she put her hands on her knees, leaned down and took a deep breath.

A footstep, and Sally sensed someone standing behind her. Rising, she began to turn her head, but in the split second she registered a tall figure, she was kicked hard in the lower back, sending her flying onto the gravel path. In shock, she lay for a moment, barely comprehending what had happened, before rolling over and sitting up.

The alleyway was clear.

What the hell was that?

There was hot stinging on her palms and chin, where gravel had scraped skin. Pain in her lower back, real pain now. Sally stood up gingerly, brushing down her top, wiping the dirt and gravel off her front.

She wavered on her feet. Her Garmin watch was cracked – she stared at it for a few seconds, unthinking. Her phone was in her back pocket and she was relieved to note it was undamaged. What to do? She rubbed at her eyes: maybe if she'd had her glasses on, she might have seen more clearly who had been behind her. A dark figure, tall – tallish? She tried to remember if she'd heard footsteps and recalled that yes, she had. Quick steps, not running, and then the sound of the pub door closing again. Sally took slow deep breaths to calm her mind.

Why had someone just kicked her in the back?

She could walk right back into the pub now and tell someone. Her friends were inside. The other cop, Kyle, might still be there. The lights under the side door were inviting her in.

Instead, she just stood there, felt hot tears come. The street was at the other end of the alleyway and she walked towards it, then onto the deserted main road, then left and then right. At the start of the dirt track that led to her house, Sally leaned on a tree and pulled out her phone, texting her friends that she'd already gone home. No need for a reason with Corina and Jac.

Holding back sobs, she remembered the glee she'd felt at finding out that Kyle the police officer was older than her. What an idiot she'd been. So smug at being the boss of her own station at twenty-four, and yet someone kicks her like they would a stray dog.

Some Senior Constable she was.

Sally walked with a dullness, each step in time with her throbbing back. She wasn't scared, out in the bush, at serial killer o'clock. If anything, Sally's prevailing emotion on the walk home and when she stumbled, sore and sad, into bed, was shame.

CHAPTER 10

Ten years earlier

The sole hiker looked up from his low chair to where Russell and Kate had just assembled Russell's tent. They made their introductions; the man's name was Ewan.

'Where you headed?' he asked.

'Alpine Road via the Plunge Pools, the Hangar and Dargie camp,' Russell said. 'You?'

'I came out the same way as you along the Razor saddle but I'm headed back tomorrow,' the man said. 'There's bad weather coming.'

'Really?' Kate frowned. She hadn't seen any warnings on the Bureau page. But had she looked just before they started out? She shook her head, trying to remember. Of course she had! Of course.

'Yeah, cold front moving in. Make sure you've got warm gear – and if you're really intent on getting to the Hangar, then I'd leave as early as you can on your last morning. The walk to Dargie will be icy.'

'I brought a sleeping bag liner,' Russell told him. 'It's called an Ultimate Thermal Insulator. Cost me eighty bucks, but with a name like that, how could I not buy it? It's like something from *The Terminator*.'

Ewan smiled, leaned forward in his chair. 'Yeah, it does sound a bit like that.'

Kate looked at Russell, who was grinning now, aiming for genial. He was the kind of man who was more at ease in the company of males. Kate was sure he'd prepared that *Terminator* joke earlier, maybe even said it aloud to a few guys at work.

She asked Ewan if he'd heard the gunshot.

He nodded. 'And yesterday too, I heard another one.'

'Must be shooters in the region,' she said. 'Hopefully they'll be gone soon.'

'Not the season for shooting. But yeah, could be, I suppose, illegal hunts.'

Ewan was a bit of a dick, Kate thought, disliking him. 'When do you think the cold front will hit?'

'Tomorrow evening? Make sure you've either set up camp early or, better still, you're off the mountain. Some people' – he subtly tipped his head towards Russell – 'might find it hard-going, walking back in difficult conditions.'

Russell chatted to Ewan more about his gear while Kate ran through the preparations she'd made, reassuring herself that she'd made the right call to come. Usually, she brought read-outs of the weather and made a final decision at morning tea, which was, despite what she'd told her group, the last place to get reception. She hadn't this time. It had all been too rushed – she hadn't been in the right headspace. But even so, she thought as she ran an eye over Russell's tent, she *had* checked the weather before she left. She'd spoken to her husband about it and they'd both agreed: fine weather for hiking, if a little cool. She had the sat phone on her if she really needed to make sure. There were only two nights to go after this one – it would be fine. What did this lone hiker know? It would be fine.

Kate gave a brief nod and looked across the mountains at the dark evening sky. It wouldn't hurt to check. She walked over to where she'd unzipped one of her dry bags from her larger pack and rummaged through the inside pocket. There it was, her satellite phone: Ric had given it to her years before when she used to hike for days on end, often solo. He'd worry about her in the wild, he said. Anything could happen! He loved bushwalking but wasn't as keen on thru-hikes, the lugging of packs and staying overnight, as she was. For her thirtieth birthday, he'd presented her with a pocketknife with her name engraved on it. Other women might laugh, but for her it was the perfect gift.

Now, she looked at the sat phone and, wincing at how much it would cost her, she dialled home, guessing that any number of satellites would be passing overhead to pick up her signal. There had been times when she'd had to wait a few minutes for good enough reception, but this time, after the first couple of rings, her call was answered.

'What's wrong?' her friend Nerissa asked. 'Why are you calling?'

'Nothing's wrong,' Kate reassured her. 'I've just heard about some weather coming in – do you know anything about it?'

In the background, she heard clicking as Nerissa searched the Bureau of Meteorology site.

'Nothing you can't handle,' Nerissa answered after a few moments. 'Bit of rain, some wind. Looks like the hard stuff's coming in on Wednesday night – gale force from the south – but you'll be back by then, won't you?'

A second pause. 'Yeah.' Conscious of the time and cost of the call, Kate hurried it along. 'Everything fine at home? Ric okay?'

'Yeah, we're trying some soup. Aiming for an early night.'

'Good. Thanks, Nerissa.'

Kate put the phone back in its spot in her day pack. Weather coming in tomorrow night – she wished she'd known. She cursed herself again for not checking properly just before they'd left. Foolish! But to have to turn back in the morning? It would mean tramping back over the Razor the way they'd come and then having to wait for hours and hours for someone to bring the van around to pick them up. Maybe even a day.

'Which way's the front door?' Russell was fighting with the fly, getting himself tangled in guy ropes and trying without success to lay it over the top of his constructed tent.

Kate moved over to help him, then assisted Lyn and Brooke with theirs.

While the hikers blew up their sleeping mats and set up their beds, Kate went about making dinner. *No use worrying about the weather now*, she thought. *I'll make a decision in the morning*. What was it Ric used to say about footy? *Take it step by step: one game at a time*.

Now, she looked at the Trangia. *Focus on the meal*. Hikers liked their food on walks. It was important to give them something hearty, make them feel as if they'd earned it.

'Dinner!' she called to her group, and they walked over, eager.

Lyn had her hands shoved deep into her pockets. 'It's much colder than I thought. I forgot gloves.'

'I've got a spare pair,' Kate said. 'I'll give them to you after we eat.'

Brooke beamed at the sight of the food all set out. 'It's a feast!' Somehow, after the long walk, she was still fresh and lovely, like a model in a catalogue for vitamins.

'I'm starved.' Russell rubbed one of his calves. 'Normally pasta doesn't appeal, but I have to admit, this looks great.'

It wasn't fancy, but the meal was filling, and hot. The hikers sat back and ate with noisy enthusiasm.

'So, tell me, Brooke,' Lyn said in between mouthfuls. 'I've been dying to ask. Are you an actor? I recognise your face.'

Brooke smiled; this was no doubt something she heard all the time.

'Ha! I wish.' Brooke flicked a glossy black lock behind her ear. 'I was on *Love and Fortune* a year ago. Maybe you saw it.'

'Oh yes!' Lyn said. 'I knew it! You got into the final stages, didn't you – and then that girl named . . . named . . .'

'Kitten.'

'Yes, Kitten, she won.'

'Kitten?' Kate said. 'Was that her real name?'

'Yeah.' Brooke put down her plate. 'Well, she said it was. You never really know in shows like that, and not many of us keep in contact once the cameras stop rolling. I did make one friend out of it all. Ruby Heath. She was on the show with me.'

'My wife loves those shows,' Russell said. 'She's obsessed!'

'I watch them all the time!' Lyn said. 'I can't help myself.'

'Guilty pleasures.' Brooke smiled.

'What happened to Ruby?' Lyn's forehead creased. 'Did she get kicked out?'

'Yep. Kicked out because it was revealed she had a boyfriend on the outside.'

'Drama!'

'Oh yeah, the producers loved it.'

Kate closed her eyes for a moment. Besides the footy, she rarely watched TV.

'Why would she go on the show in the first place then?' Russell looked puzzled. 'Isn't the whole point of it to meet someone?'

Brooke gave a short laugh. 'Maybe one or two go into it for those reasons, but mainly it's for fame, or to boost your business. That's why I wanted to get on the show – I thought it would help with my PR stuff. I've got an online business selling beauty products.'

'And did it help?'

'No, not really.'

Kate studied the younger woman. With her dark hair tied back, her perfect skin and rosebud mouth, Brooke's good looks could easily distract from the way the young woman often chewed at her lip, and the dark shadows under her eyes.

'The thing is,' Brooke continued, 'those shows often attract really weird types. Some of them can become fixated.' For a moment, the only sound was the four of them scraping their forks across the plastic bowls. Then Brooke spoke again. 'Actually, I've got a bit of a stalker.'

Lyn caught Kate's eye, raising her brows. 'What?! Like someone following you?'

Brooke studied her bowl. She'd barely eaten a thing. 'Sort of. I'm never quite sure. It's mainly harassing phone calls and messages on my socials. And before that, constant fan mail. But . . . a few weeks ago, outside my apartment, I thought I saw someone hiding near my neighbour's car. By the time I'd gone back inside and called the police, the person had gone.'

'What did the police do?' Lyn asked.

'Not much they could do,' Brooke answered. 'I didn't get a good sighting of who it was – it was dark, so that wasn't any use to them. Another time I thought that maybe . . . well, maybe someone had been in my apartment.'

The group was silent for a moment.

'That's so scary,' Lyn said. 'You poor thing.'

'You'd be surprised at how common it is.' Brooke shook her head. 'The police told me one in five women get stalked. It's even higher if you're a so-called celebrity.'

'Jesus,' Russell said.

'That's showbiz.' Brooke aimed for a light tone, made jazz hands in the air.

'Maybe you should give it up.' The voice made them all turn, and Kate was surprised to see the other hiker, Ewan, sitting to the back of Russell, the beam from his headtorch shining directly on their faces.

'Whoa!' Russell said, holding his hands up to his eyes. 'You scared me!'

'Sorry.'

Ewan didn't sound sorry. The beam from his headtorch turned down to his hands, where he was sewing something.

'What're you doing?' Kate asked.

'Hole in my liner,' the man said, intent on his task. 'This one has been with me for years, so I'm patching it up. Nearly finished.'

'I *have* given it up,' Brooke continued as if Ewan hadn't spoken, staring into the night. 'I've got a business now.'

'Reality TV, social media, celebrity magazines,' Ewan said, collecting his liner and rising. 'All a waste of time.' He flicked his headlamp off. 'None of it is real. It's a pack of lies.'

An hour later, Kate clenched her hands into fists and snuggled into her sleeping bag, thinking about truth and lies. She hadn't told the group that she'd lied to her boss at the nursery so she could lead this hike. She'd lied to the group about this being the tail end of the hunting season, to Lyn about having a spare pair of gloves, and about how lucky they were to see the wedge-tailed eagle. It wasn't rare at all.

Wind whipped at the tent, and Kate burrowed deeper into her bag. Lately, she'd lied about a lot of things.

CHAPTER 11

Once she'd waved her friends goodbye on Saturday morning, Sally examined her back in the mirror. An ugly bruise was beginning to show, grey and purple. It hurt to touch, but not as much as the stinging on her palms and under her chin. She checked that all the little bits of gravel had been removed before dabbing antiseptic on the grazes.

She'd told Corina and Jac she'd fallen over while getting fresh air – then decided to do a runner home. She didn't want to tell them that she'd been attacked in the alleyway. A kick to the lower back? Why would anyone do such a pointless thing? If this had happened to someone else, she'd tell them to report it. She'd calmly explain that it was assault, that the police would find out who'd done it.

She examined the bruise once more. Definitely a boot, size 11 or bigger. The rounded shape at the top leaned to the right. A left footer? She washed her hands, and as the hot water seared into her graze, tears pricked her eyes. Shame, injury and a hangover: she was meant to be a public figure of trust, and she'd been so off

84

her face at the local pub she'd done the freaking Cossack dance. In front of *everyone*.

Fresh air would help. Just a walk in the bush to clear her mind. Outside, it was bright and cold. She took a few deep breaths.

Wanting to steer away from town, she headed right, further down the dirt road, and then left, past a paddock to where the farming land turned to bush. As her addled brain began to clear, she tried to make sense of the night. What had happened? She'd gone outside for some air, leaned against a low wall, felt someone behind her, and then *wham!* She was on her knees, and then her front. It was a solid kick too, full booted. The embarrassment rose up again. If she were a character in a movie, she'd have turned around and belted the guy, maybe even jumped on him from the top of the wall and crushed his neck between her thighs. But that was the movies, not real life.

She ran her mind over the people in the pub, scanning the faces – it had mainly been tourists, she thought. No one she remembered having a run-in with at the station, no one with a grudge about a fine or warning she'd handed out. She'd met Kyle, her soon-to-be colleague, the netballer and her friend. The teacher Glen, of course, who'd done the worm, and her best friends, Corina and Jac. No one else she could think of.

Sally came to a fork in the path: one track headed up and to the right; the other continued straight back towards the paddocks. Without much thought, she chose upwards. After ten minutes, she had to stop, heart pounding, pain in her thighs. The view was impressive: the town below was hugged into the valley as if it was being nestled there by the mountain. She couldn't make out her house, but she could see Don's chimney, the main street, the school and the police station. In the bush, somewhere below her and to the right, a dirt bike was careening through the trees.

High pitched and whining, it sounded like a spoilt kid at a party. She checked the time: still another hour or so till she had to be at work. Deciding to push on, she followed the path further up, over a creek and deeper into the bush. It was quieter here and so still. Even the dirt bike whine was gone.

Briefly, she wondered whether she was on private property or in the National Park. It was impossible to tell; she hadn't crossed any fences or seen any signs. The path continued through thick trees and a wall of ferns, which brushed like trailing fingers as she passed.

And then, something.

A footstep? But there was nothing, nobody around.

She began walking again, her breathing loud in the still of the bush.

Again. She heard it, this time distinct – two steps.

Whipping around, Sally called out, 'Hello?'

The bush gave nothing away. She blinked a couple of times, rubbing at the corner of her eye, then leaned forward, peering into the bush. And through the thick foliage, not fifty metres away, she saw what looked like a small wooden structure.

'Hello?' she called again.

There was a crash in the bush to her right and a kangaroo darted away at speed, melting into the undergrowth.

Sally held her breath for one terrified moment, and then exhaled slowly while gazing at the wooden structure. It looked like a little hut with a battered door. She leaned closer still, peering through the trees at it, when the door was suddenly thrust open and a man appeared.

Sally stepped back onto the track.

'Fucken tourist!'

He hadn't seen her. Or had he?

'Fucken trespasser!' The man raised an imaginary gun and levelled it directly at her, pretending to peer through a scope. 'Bang!' he cried out. 'Bang, bang!'

Sally turned and ran.

The wall of ferns this time felt clasping rather than tickling, and tree branches scraped at her hair as she sped through the bush. There was another crash behind her, and she did not stop to look or to consider the possibility of who or what it was.

Get away, get away, she thought as she ran, breath growing ragged, chest bursting, the pain in her back forgotten.

Finally, she reached the clearing. Only there did she stop, her hands on her knees, panting. *Who the hell was that?*

An hour later, showered and dressed, a little calmer, she pulled out of her driveway to head to work. After the attack the night before, it was no surprise that she'd got such a fright, but now Sally had managed to convince herself that the man in the bush had been a local, wanting to scare her off.

Don was in his front garden again, the mower parts still in pieces. She slowed. 'Hey, Don!' she called out, and he waved.

'What's up?' He tilted his hat up to see her more clearly.

'You know the bush path up the back of the paddock down the end of this road – the one that goes up, not across? I walked it today – went about two or three k's up it before I turned around. Pretty thick bush – is it National Park, or what?'

Don ran a greasy hand across his forehead. 'You would have been heading into the Farley property at the start . . .' He nodded, thinking. 'Then over the creek – that's where it leads into the National Park, yes. Nice bit of country.'

'It really is,' Sally said. *Scary locals notwithstanding.* 'Well, I'll be—'

'And of course,' the old man continued, 'you would have been right on the border, or in Durant land as you went on.'

A dark flutter in her chest. 'Durant land? All the way out there?'

'That's where their property extends to, you know. It's right around the base where you were and up into the mountain, almost to the top of the Razor. Acres and acres of it – half not fenced off properly. They own a bucket of land around here.'

'I thought I saw a hut or something up there.'

'Doesn't surprise me. You can find all kinds of huts in the bush, illegal mostly. Hunters, kids, teenagers use them. Homeless types – we used to call them swaggies.'

'Thanks, Don.'

But Don hadn't finished. 'Be best to stay clear of the Durant land, Sally. You never know when they're out there stalking.'

CHAPTER 12

Ten years earlier

Kate woke just after six to a cold morning, the chilly air and clouds hinting at rain.

During breakfast, the group each took turns to discuss the quality of their sleep: the buoyancy of their air mattress, whether they were noisy or not, if their sleeping bags kept them warm.

Kate only half listened, busying herself with preparing the day's food, checking the sat phone for any calls (none), and readying herself for the day's walk. After a moment's thought, she put the phone, the snacks and an extra merino long-sleeve top in the section of her backpack that could be taken off to use as a day pack. That way, she'd have the phone close by and wouldn't have to scramble for it if it rang.

Ewan from the night before had already left. He'd been eager to escape the wild weather, but now, looking up at the sky, Kate could only sense light rain in the air. After they'd eaten, and when the tents were dismantled and backpacks strapped on, the group set off, almost immediately passing an elderly couple who were walking at speed from the other direction.

'Where've you come from?' There was a touch of swagger in the casual way Russell asked it: the seasoned hiker, sussing out how far everyone had walked, whether they were quicker, more efficient.

'The Hangar,' the woman said. 'It was very muddy. If you've got a ground sheet, use it!'

'Will do,' Russell said as he walked past them. 'Thanks.'

'And don't bother with Devil's Head, we just went up there and it's totally overcast, you can't see a thing!'

'Pity,' Russell said, his voice pleased. 'I was looking forward to it.'

'Good morning!' Brooke was next to greet them. 'Isn't it beautiful?'

'Oh yes,' the woman agreed. 'Have you come across the hunter?'

'What?' Kate asked, sharply.

'That hunter. He was just standing there in the bushes on the side of the path this morning. Didn't say a thing. We thought he might be making his way here.'

Kate felt a twist of unease. 'Probably staking out an animal.' *That gunshot yesterday.*

'He gave us the shock of our lives!' the woman's partner said. 'Not good for tourism, if you ask me.'

'No.'

Foregoing Devil's Head, they walked on, Lyn in the lead, then Brooke, then Russell, and finally Kate. She generally preferred walking behind the pack. *It's what wolves do*, she thought, stepping over a dead log. In her Outdoor Ed days, friends liked to talk about wolf formations, the deliberate way they arranged their groups.

'How come you always walk at the back?' Russell asked. He'd stopped in front of her, wiping his forehead.

Kate looked up, startled. Had she been thinking aloud? She'd been so tired lately that it wouldn't surprise her. 'Did I just say something?'

'No – what? No, I was wondering why you always walk at the back. I would have thought you'd be up the front, being the guide and all.'

Kate searched for any hint of accusation in Russell's voice but could find none. The older man probably just needed an excuse to stop for a moment to catch his breath.

'Well,' she said, 'I was just thinking about that. It's been observed that it's how wolves arrange themselves when they're on the move.'

'Wolves?' Russell said, eyebrows raised. 'You take your cues from wild dogs?'

'In some instances, yeah.'

Russell waited. Kate wanted to keep moving, but the man wasn't budging. She took out her drink bottle and had a long sip. 'In wolf formations, the older wolves tend to lead; the others stay behind them.'

'What, so they get eaten first if a bear attacks?' Russell looked in front of him, to where Lyn and Brooke had now stopped, waiting for them to catch up.

'No. The other wolves know that the older ones will fight to the death for them – they'll probably lose, but it will give the rest of the pack time to get ready, and it will tire the enemy.'

Russell indicated for her to continue.

'Next in the group are the young, fit males, the ones with the most energy. After that is the largest group: the females, the pregnant wolves and the cubs. They're the weakest group for sure, but they are the pack's future. They're the most precious asset, and everyone knows it. They need to be safeguarded at all costs.'

Russell whistled through his teeth and started walking again, before stopping after a few steps. 'Hang on,' he said. 'So where does that leave me?' He nodded to the women in front of him. 'Lyn's the older wolf, Brooke's the strong young one, and I'm what – the pregnant female?'

Kate laughed. 'I haven't told you the best bit,' she said, beginning to walk on. 'At the very back of the wolf pack and following them from a distance is one lone wolf: the leader, the one with the most experience. Their ultimate protector.'

'And that's you?' Russell seemed impressed.

Kate made a show of looking behind her and then back again. 'Well, I can't see anyone else.'

Ninety minutes later, they were making slow progress along the incline when a young man, tall and thin, approached them on the path.

'Hi, Kate,' he said. 'What's up?'

It took a second for her to recognise who it was with the bright sunlight spearing down behind him. 'Jim, hi!'

'You all okay?' the young man asked, his eyes on Russell's heaving frame.

'All good. We're on our way to the Hangar. Just taking it slow. How bad's the track further on?'

'It's not too bad. Go easy on the turns, they're a bit sludgy.'

Kate frowned. 'Perhaps I should take the Jagged Ridge trail?'

'I wouldn't,' Jim warned. 'It hasn't been maintained for months.'

Kate was silent. She'd actually walked it three weeks prior and found it in quite good shape, track still formed, the camping spot pleasant and secluded. It would be easy enough to get to there. Most importantly, the route that way was much shorter as it ran diagonally down the mountain, missing all the peaks and rises of the Saddle. Less scenic for sure, but shorter. A whole day shorter.

'There's a lot of traffic this weekend,' she said.

'It'll ease – you'll have the school kids coming tomorrow, and after that it should be fine.'

'Anything else to be aware of?'

'Saw a copperhead just back there. It slithered off. Nothing to worry about.'

'Okay then.' Kate smiled at Jim. 'We'll be off. Let you get on with it.'

'Say g'day to Ric.'

'Will do, and say hi to your mum and dad.'

Jim gave them all a smile, and a quick glance at Brooke, and then strode onward.

'Hey, Jim!' Kate called him back. 'Have you heard those gunshots? What's going on?'

He turned. 'My guess is a rogue deer hunter. They come up here, deck themselves in camo and think they're in some *Rambo* movie.'

'Crazy.'

'Well' – the young man waved goodbye a second time – 'enjoy. And hope you beat the rain! Hate to have to come back here and rescue you all.'

'No chance of that, Jim.' Kate waved back. 'We've got it all under control.'

Brooke stopped beside her to unlace a boot and wriggle her foot around. 'He wasn't bad. Maybe I should move here.'

'Don't.' Kate smiled. 'He's only nineteen! He's a local from Edenville, the small town at the bottom of the mountain. First year with Parks Victoria. He's a quiet kid, you might scare him off.'

Brooke looked behind her, to where Jim's retreating body moved at ease along the path. 'Wouldn't it be nice to have someone to go walking with in places like this?'

Yes, Kate thought. *It would be.*

She pointed at Brooke's wriggling toes. 'Is your foot okay?'

Brooke nodded, fitted her foot back into her boot and began tying the laces.

As the other hikers stopped to wait, Lyn spoke up. 'My husband and I used to like bushwalking. Not overnight hikes or anything, just walks in the mountains. It was one of the things I missed most about him when he died.'

Kate stopped, felt the threat of hot tears. She waited a moment to regain her composure, adjusted her hat and moved on.

CHAPTER 13

The phone was ringing when Sally entered the station. Pat Kennedy.

'I just arrived,' she said, looking at her watch. 'I'm on time. Remember, I'm only on half a day today.'

'Wasn't checking up on you, Sally,' Pat said with a laugh. 'I'm just reminding you that we'll be sending another cop to your station as promised. Just for the week, to tide over this anniversary business. He'll arrive on Monday.'

'Yeah, I met him last night.' Sally opened her laptop. 'Kyle.'

'At the pub, was it? Good night?' Was there a note of reproach there? Or was her embarrassment turning into paranoia? No. If anything, Sally detected a wistfulness in Pat's voice. Older people often sounded like this when they asked her how her nights went. Keen listeners to her tales of vodka shots and dancing and people she'd seen out; she sensed them inserting themselves into the scene, watching their younger selves on the dance floor, buying drinks.

Should she report last night's assault to Pat? She really should. She would advise anyone else to. Pat was a good cop, a decent boss.

'It was okay,' she said finally.

'Good.' Pat sounded disappointed. 'Well, anyway, Kyle will help you in coordinating any media and crowds that come to town. We're also keeping an eye on the river levels. They're looking stable at the moment, but you never know.'

'But I'm in charge, right?'

'You're the senior officer, and it's your station – so yes. You are.'

'Right.' Sally nodded with satisfaction. 'Good.'

'Also – and you're not going to like this – Neil Durant is back in town. Traffic police pulled him over when his number plate came up.'

'Why would his number plate come up?'

'Robbery: did some time a few years back. He's no longer on parole, but we track him even so.'

'Based on what?'

'Based on what? There's always something to base things on. Broken headlight, crack in the windscreen, speeding.'

Sally felt her bruise again; it was rubbing against the waistband of her pants. She studied the grazes on her hands.

'So, watch out for Neil, okay? I'll get Kyle to send you through an image of him. He's changed a bit since his youth. My bet, he's in town to stir up trouble with the old harassment allegation now that some idiot in the media's been giving him attention.'

'Rob Gains.'

'Eh?'

'Rob Gains – he's the journo who called me asking about the ten-year anniversary. Laura Wynter is making some sort of doco about the murders.'

'He'll be speaking to Neil and Lex then. This is all we need.'

'Lex has already spoken to him, plus, he's doing a little digging of his own.'

'He won't find anything.' Pat sounded tired of the subject.

Sally flicked through her work emails. 'Kyle's sent me something just now. Looks like there's a Facebook group forming, relatives and friends of the people murdered ten years ago . . . Oh, hang on, they're coming up here for a vigil.'

'Shit,' Pat said. 'Forward that to me.'

'It'll be busy in town next week; the primary school is putting on a fete that weekend too.'

Pat muttered something, then reminded her to keep him updated.

Outside, it was starting to rain again. 'Maybe the town will be flooded in so no one can get here,' Sally suggested.

'Start praying,' Pat growled, and hung up.

GRIEVING FAMILIES RETURN TO SITE OF THEIR PAIN FOR A VIGIL TO HONOUR THEIR LOVED ONES

'My daughter was a shining light,' Brooke Arruda's mother Inez says. 'We miss her every day.'

Sally leaned over the front desk of reception, reading the newspaper article Kyle had sent through. A photo accompanied the brief article: two adults, grief written plain on their faces, leaning into one another for support: Inez Arruda and Donna Walker, Russell's widow.

The vigil will take place on the weekend anniversary of the murders at the beginning of the Razor walk. Representatives of all families will be present in what will no doubt prove to be a moving vigil.

Sally sat back. What the hell? They wanted to hold the vigil at the start of the walk itself? It was at least a forty-five-minute drive to get up the mountain, winding roads and tricky turns. Who was driving them up?

The rain was turning heavier now, a sharp burst of it drumming on the tin roof. The little room felt suffocating in the humidity. What was this? A cop station in Cairns? For the second time since she'd been in the station, Sally turned the air con on. *To hell with budget cuts*, she thought. *I'm dying here.*

She looked at the photo of the family members again, wondered briefly what a vigil involved: singing, prayers? And whose idea was this one? But then in a flash, she thought of Laura Wynter, sole survivor, who was descending on Edenville with a camera crew. *What's the bet she's the one behind all of this*, Sally thought, conjuring up Laura's TV-ready face, her cropped brown hair, her intelligent, ironic smile.

And the news that Neil Durant was back in town – that was convenient for her. She wanted to speak to him, if she was going to clear up those harassment allegations. She called Lex: again no answer, and again no option to leave a message.

Her phone pinged as she hung up.

Corina: **You ok???**

Sally sent back the thumbs-up emoji. Then, after a moment, she typed back: **Why????**

U v quiet this morn. Did that old creep at the pub upset you???

Sally pushed 'call back'. After two rings, her friend answered. 'What old creep?'

'The one who spoke to you just before you went outside – and, you know, ditched us. Don't you remember him?'

Sally frowned, concentrating. She had been drunk, but not memory-loss drunk. 'I remember the whole night – I mustn't have seen or heard him.'

'It was pretty crowded,' Corina agreed.

'So, what did this person look like?'

'I dunno. Old? Red-faced, a beanie, in his seventies? Nose like eight blueberries. Lecherous divorcé vibe.'

'What'd he say to me?'

'Said something about "bastard cops" or "another bastard cop" when you walked past. Jac heard it and told him to shove off, and that other guy, the one who did the worm, he told him to shut the hell up. He's good-looking, that worm guy, isn't he?'

'He's a teacher. Name's Glen,' Sally said, distracted. 'Teaches Grade Six.'

'Right. So, you okay, Sal?'

'Yeah.'

'Well, I hope you find out who that arsehole bloke is.'

'I know who it is.' Sally stared at the photo Pat had asked Kyle to send through.

Neil Durant. The man at the hut.

CHAPTER 14

Shit heap. There was no other way to describe Lex's house.

Sally's friend Amelia would say that the house had a bad aura, that the past was present in this house, that there were ghosts with important things to tell. Amelia was mostly off her tree, but Sally sometimes listened.

She got out of her vehicle slowly, and called in a soothing voice for the dogs that were chained up in the shade not to maul her to death. There was a low grumble in their throats when she passed them.

As she negotiated the treacherous porch steps again, one almost gave way. The second to last one had a huge crack in it. You took your life into your hands just getting to the front door in this place.

Lex answered, waving off his growling dogs. 'They don't bite,' he said, face at the door. 'Well, not always. Here, doggos!' he called to them. 'Settle down!'

'Can I come in, Lex?'

Lex stood aside. Weak light filtered in from a dirty skylight. The hall was cold and uninviting.

'In here.' Her host walked into the front room again, the one with the photos and the rusting tools. 'You want a drink or something? A bickie or a smoke?' Lex shifted on his feet. 'Might not have any bickies, mind.'

'No thanks, I'm right. Hey, don't you ever answer your phone? I've been calling and calling you.'

'Been up the bush.'

'Right.' Sally sniffed, not wholly convinced. 'How's the arm?'

'Better.' Lex rolled up his flannelette shirt sleeve and showed her. The skin was still red and sore, but not weeping.

'Got to stop scratching it.' Sally felt a prickle on her own arm. 'The more you scratch, the worse it gets.'

'Whole family suffers from it,' Lex said. 'Like a pack of dogs with fleas.'

Sally's eyes fell to the photos again, while unconsciously scratching her shoulder. 'How many were there of you again?'

'In total?' Lex rattled off the names: 'Neil, Bill, me, Annie, Faith. We also had some others who came from time to time – cousins and uncles and that.'

'Where are they all?'

'Bill's dead, you know that.' Lex's voice was flat. 'Faith died when she was a little kid – leukaemia. Annie got cancer too, and we barely hear from her now. The cousins mostly live in Sale.'

'Neil?'

'Neil's back.' Lex looked directly at her for the first time.

'Is he here with you now?'

'Not now, he went into Wexton. But he's staying here, yeah. It's his home too.'

Sally held up her hands, showing Lex the gravel rashes. She pointed to her chin. 'Someone attacked me at the Snow Lights pub last night, right after your brother called me a bastard cop. Know anything about that, Lex?'

Lex's face was unreadable in the dim light. 'I dunno. Never go to that pub.'

'Was your brother there last night?'

'I'm not his fucken minder,' he snapped.

Sally squared her shoulders, decided to change tack. 'Is Neil back for the anniversary? I saw him coming out of a hut on your property. He pretended to shoot at me.'

'That hut's ours. You were on our land.'

'I didn't see a fence.'

Lex scratched his arm. Sally scratched hers.

'So what if Neil is back for the anniversary,' Lex said. 'It's not just the anniversary of the murders, you know. It was also the death of our family.'

He had the good grace to turn away as he spoke. The words clearly weren't his; Sally could tell he didn't like saying them.

'Neil says that, does he?'

'Not Neil.'

'A journalist then? Rob Gains?'

'Well, it's not far from the truth.'

'How so?'

'Bill's dead: everyone blames him, and then the police come after our family. Again. Cops never let up; never, ever let up.'

The room smelled vaguely of rust and damp. Sally had an urge to reach over and pull the window up, despite the cold. How could Lex stand this place?

'Why stay here then?' she asked for a second time.

There was a long pause. 'There's spots there' – he pointed out the window – 'that hardly anyone knows about. The trees, the creeks, secret places only we know about.'

They both turned to the grimy window, through which the thick bush was just visible, so close to the house, pressing in. It was unsettling.

'And family,' Lex said, more firmly. 'They're here, even the ones who are gone.' His parents, Sally remembered. His little sister. Bill, his brother: Lex felt them all, here, on this property.

She'd never known that sort of attachment to place. Moving around with her mother, to this boyfriend and that and then boarding school. What must it feel like, she wondered, to feel so grounded that you can't leave, no matter how unwelcome people make you feel?

'You and Neil close, Lex?'

'He's my brother, what can you do? Doesn't mean we have to be best friends.' Lex went to scratch his arm, then stopped.

Sally turned to leave. 'Can you please ask Neil to come and see me at the station when he gets back? I want to look into these harassment allegations. We're taking them seriously, Lex, I hope you know that.'

The man muttered something, staring at his hands.

She waited, then stepped from the dusty room into the cold hallway again.

'And what about the charges against Bill?' Lex's gravelly voice rose. 'You going to look into those too?'

She sighed. 'Do you have anything new to add? Like, really new?'

The man was silent again. He sniffed, then spoke. 'What about the fact that one of the victims, the older lady, was married to ex-military, some sort of hero. I know he died before the murders, but he would have known his guns, would have known types who knew their guns. He spent a bit of time here, brought friends up this way. Did anyone ever look into that?'

'Investigation details are not always for public consumption,' Sally said automatically, even as her mind raced.

'I told you. I do my investigations too,' he said. 'There's a lot you can find out on the world wide web.'

'Yeah,' Sally said, thinking.

'Bill didn't do it,' Lex insisted, jaw set. 'I've thought about it more and more. Why would he? *Why?* He could have shot hundreds of hikers over the years, and he never did. Why that time?'

'It's evidence we need, Lex, and it's evidence they found. There was enough for a conviction, even after Bill's death. And really – if he didn't do it, why kill himself?'

'Maybe he didn't.'

'What?' Sally frowned. 'Are you suggesting that Bill was murdered too?'

Lex rubbed at the corner of his eye with a dirty finger before raising both arms in a gesture of helplessness.

'I'm doing research of my own,' he said again, firm. 'And when I find something, that Gains bloke from the press will be the first one I tell.'

CHAPTER 15

Bill Durant was the sixth victim, not the murderer? What evidence did Lex have? Sally stared at the road ahead, thinking hard. His argument was flimsy at best. That his brother didn't usually shoot with a 30-30; that he hadn't shot anyone before?

Yet, unlike the police, Lex was also looking at the murder victims themselves. Was there anyone in their lives who might have wanted them dead? It didn't mean anything that Lyn Howlett's husband was ex-military and was familiar with this area, because he was dead before the massacre. It changed nothing. But even so, it highlighted how little the police knew about the hikers who'd died.

Cover all bases, that was what she'd always been taught in training. Be methodical. Sally drummed on the steering wheel, nodding to herself: well, she would do just that. If Lex was researching the victims, so would she.

Sally was approaching the turn-off to Wexton. Her half day of policing was almost over, but with renewed energy, she took the exit, driving a further ten kilometres till she pulled up at the sign for the Native Gardens Nursery, where the guide Kate Barone had worked. There was a rushing noise in the air, and it took her a moment to realise that it was the sound of the Garrong River, mutinous in its rushing silver hue. Dark trees bent over the water, and behind it all, the Razor, only half exposed; dominant, terrible even, in the grey sky.

In the reception area of the nursery, a sturdy woman in her fifties, with dry curly hair and a weather-beaten face, was talking intently to a customer about Superb Grevilleas. 'Frost and drought tolerant: low maintenance, pretty all year round.'

'Sounds like my kind of woman,' the old man quipped, and the woman laughed politely.

'I'll take four for the front,' he said. 'And a couple of the knobby club rushes, because you can never have too many of those.'

'No, you cannot,' the woman agreed.

The man turned to Sally as the assistant tallied up his goods. 'Getting the garden done up for my daughter's wedding,' he explained. 'She wants the ceremony' – he curled his fingers into quotation marks – '"low key", which is shorthand for just as expensive but with fewer people.'

'Oh no, is it?' Sally was mildly amused. A big wedding, with all its white trimmings, had never consumed her like it did some girls. She'd seen the photos of her mother's two weddings: the first at a cheap reception centre – a boozy do with mullets and tatts; and the second a big Catholic affair, with flower girls and a three-tiered cake. It was enough to put her off the whole idea.

'Yep,' the man said, collecting his plants. 'My daughter's the modern type – but not enough to pay for it herself.' He stumbled out of the shop, weighed down by plants and thoughts of a hefty wedding bill. Sally shut the door after him.

'How can I help?' the shop worker asked, as she wiped a hand across her forehead, leaving a smear of dirt. 'If you've just moved into the new subdivision up the road, I'd encourage more natives and less lawn!'

'I'm Senior Constable Sally White, from Edenville.'

The woman paused, then smiled in recognition. 'That's right! I thought I recognised you. You're the new policewoman. Last time you were here you dealt with my husband, not me. Got to say, it's nice to have a friendly face in the station rather than some surly man giving you what for.'

Was it a compliment for a cop to be called friendly? Sally wondered. She was often called friendly. Sometimes even 'warm'. All the best female cops on TV had excellent resting bitch face. She'd have to practise hers.

'I'm wondering if there is anyone I can talk to regarding Kate Barone, the woman who was killed in the—'

'Kate!' The woman pushed her hair behind her ears. 'She worked with me for years – I'm Nerissa. My husband Roland and I were very close with Kate and Ric.'

Sally gave a nod.

'What happened to her up there on the mountain, it's just . . . I mean, how . . . how could anyone do such a thing?' Nerissa removed the price card from an outdoor chair and slumped down into it, gesturing for Sally to take the other one. 'Geez. A torture rack would be more comfortable,' she moaned.

Sally sat on the other iron chair and grimaced. 'I'm sorry to bring this all up again, but we're going over the original investigation, and I wonder if I could ask you a few questions?'

'Why?' the woman said, a little sharply. Then: 'I mean, why bother?'

'It's routine,' Sally answered, feeling the cold metal bars of the seat cutting into her legs. 'Because of the anniversary.'

Nerissa didn't seem to find that odd. 'Ten years ago this week. I haven't stopped thinking about it. I miss Kate so much.'

Sally waited.

'Kate called me, you know, the day before she died. To ask about the weather, of all things. She couldn't get the internet up there on the top of the Razor, but she had a satellite phone, so she called. I was so worried when I heard it was her!'

'Why?'

'Sat phone calls are so expensive! I thought there must be something wrong, but no, it was just Kate checking the forecast.'

'Diligent of her.'

'Well, yes.' Nerissa paused. 'Normally, she would have been on top of all that – she was the guide, as you know – but she'd been so distracted, what with Ric and all.'

'He was ill, wasn't he?'

'Very. Pancreatic cancer. I was actually with him when she called. I told her I'd given him some dinner. It was soup – that was all he could handle at that stage.'

A gentle wind set some wooden chimes jangling. Sally could see their price tag: $68 for a set of two.

'When she was on her hikes,' Nerissa continued, 'a few of us used to help out with Ric – just take him his meals, sit with him and whatnot.' The woman had a kind face, lined now in sorrow.

'If Ric was so ill,' Sally said slowly, 'how come Kate led the hikes, and that one in particular? Did she not like to be around him when he was so sick, or did she maybe need a break?'

'No.' Nerissa looked shocked at the idea. 'No, no, it wasn't like that at all. Kate would have stayed with Ric every moment if she could. She was the most loving . . . the most dedicated . . .'

107

Sally waited, while the older woman fished about in her pocket for a tissue. Unable to find one, Nerissa turned aside and, undeterred, snotted into a clump of poa.

Sally suppressed a gag.

'Kate and I did Outdoor Ed in Bendigo,' Nerissa continued, wiping her hands on her jeans.

'Right.' *Right.*

'That's how we met. We spent hours rock climbing and bush-walking when we were younger. Tasmania, the Grampians, the Bibbulmun . . . I've got so many good memories of her.'

'So,' Sally tried again, 'why did Kate choose to go away when her husband was so sick?'

'Because they needed the money.' Nerissa sniffed loudly. 'Kate and Ric tried *everything* for his treatment. She was banking on this new pill from America, and it cost a bomb. We'd had fund-raisers at the footy club, she'd mortgaged the house and sold most of their land – really, they had nothing left, and so Kate was taking on all these hikes, even when she was supposed to be working here! She was getting a bit frantic about it at the end, trying to do too much. I covered for her that last time; we said she had a funeral to go to.' Nerissa gave a sad smile. 'Yeah, like her own funeral. Who would have thought she'd be dead before Ric?'

Sally sat as still as she could, just listening.

'After Kate was killed, Ric took a turn for the worse, moved up to his brother's in Queensland and refused all treatment.'

'Oh, that's awful.' Sally was aware that didn't sound very professional, but at this point, she didn't care.

'Yeah.' Nerissa looked down at her hands. 'I just keep remem-bering that last phone call I had with her. She asked me about the weather; I told her there was some bad stuff on the way, but nothing she couldn't handle. In any case, what could she have done? I've heard people say she should have called off the hike because of the weather. But who knows? Maybe the people on the trip wanted to keep going. If the hikers had turned back after just one night, they might have asked for a refund, and Kate really needed the cash for that medication.' The woman picked up a stray leaf from the floor and studied it. 'So, she took them to the Precipice – a good plan too; it's a shortcut, and the campsite is quite nice. At least, it was. I haven't been there since the . . . since she was . . .'

'Yes.'

'And anyway' – Nerissa sounded as if she'd mounted the defence before – 'it's not as if Kate didn't know what she was doing – she was an amazing guide! When she was twenty-one, Kate walked the entire AAWT on her own.'

Sally raised her eyebrows in admiration. The Australian Alps Walking Track was over six hundred kilometres through the Alps, all the way from Canberra to Walhalla, in Gippsland.

'We were so proud of her,' Nerissa continued. 'We'd all talked about doing it – but Kate actually went and did it, and on her own. She used to write a blog about hiking years ago. Remember when blogs were in fashion?'

Sally did not.

'At her funeral, we read out a couple of the most popular entries. We all thought she should get them published, or send them off to *Great Walks* or *Wild*. Everyone was always telling her she should have been a nature writer, but she'd just laugh it off, she was so modest. In the end, a group of us put them together in a little book we made. I could show it to you, if you like.'

'I'll have a look, that would be great.' Sally smiled politely. She had no intention of reading the homemade book, but it seemed rude not to accept the offer.

Nerissa threw down the leaf and hurried out the back of the store. Sally looked around. A nice place to work in, she thought. Surrounded by greenery, the smell of dirt and growth. No worries about being too young, or too inexperienced, or just not good enough. In a place like this, surely such pressures were non-existent. *Yes,* she briefly daydreamed, *snotting aside, I could work here. Pack in police work and get a job with plants.*

Nerissa returned, more composed. 'It's great to have someone like you locally, maintaining law and order. And I heard you had a good time at the pub?' The pleasant tone was now overlaid with a touch of slyness.

'Not much you can get away with here.' Sally took the thin book offered to her.

'Hey, we've all been there.' Nerissa gave a brief laugh. 'And who doesn't love Boney M.?'

CHAPTER 16

Ten years earlier

It was always a treat to introduce hikers to the Ladies Baths. After hours of steady hiking and the bleak winds of the mountain plains, the tall Alpine ash and Garrong River offered a welcome respite. In this place, the rushing water narrowed into a shallow granite gorge, before plunging down four metres into a series of deep pools below. Formally called the Plunge Pools, but known to locals and regular hikers as the Ladies Baths, it was an idyllic place to rest.

Once again, Kate set up her Trangia and made cups of tea. Brooke and Lyn took off their shoes and dangled their feet in the cool water, while Russell lay under a tree, his legs and arms splayed in supplication to the elements. Normally, Kate liked to strip off and jump in the deepest pool. But not today; it was too cool, and the weather, while not yet dire, wasn't looking great. If she were on her own, she'd power on, not worried – she'd camped in the snow many times – but with this lot, it was different.

'Kate!' Lyn called. 'Can you come and have a look at this?'

Kate turned off the Trangia and wandered over to where the women were inspecting their feet.

'Brooke's got a blister.'

Kate groaned. *Blisters!* The curse of the hiker.

The young woman was inspecting the base of her heel. 'It's not that bad,' she winced, through gritted teeth, pointing to an angry red circle the size of a twenty-cent piece. 'It's been sore, but not *that* sore,' Brooke continued gamely. 'It was only when I took my sock off that I realised how bad it was.'

'That's because your sock probably now has a big patch of your skin on it,' Lyn said.

Kate looked up at the sky, closed her eyes for a second. 'Why didn't you tell me this when we last stopped, Brooke?' she asked mildly. 'It's only going to get worse, and we've got a climb back up now and then it's another long walk to the Hangar campsite.'

'Like I said, it didn't hurt that much,' Brooke protested. 'And I wasn't going to slow everyone down on the walk because of one tiny blister.'

Ahh, famous last words. One tiny blister. Kate wouldn't be surprised to learn that one tiny blister had brought down whole cities, armies, civilisations. Within the walking community, everyone knew: a bad blister reduced mobility, concentration and enjoyment, not only for the person suffering with it, but for everyone around them too.

'It was your new boots,' Lyn offered. 'You probably didn't wear them in enough.'

No shit, Sherlock. Kate walked back to the Trangia and turned the heat up again, options swirling in her head.

They could continue back up the path from the Ladies Baths to the ridge again, and hike the rest of the day on the Razor, maybe three more hours, to the Hangar. That was the original plan. *Or*, Kate thought, slowly pouring boiling water into each of their mugs, *we could take the rarely used Jagged Ridge trail, and camp at the Precipice site tonight.* It would mean walking for longer this afternoon – but they'd cut out one night and one whole day of walking. Besides, there was this weather front to consider too . . .

She called them over. Lyn came first, then Brooke – still barefoot and hobbling – and finally Russell, who looked as if he'd just been woken from a deep sleep.

'I'm thinking,' Kate began hesitantly, 'what with the weather and Brooke's blister, that we should cut our hike short. I know another route that sidesteps walking across the top of the Razor and instead leads us right to the front of it, and from there, down to Alpine Road. There's a campsite we can stop at tonight. It means walking for a bit more today, but there *is* a steep section and we'll take it slow and steady. And tomorrow it's only a short walk down the valley to the road. We can get to the Jagged Ridge trail from here.'

There was a moment's silence.

'What's the weather look like?' Lyn asked.

'It may not get really bad till tomorrow night' – she paused, aware that she was fudging the facts of what Nerissa had told her – 'but if we take this option, we'll be home in our own beds by then.'

Russell held his hands up in the air. 'I'll say yes to that,' he said. 'Not that you'd notice, but I'm not that fit.'

Kate smiled, nodded.

'My foot is starting to hurt now,' Brooke admitted. 'As much as I hate to say it, maybe it is the best option.'

'Well,' Lyn shrugged, 'I can't do it on my own, so I guess I'll have to agree.'

'I'm sorry, everyone,' Brooke said, miserable.

'You may not get any money back from the company,' Kate warned, yet another lie rolling easily off her tongue. 'They're very strict with things like that.' Brooke and Russell muttered that wasn't a problem, which was a relief as there was no way she could reimburse them all for the shortened hike. In normal circumstances, maybe – but now, at this time, she needed every cent she could get.

'It's why my husband mainly liked to hike on his own.' Lyn drank her tea. 'He said when you only have yourself to rely on, there's no one to blame, no one to owe.'

'He sounds like a really fun bloke.' Russell snorted into his mug of tea, and Lyn chuckled.

'Okay then, sorted,' Kate said, firm. She felt a tremor of pleasure – she'd be getting home one day early, to Ric. 'Brooke, you'll need to take it easy from now on. We'll be walking slow. I'll carry some stuff from your pack to make it a bit lighter for you.'

Lyn volunteered to take more of the load too, and, after a moment's hesitation, so did Russell.

While the rest were finishing their tea and biscuits, Kate taped up Brooke's blistered foot. As gently as she could, she covered the wound before helping the younger hiker put her sock on.

'You're like a nurse,' Brooke said with a smile. 'So kind.'

'I've had plenty of experience with blisters.'

'I know we have to leave the trip early, but I'm still sad about it. Yesterday, when I was walking, I had hours – whole hours – when I didn't think about that stupid person harassing me.'

'It's the best, isn't it?' Kate said carefully, sensing the other woman's need to confide. 'You're only concentrating on putting one foot in front of the other. You're forced to take a break.'

'Yeah, and your head is so clear up here. I thought, you know what? I'm not going to let that idiot scare me. Life's too short – I'm going to work harder on getting him arrested or whatever they do with stalkers these days.'

'That's the spirit!' Kate grinned. 'Okay,' she said, rising then helping Brooke up. 'See how that feels.'

There was a crack of twigs behind and to the left of them. Kate looked about, frowning.

'Did you hear something just now?' she asked, eyes searching their surroundings.

'Nope,' Brooke said, gathering up her pack and setting off.

Kate hesitated a moment, before hitching her own pack and following.

CHAPTER 17

As she drove back to Edenville, Sally passed the football oval, where dozens of cars were parked along the boundary. She slowed, looking out the passenger window at the scoreboard: the Mountain Men were winning: 76–53, fourth quarter. A goal was scored, and she beeped her horn in time with everyone else, hoping the netballers were winning too.

Shortly after moving to the town, Sally had joined the Mountaineers – the local netball team. She'd been playing Wing Attack regularly in B division. It was a good sport, netball: the speed of it, the toughness. Sally liked her teammates and hoped they were beginning to see beyond the local-cop tag.

A wild cheer rang up from the oval, and Sally was reminded that the football/netball presentations were on Tuesday night. She and Jim had tickets to attend.

Back home, Sally returned a missed call from Jim. He was driving down the Razor and was tired after his days walking along the Saddle. There were loads of people out, he said, trying to get in a hike before the cooler weather arrived. The rain hadn't put as many people off as he'd thought. He was going to try to catch the last few minutes of the footy and then head to his own place to sleep. Did she mind if they skipped dinner at the pub?

She did not. In fact, it suited her to have a quiet night in.

Jim asked her how Friday night with her mates had gone, and listened politely as she told him how much fun it had been, how much the girls had loved being at the pub, and how good it was to see them again.

'Sounds great.'

'It was.' If her voice sounded a touch too high when she spoke, he didn't seem to notice. 'It really was.'

'Well,' he said after a pause, 'maybe I'll drop in tomorrow?'

'Yep, do that.'

They hung up, and Sally looked outside. So dark now. In the valley, night came fast.

She touched the lower part of her back. It was still tender. Twisting around, she studied the bruise in the bathroom mirror: a dark grey with yellow at the edges – and yes, the curved shape of the top of a boot. Feelings of humiliation returned.

Following a long shower, she dressed in her pyjamas and sat in bed with an apple for dinner. Out of habit, she scrolled mindlessly through TikTok for half an hour, then turned off her phone and, reaching over to the side of her bed, picked up the homemade book Nerissa had lent her. Inside was a series of articles, neatly typed, with borders and sub-headings. Sally skimmed over the papers, tired: 'How to light fires when your wood is damp'. 'How to fashion a camp oven from rubbish'. 'Nifty tricks to make your pack lighter'. And another: 'Hidden Huts of the High Country'.

At this, Sally sat up. There, in the middle of the page, was a direct mention of the enigmatic Precipice, where Kate's life had ended. When people spoke about the crag, they used vaguely supernatural terms like 'mysterious' and 'eerie'. On the Precipice, it was said, the wind, searing through hidden caves and crevices, created a terrifying, human-like wailing sound. And now, of course, the towering jagged cliff was known for the five people who'd been murdered underneath it. There were no signs to the Precipice now.

In the article, Kate mentioned a clearing good for camping and had included a neat mud map. It must have been at this campsite, Sally thought, where the first three killings occurred. Brooke and Tom had died about four hundred metres away, close to where Jim had found Laura Wynter. Bill Durant had shot himself on a small ridge just above where the tents were pitched.

Kate had written:

The Precipice itself is not easily accessed. From the campsite, take the track heading south and then loop around to where the cliff makes a sharp ascent. Here, you'll find a vertical chimney between boulders, which you'll need to climb. Start by putting your left foot and hand on one side of the rock wall with the right hand and foot on the other, in the shape of a starfish. Press and push your feet and hands outward. There are some good edges to use as foot and handholds. Pull down on holds above so you can move up one foot at a time. Next time, I hope to fix a rope from the top to help with hauling packs up.

Sally made a whistling sound through her teeth. Impressive! It was like something from an old adventure book. She put down her apple and continued reading.

At the top of the chimney there is a small ledge to negotiate, and then one more short climb to the top where you'll find a large flat rock perhaps ten metres in diameter. The views from this 'roof' are superb, all over the valley. Beware in fog or poor weather, though, as the cliffs on either side are steep, and will most certainly result in death if you slip. Trust your instincts!

'Wow,' Sally said aloud. 'Puts the old jog round the paddock to shame.'

There are two choices to make for your descent. Climb down the way you came, back along the ledge, down the chimney, and make your way to the campground. The more perilous route (but far more exciting too, in my opinion), is to jump across a crevice at the east side of the top of the flat rock – one metre in distance!

Sally slammed the little book shut. This wasn't in any of the current guidebooks. Would Jim know about this track? She closed her eyes, imagining the spiral down the rock, like the slide in *The Folk of the Faraway Tree*, only much more terrifying, and not that far away.

And there was something about the way Kate wrote: the clear and precise language, her practical enthusiasm. It spoke to Sally in a way that so many books had not.

When sleep finally came, Sally dreamed of the vertical chimney. Up and up and up she was climbing, but the top never came. In the morning, when she woke, disorientated and exhausted, her hands were gripped tight as if clinging to an imaginary rope.

CHAPTER 18

Despite its newfound wealth and the influx of city people, Edenville still retained a Day of Rest mentality on Sundays. In the main street, only the coffee shop was open, and in the distance Sally could see Lex's car parked nearby. He'd be having his ritual morning brew, she thought, and as if in response, a wiry arm appeared out of the driver's side window, throwing a disposable cup into a kerbside bin. He pulled out before she could get to him. Pity: she would have liked to ask him again where Neil was. He still hadn't responded to her call.

Sally preferred tea to coffee. Victorians liked to tell her it was because she'd grown up in Adelaide and not in Melbourne, but Sally thought it was just because she *preferred tea*. People were always telling her the reasons for her choices.

In the coffee shop, she bought an apple scroll and a chocolate milk. No particular reason for the choice; she just liked the taste.

The cafe owner was named Marie Therese, though she preferred just Therese. She was a small woman from Portstewart in Northern Ireland. It apparently had one of the best beaches in the world, but you could only swim one day a year. The rest of the time, Therese said, it was like being stuck in an ice cube.

'Does Lex Durant come here every day for a coffee?' Sally asked, after they'd chatted about the weather, the town, how busy she'd been.

'Oh yes,' Therese said. 'Every morning, no matter the day. I always give him a coffee and write him a little note on the lid. It's just something I do.'

It was pleasing, listening to the way Therese spoke. Her Rs were like a friendly pirate – Sally could listen to her all day. But not today.

'What's he like?'

Therese pursed her lips and began arranging cups next to the coffee machine. 'Why would you want to know a thing like that?'

Sally paused. Why *did* she want to know? She decided to be honest. Half honest. 'Lex asked me to look into something for him.'

'I see.' Therese's shoulders relaxed as she moved on to polishing the wooden benchtop with a tea towel.

'Let me tell you this, then. I've only been in this town for three years, but from everything I've seen, Lex Durant is an old sweetheart.'

Sally choked on her chocolate milk. *A sweetheart?* That old man in the decrepit house, skin peeling off him like snow? She'd have understood if Therese had said 'no trouble' or even 'harmless', but *sweetheart?*

'He's from a large family, sisters and brothers, no money, loads of fights and alcohol.' Therese pursed her lips. 'That and the constant worries about the police – is it any wonder the poor man's a wreck?'

'Does he say much about the police?'

'He's talking to a girl who spent her youth in Belfast!' Therese gave her tea towel a decisive flick. 'I know a thing or two about trouble with the authorities.'

Sally waited.

'And no,' the cafe owner relented, 'Lex doesn't say anything in particular. He doesn't say much at all.'

'What about Bill Durant, did you know him?'

'No – as I say, I've only been here three years.'

'There's Neil Durant too, does he ever come in?'

'Sorry, love, Lex is the only Durant to buy coffee. Every morning like clockwork.'

'Wonder why he doesn't have his coffee in here,' Sally murmured. There were nice round tables, a bench seat by the window, fresh flowers. 'Every day he seems to drink it in his car.'

'Oh, love.' Therese gave a wry laugh. 'When you're brought up with nothing, when your family's the local mess – you don't feel right in places like this, where people can gawk at you and gossip under their breaths. You've never been poor, have you?'

Sally opened her mouth to respond, then closed it. Why bother? It was true, she'd never *really* been without: on the contrary, and thanks to Angelo, she'd mostly had whatever she needed. A home, boarding school, nice clothes. There was no point in relaying to Therese that for four years, from age six to ten, it had just been her and her mother, after her biological father had finally left for good. No point in telling Therese about those four years of couch-surfing, renting old caravans and sleeping in the car. The edge of it, the vague anxiety which lingered – no need to tell her that. It had only been four years, after all. Sometimes it was fun.

*

Standing outside the cafe now, Sally finished the rest of her drink and took a bite out of her apple scroll, enjoying the quiet Sunday morning. A pair of teenage girls walking in front whispered intently to one another; a young mother passed her and said hello. The Snow Lights pub was across the road. Sally stopped, took another bite of the scroll, and considered it. The alleyway she'd stumbled out of on Friday night was directly opposite. No sunlight there, a pothole out the front.

The apple scroll wasn't tasty any more. She turfed the rest into a garden bed – a bird could eat it – then crossed the road and stood in front of the dark rectangular space, taking note of its length, the skip at the very back, the big door to the side of the pub, and the single step leading down from it. She walked up into the alley, close to the wall. When she came to the spot where she'd leaned over, trying not to vomit, Sally stopped.

The chance of a footprint now was next to zero, but Sally searched for other clues. Small items which the attacker may have dropped – receipts, a cigarette butt, a bottle top, anything. But there was nothing. The crime scene was totally compromised, and again the voice in her head chastised her for not reporting it straight away.

She took a few photos of the scene, all different angles, up close and further away. Squatting down again, she examined the ground one more time. Its surface was red brick buried underneath years of dirt and grime. Sally stepped back, then zoomed in with her phone, took some more shots. Beside the door that led to the pub was a broken red brick, and she moved it with her foot. Something white there, clinging beside it. Tissues. She bent down to look more closely. One piece was a tissue, yes – but the other was a crumpled piece of paper. She used the long sleeves of her top to cover her fingers and pick it up. It was a little soggy, but the brick had kept it mostly dry. And something was written on it. She bent her head down close to the paper, squinting her eyes to read. There were four words that she could make out: *Whispe, Snow, Lexi, Hog.* The other words were a blue, inky mess. The paper meant little, and yet – *Lexi.*

If she'd reported it in the first place, she could have asked someone from Forensics to look at the note – just as a quick favour. But now, it was probably too late.

No, it's not, a voice inside her nagged. *That's not what you'd tell anyone else.*

Frowning, she pocketed the piece of paper and walked out of the cold laneway into the relative warmth of the main street.

Once home again, Sally sat at her small dining table, in front of the big windows that offered an impressive view of the Razor. *Whispe, Snow, Lexi, Hog.* She wrote them down on the back of an envelope. Was that a 'c' after the 'i' in 'Lexi'? Hard to tell. The words read like a list, and while Sally wasn't optimistic that it had anything to do with her assault, she fed the words into Google, and read the entries for sites on Lexi the Pet Pig, and a band named Snow Hogs (which actually looked pretty good). Next, she typed the words individually, came up with nothing. Someone was probably writing suggestions for what to call their dog, she thought. Dropped the list when they went to fish out a tissue.

Discouraged, Sally returned to thinking about the Mountain Murder enquiries. Her meeting with Nerissa at the nursery hadn't yielded anything in particular, but it was interesting that Kate's hiking tours were a side hustle to her more regular work, and that she was desperately trying to raise money for her husband's treatment. Her blogs read like she was deeply familiar with Mount Razor and capable in the bush, and yet she hadn't even properly checked the weather before setting out. What else had Kate Barone overlooked?

Sally reminded herself of the lessons from training. *Cover all bases. Be methodical.* She made a list of what she needed to do in the coming week, at the top of which was interviewing the loved ones of the other victims, to make sure there was nothing the old investigation had missed. Some would be arriving for the vigil, but Sally wanted to speak to them before they were together again, and without the press watching on.

From the recent contact details she'd looked up, most of the next-of-kin were living in Melbourne. Tom's elderly parents had passed away two years after their only child's death. There was a photo of them being greeted by the Vice Chancellor of Melbourne Uni. Sally stared at them, their faces etched in sorrow, their backs stooped, grief an invisible burden they'd now always carry. Poor parents, poor Tom. He'd moved from Surrey in the UK to Melbourne to study medicine, and quickly become interested in Australian bushwalking.

Despite it being a Sunday, Sally sent Pat an email, letting him know that she'd like to visit the family members. All the better to placate the Durants, she wrote, if she could outline how thorough she'd been. Plus, it wouldn't take long: one day for Lyn and Brooke's contacts, another for Russell's, and then phone calls to Tom's remaining relatives in England. She'd already ticked off Kate Barone's friend Nerissa, but would make enquiries about others who knew her well. Perhaps Glen could help with that.

She wanted to type, *And what if Lex is right? What if Bill didn't kill those people?* But she snatched her fingers back from the keyboard, as if from a flame. Pat would only lecture her again about not being on the mountain when it happened. Make her feel like a silly little girl. Like Lex, she'd conduct her own research. No need yet for anyone else to be aware of her niggling concerns.

And the piece of paper she'd picked out from under the brick in the alleyway. Should she mention it? Her fingers crept back to the keys, wondering what to write, when her phone buzzed.

It was her mother, Deb, 'just calling for a chat'. Sally listened as Deb told her about a new course on memoir writing she'd signed up for. 'I have so many stories!' she exclaimed. 'It's been cathartic jotting them down – the modelling days, the treatment we used to get from the old television executives! That one who flew me to Port Douglas for lunch and asked me to be his wife for *when he was in Australia* – can you imagine! No hashtag MeToo in those days!' Sally wondered briefly if her mother would mention in her memoir the weeks they'd spent sleeping in their car near Glenelg. Her mother had pretended they were having a holiday by the beach, but it didn't much feel like one when they were both crying most nights.

'Look, Mum,' Sally butted in, 'I'm trying to get some work done. Can I ring you back?'

'Oh, sorry! Yes, look – I was just calling to say that I'm coming up to visit you tomorrow. I haven't seen you in ages!'

Typical – Sally was about to have one of the busiest weeks since she'd got here, and this was the time Deb chose to invite herself to Edenville. She'd only been once before, on the guise of helping her daughter move, when in actual fact, Deb had spent most of her time sitting on a pile of boxes, smoking and telling Jim funny stories. Still, Sally felt an old longing rise up for her mum's company. She felt the bruise on her back, its tenderness, sore rather than painful. She wanted to see her crazy mum, but . . .

'I've got dinner at Jim's parents' house tomorrow – we go every Monday night.'

'Maybe I could come,' Deb suggested. 'Isn't it time I met his parents? It'll be fun!'

'It won't be that much fun.' Sally imagined her mother playing the Brear family's beloved board games. *Cringe.*

'I'll be on my best behaviour – the perfect mother. I'll wear pearls, and I promise not to swear. Tell Jim's family I'll bring the wine.'

'They don't drink, Mum.'

'No, but I do.'

CHAPTER 19

Sally arrived at the station early on Monday morning to discover another police vehicle already parked out the front. Inside, the radio was on, and someone was talking loudly on the phone. Hanging her coat on the rack inside, she called out a cheery hello.

Kyle greeted her from behind the reception counter. 'Oh!' He looked surprised. 'Hi.'

'Morning, Kyle. What's going on?' She walked slowly to the small office behind reception, where the constable had already made a space for himself on a spare desk near the window.

'I didn't move any of your stuff.' Kyle followed her. 'Is it okay that I set up my laptop there?'

His boyish features and anxious manner again tricked Sally into thinking that he was younger than he was. She reminded herself that while he was in fact one year older, *she* had senior status.

'Yeah, course it is. It's not as if I own the place.' She *had* felt as if she owned it though. Now, with a second person in it, the small station felt as crowded as a city office. 'What's Pat want you to do here exactly?'

'Well' – Kyle shrugged – 'he said that you already had it all planned out.'

'Did he really?'

'Yeah, and he told me that I should take care of the normal station stuff, as well as assist you in reviewing the old cop files, just to make sure everything's legit when the media start hammering us.'

'Right.'

'He suggested that I should make a start on those original harassment accusations, maybe talk to some of the old coppers.'

'Did he?' For a moment Sally was stumped, pleased that her boss was so promptly onto her concerns. 'That's great, Kyle.'

'Pat said you might be away doing interviews and stuff.'

Sally stood up straight. So, Pat had approved it all then? 'Yes. I need to go to Melbourne – I'll be gone most of the day, but you can catch me at any time.'

'Sure. Hey, what happened to you on Friday night? I didn't see you after you did that dance.'

Sally kept her head down. 'I left straight after. Got bored,' she muttered.

'Well, it was seriously impressive.' Sally looked up to see Kyle holding his forearms together, in an approximation of her moves. There was no malice in it though.

She tried to make her voice sound older when she answered, 'Years of practice.'

On the drive down the Hume, Sally listened to a podcast about intermittent fasting. It was very interesting, she thought, as she opened a small packet of M&M'S. *I should try that one day.*

As the land flattened and grew brown, she put on Cold War Kids, then went old school with the Smashing Pumpkins.

The news on ABC was mostly worrying; the climate was a mess. She listened to some Waifs.

By the time Sally reached Melbourne, traffic on the ring road was coiled like a snake getting ready to eat itself. She checked her phone. No messages from Kyle back at the station.

Obeying the snooty voice on her satnav, Sally drove first through a leafy burb with grand old houses and gardens, then through one with massive mansions and three-car garages, and finally another that contained a little bit of both.

Her route took her past a generous Californian bungalow, complete with leadlight windows and a shady porch: Lyn Howlett's former house.

With the salmon gum on the verge and the neat row of lilly pillies on the side fence, it looked like a well-loved home. This was where Lyn had raised her son, and where she'd lived with her husband Terry. The husband whom Lex said had been in the military and 'spent a bit of time here, brought friends up this way'. *Which friends?* Sally wondered as she drove slowly past. *And where in the High Country did he spend his time?*

Minutes later, Sally had parked her car a block away and was walking along the street, towards a row of shops. A lone man sat outside a cafe just a block away, phone placed strategically on the table in front of him.

'Martin?' Sally asked.

'Yes, you must be the senior constable.'

'Sally White.'

'I thought it would be someone more senior.'

'Sorry, just me.' She smiled thinly and sat down, nodding towards his phone. 'Are you taping this?'

'What? No. Why?'

'No reason, I was joking.'

'Oh.' Martin looked at her strangely. 'Right.'

An uncomfortable beat followed.

'I've got a meeting shortly,' Martin said. 'This won't take long, will it?'

'No, not at all.' Sally was relieved to begin. 'Can we just start by talking about your mum, maybe what sort of person she was?'

The man seemed to shrink. 'She was a normal mother, I suppose. You know, busy, kind. I had a good upbringing. Her and Dad mostly got along well. Holidays by the beach, camping, Christmas with cousins – all the normal stuff.'

Sally didn't know about all the normal stuff. But once again, she must have looked like someone who did.

'Except, then,' Martin continued, 'after she died, I found out that she'd been frittering away all her money.'

Sally pulled out her phone. 'Really?' she asked. 'How did you find that out?'

'The will, for starters,' Martin said, flat. 'There was hardly anything left in it. Or her bank balance. She'd been quite well off when Dad died, and she'd already sold our home, so it was a bit of a shock that there wasn't much left, I can tell you.'

'Right.' Sally made some notes. 'How long after your father died did Lyn sell the home?'

'I don't know. Two years? I told the police this when they first came around.' Martin looked at her in some annoyance.

But they already had the killer, Sally thought. *They wouldn't have been interested . . .*

'And your father, he received a big payout after that accident, didn't he?' It had been astonishing to read old newspaper reports about how Terry, Lyn's husband, had saved a truck driver from his burning vehicle on the Princes Highway one year before his own fatal heart attack. Terry and one other man had not hesitated to leave their own cars and rush to the scene of the accident, risking their lives to save a young father. The owner of the trucking company, a multi-millionaire, had awarded each man $200,000.

'He did. But he would have spent it quickly enough. Dad bought a done-up Mustang.'

'Right.' Sally wrote it down. 'Was Lyn in any sort of trouble, legal or otherwise?'

'None that I know of. I did ask her once if she had any money worries, when a real estate agent friend told me that she'd asked him how much she could get for the unit she was living in – the one she'd bought after the sale of the house.' Martin tugged at the sleeves of his shirt. 'But she just said she had everything under control and not to worry. So I didn't.'

He seemed distracted now, uncomfortable with the subject.

'How did your mother seem just before she died? Was she happy, excited about the walk?'

Martin checked the time on his phone and winced theatrically. 'I should get going.'

'Martin? Was your mother in good spirits before she went on the hike?'

'I hadn't seen her for a while, I really couldn't say.' He coughed lightly.

'But you'd spoken to her?'

'Well, I spoke to her a few weeks – no, a month or so before that, when I'd learned she'd been to the real estate agent.'

Sally looked at the man. The only interaction he'd had with his mother in months was to ask her whether she was about to sell off her unit?

Martin read her expression. 'I've got my own family, and I was very busy.'

Sally stayed silent.

'I should have called her more often,' he admitted weakly.

'Was your mother giving money to anyone in particular?'

'No, she didn't talk about it much when I asked her. She said everything was fine. I was angry, I suppose. In hindsight . . .'

His flushed face and the way he grappled with his answers almost made Sally feel sorry for him. Almost. She looked at her notes.

'Was your mother single?'

'Of course!' He gave a brief laugh in disbelief. 'I mean, Dad died five years before she was murdered. But,' he added for emphasis, 'she was fifty-five years old – she's hardly going to be gallivanting about, picking up men.'

'Mick Jagger has a seven-year-old.' Sally had read it online somewhere.

'What?'

'Just saying.'

The man scowled and looked down at his phone again.

'Did Lyn have any close friends?'

'She was very pally with her neighbour, I know that. They played cards together. Ha! Probably handed out money to him too.'

'Do you have the name of the neighbour Lyn was friendly with?'

'Why do you care?' Martin shook his head. 'They got the killer, didn't they?'

Sally waited.

'Kevin Brophie,' he said, resigned. 'He's the one nearest the gum tree on our old street. Got the chaotic front garden.' He stood. 'Is that it? Anything else?'

'Just one more thing: have you been contacted by Laura Wynter? She was there on the night of the murders.'

'I've had one message from her, she's organising some vigil on the mountain. I haven't responded. I'm not interested.'

So it was Laura who organised it, Sally thought. *Anything to boost her career.*

'Right. Well, thank you, Martin,' she said sweetly. 'You've been brilliant.'

Despite being a bloody awful son.

Back at Lyn's old house, Sally parked in front of the salmon gum. An elderly dog was asleep in a basket at the end of the neighbour's porch. It raised its head and tried to stand when she knocked on the door.

'Stay there, old mate,' Sally soothed. 'Have a rest.'

But the golden retriever would not be persuaded. It stood and then walked in a wonky fashion towards her, like an ancient host, determined to be polite. She held her hand out and patted its smooth, bony head.

'That's Sue.' Lyn's old neighbour had opened the door. 'She's the concierge of the house.'

'And a good one too.' Sue sat down and thumped her tail on the wooden floor, as if proud of the compliment. 'I love your garden.'

'Thank you, but it's a little wild. The trees have skyrocketed with all this rain, and that fig is getting too big for its boots. How can I help?'

'I'm Senior Constable Sally White from the Edenville station. I'm here to talk about Lyn Howlett. I've just had coffee with her son Martin, and he said you were good friends with her.'

'Martin.' The man's mouth turned down. 'Right.'

'Can I ask you a few quick questions about Lyn? We're going over the original investigation, just reviewing the case.'

The man studied her a moment before nodding. 'I'm Kevin. And yes, Lyn was a good friend. Come in.'

He turned and walked down the hall, the ever-loyal Sue at his heels. When they reached the kitchen, a rich aroma of tomatoes filled the air. There were pots bubbling on the stove, full of red liquid.

'I'm making relish,' Kevin explained. 'Do it every year.'

'It smells great.'

'Turn the heat down a bit, can you, love, while I get Sue to her bed.'

Sally did as she was asked, and then, as Kevin helped the dog onto a comfortable mattress in the corner of the room, found a wooden spoon and stirred the pots. Kevin made them both a cup of tea, and they sat down at a small table overlooking the vibrant back yard.

'I knew her husband before they got together. We were in the army together. He was going out with another girl, but fell for Lynnie hook, line and sinker. Lyn worked with my partner at the time, and we all became friends.'

Sally's tea was too strong. It needed milk, but she didn't want to interrupt Kevin's story.

'When they bought that house next door, I bought this one. Cheap as chips back then. Few years later, my partner up and left me, and I've been here on my own ever since.'

The man pulled a packet of tobacco out of his chest pocket and indicated if she'd mind him smoking. She shook her head, glad of the open window beside her.

'What was Lyn's husband like?'

'Terry? Heart of gold, but he liked the drink too much. He'd make all these promises he couldn't keep, let people down. He did know some dodgy types in his time. Got into scrapes.

Went to court at one stage for aiding and abetting a theft – but he was never convicted, and the experience scared the bejesus out of him.' Kevin gave a chuckle. 'Terry was always best when he was in nature; it calmed him. Even before he met Lyn, he used to spend time in the High Country, said he felt free in the mountains. Then he met Lynnie, and he'd take her camping there too. Some of the places he went: the way he described them!'

Sally thought of Lex's investigation into Terry. 'You said Terry knew some dodgy types. Was there anyone who could have held a grudge towards him or his family?'

Kevin got up to stir the pots again. 'I doubt it. Terry might have been a bit of a tearabout, but he was a lovable bloke. I mean, he was a hero for a while there in the press!'

Sally nodded.

'Whatever his flaws,' Kevin continued, 'Terry wasn't one to bear a grudge, and I doubt anyone ever felt that way about him.' He checked each pan, looking into them with care, murmuring instructions to himself.

'You like relish?' he asked after a moment.

'I do.'

'Might have to find you a glass jar to put some in. Don't have labels or anything . . .'

Sally tried to steer the conversation back to the case. 'You don't know if Terry ever met Neil or Bill Durant when he was up in the mountains, do you?' *Long shot, I know, but—*

'Now, funny you say that – because after that man killed Lynnie, I looked him up: Bill Durant. And you know what?'

'What?'

'I don't think he ever mentioned him.'

'Oh.'

'But . . .' Kevin's eyes crept to the stove again.

136

'Yes?' Sally felt like snapping her fingers to get his attention back.

'But Terry did mention a big family, all shooters, who roamed the Razor as if it was their own. I'd hedge my bets that it was the Durant family. Terry didn't know them per se – more *of* them. He said they were from Edenville and were pretty wild, but Terry of course passed no judgement. He'd been a bit wild too, over the years. Girls, you know – they loved him.'

Terry had known the Durants. Or at least known *of* them. Sally could hardly believe it: the first real link between Bill and one of the victims.

'So, you and Lyn remained friends after Terry died?'

'Oh yes. Even after she moved to her new place, I still saw her regularly.'

Sally took a sip of her tea. 'Her son mentioned that Lyn was spending lots of money before she died. Did you know anything about that?'

'I did!' Kevin slammed his cup down, splashing liquid across the table. 'Lyn was scammed online, and she felt terrible about it!'

'Oh.' Sally was taken aback. 'Martin didn't say anything about that.'

'No, Lyn didn't want to worry him.' Kevin shook his head. 'She was so embarrassed. But she had it under control, she really did.'

'What happened?' Sally picked up her phone once more and indicated to Kevin that she was going to take notes. He nodded.

'Online scammers,' he said. 'Professional. It was tragic. She'd reported it to the police, but nothing was ever done about it, as far as we knew. She lost thousands, tens of thousands – that's why she sold her house next door. But she was on her way to getting most, or some of it, back.'

'How did they scam her, do you know?'

'From what she told me, it started when she got a message from Microsoft on her computer saying that there was some sort of glitch, and she'd be susceptible to scams if she didn't let them run a program to check for problems. She believed it, and next minute whoever it was had control over her accounts. She didn't even notice at first, till her bank rang to ask about the irregular withdrawals. She told them not to worry, because she'd been buying some stuff online and putting money towards a big holiday. By the time she *did* realise – after a second call – there was almost $100,000 gone.'

'Crikey!'

'Exactly.' From her bed in the corner, Sue gave a short bark in agreement. 'Lyn was confident that the Fraud people were going to get her money back. But then she died, and the investigation died too, I guess.'

Sally jotted down what Kevin was saying.

'Why did Lyn decide to go on the walk? And why there? Did she ever say?'

'That happened online too, actually. She joined a site for older women, "On Your Own but Not Alone". All very safe. They shared recipes, stories, health advice – things like that. No money involved whatsoever, thank goodness. One of them suggested the hike, and that particular guide too. There was a special deal for that weekend, I seem to remember. Too good to miss, that sort of thing.' Kevin trailed off sadly.

'How was Lyn before she went on the walk?'

'Happy. Last time she'd been up in the High Country, it was with Terry and me. We were camping near Forlorn Hope. You been there?'

'No, but my boyfriend probably has.' Sally smiled.

'Great spot, you can see a real alpine bog there – peat moss and rope brush and candle heath. There's rare skinks and frogs, and the water coming from it is the purest you've ever drunk. The brumbies and deer have created havoc, but that place is magic.'

It did sound magic. She could never understand why so many places in the High Country had names so awful they'd make you run a mile: Forlorn Hope, Mount Despair, Horrible Gap and more.

'At least,' Kevin said, 'they *were* magic. After the fires, I don't know what they look like.'

She glanced at the kitchen clock. Time to get moving.

'We only went shooting once on that camping trip,' Kevin was reminiscing. 'Lynnie didn't like us doing it.'

Sally frowned, took another sip of her tea. She was getting used to the taste. 'You went hunting?'

'Yes. When I do go, it's usually on my own. But I used to like hunting with Terry. He wasn't a cowboy.'

'What do you mean by that?'

'I mean, he knew what he was doing, and he didn't do it as part of some macho show. He wasn't into big trucks with stickers and posting photos of what he'd shot. Terry was a careful hunter and, as I said before, he loved that area. It was nature he was really into.'

The man stood and walked first to stir his pots, and then to give his dog a gentle pat on the head.

'I can't imagine you hunting,' Sally said with a smile.

'You can't?' Kevin shrugged. 'That's okay. Not all hunters are rednecks. Most of us just like to be in the outdoors, appreciate the surrounds.'

And kill.

Catching her look, Kevin gave a nod. 'What's more humane? Shooting a deer cleanly in the bush, acknowledging you've killed it, accepting the death, then using all of it for your own food. Or buying meat from the supermarket, all packaged in plastic and transported hundreds of kays? Have you ever seen a truckload of cattle being sent to the abattoir? Or sheep loaded onto a truck in forty degrees?'

'Yes, unfortunately.' The bleating, the stench of it.

'I won't go so far as to say I pray every single time I shoot a deer or a pig, but I do give thanks for the creature. And I eat almost every part of it.'

The sweet, rich smell of the tomatoes and the bitter tea, coupled with the strong tobacco scent, was making Sally feel a little strange. *Nothing is as it seems*, she thought, out of the blue. 'I have to go, Kevin. Thank you for your time. Will you call me if you think of anything else?'

'Of course.' He found her a piece of paper and pen, and she wrote her number down.

'Thanks again,' she said.

'Just a tick, wait till I get you some relish.' Sally stood in the kitchen doorway as he carefully ladled out the mixture into a jar before sealing it tightly with a red lid.

'There you go,' he said, handing it to her. 'You'll never look back.'

CHAPTER 20

70-year-old woman seeks partner to share the sunset years.

Sally was scrolling the website of 'On Your Own but Not Alone' while parked illegally near a row of shops. The site's *Meet new friends, travel, enjoy!* page was particularly depressing. What had looked initially like a space to make new acquaintances was really a dating site couched in nondescript posts, in between ads for cruises to Vanuatu.

68-year-old man looking for someone to share a life of travel and experience, read one, accompanied by an image of a distinguished senior who might well have been a lead in *The Bold and the Beautiful*. In smaller letters: *Pref younger female, aged 20–30.*

Sally rolled her eyes.

Ex-USA Navy Seal seeks female companionship.

Yeah, right. There'd be more chance of that bloke being an *actual* seal . . .

But Lyn hadn't fallen for a romantic scam. She'd been interested in friendship and social opportunities. Another page titled *Gardening, Walking, Craft!* provided more realistic opportunities: a bus tour to the National Gallery of Australia, an online talk on menopause, a guide on How to Build a Chook House. The comments on the message board were helpful, friendly. *Anyone done Pilates?* wrote @busynan. *Been told I need to strengthen my core!*

There were hundreds of followers messaging, posting recipes, sharing photos of gardens. It was easy to see how people could have been drawn to the camaraderie of the site. The tone of it was welcoming and chatty. And yes, there were advertisements for guided walks in Tasmania and along the Larapinta Trail in the NT. One was highlighting a special offer, like the deal Lyn had taken up a decade ago.

Sally flicked through her phone and found the contact number for her old colleague Detective Sergeant Brian Collins. Her first posting after police college had been in Melbourne, and her desk had been next to Brian's. They'd become friends, despite the thirty-year age gap. And although he was disparaging of most things she'd learned in college – in particular all the stuff on mental health and well-being – he said he appreciated her positive attitude, which (if he was ever prepared to admit it) meant she had good mental health and well-being.

The sergeant answered on the second ring.

'Hi Brian, you on another tea break or what?'

'Sally! How's life in *Deliverance* country?'

'What?'

'How's country life? Judging the biggest pumpkin at the show? Getting cats down from trees, are we?'

'Big talk coming from a Mallee man.'

Compulsory teasing over, Sally cut to the chase. She explained a little about Lyn and her fraud case, and asked what the process would have been once it was reported. 'Is there any way of finding out who her scammer was?'

Brian coughed, and she could hear the ever-present lozenge swishing about in his mouth. There were things she didn't miss about him.

'Once you report an online scam, Fraud investigates,' he said. 'If it's a banking fraud, then they have their own departments – a lot of online agencies do too – but if it is directly reported to the police and there is evidence of money being diverted online, then the Online Fraud squad becomes involved. But it can take a long time. There's so much of this stuff going on, they're overwhelmed. And when Lyn was murdered, they probably put the case to rest – unless one of her family members wanted it ongoing for some reason.'

'I don't think her son really knew about it.'

'Well, that's pretty common. There's a lot of shame involved in being the victim of a scam.'

Sally hesitated, then spoke. 'Can you find out for me, Brian? Like, maybe ask someone still in Fraud?'

'Yeah, I could make a few calls – just to confirm the process. Maybe, *maybe*, I could get someone to see how far your victim's case went, or if it's still active, although I seriously doubt that it is.'

In the background, Sally heard a woman cracking up laughing.

'What's going on down there?' she asked.

'Oshani's showing the others her fancy dress. There's some party they're having this weekend.'

'Oh.' Sally unpeeled a Mintie she'd found in the glovebox. She wondered what the costume was.

'You know,' Brian said, 'you could have done this yourself, Sally.'

'Yeah, I know, but I haven't been in the job that long, and if *you* ask someone, it's just . . . quicker.'

Brian didn't deny it, and there was a part of her that knew he liked being the fount of all knowledge.

'And what about your dad?' Brian persisted. 'In his new role, he could find out anything at the click of his fingers.'

'Angelo is not my dad.'

There was a pause. 'He considers you his daughter, Sally. You know that.'

'He didn't consider it much two years ago.'

'Come on, he'd just been made the Assistant Commissioner in Crime Command, and his ex-wife's ex-husband was arrested in the biggest drug haul in years!'

'Mum didn't know anything about it.'

'We know that. But Eddie Kiel had just been charged, and you know how the press likes to dig. Your mother and you would have been dragged into the mess.'

Sally snorted dismissively, even as she listened.

'The thing is,' Brian continued, 'and you *know* this, he had to distance himself from the two of you while the legal proceedings were taking place. He barely saw his other kids, either.'

Yeah, but his other kids weren't the offspring of Eddie Kiel. How often had she longed for Angelo to come and visit her then, to show everyone that *he* was her father, not Eddie, the ferrety man who befriended drug lords and bikies. The deadbeat dad who'd run off when she was only six, leaving her mother broken-hearted and broke. It would have meant so much to her if Angelo had acknowledged her publicly when he'd accepted the role of Assistant Commissioner. He'd thanked his partner and his two daughters Isabelle and Lucia – on television, no less. There'd been no mention of Sally, when *she* was just about to start her exams to become Senior Constable, the only one of his household to follow in his footsteps.

'He needed to protect you, Sally,' Brian went on. 'Eddie Kiel ran in dangerous crowds. We always try to protect the families of the accused.'

'Do we?' Sally thought briefly of Lex and his siblings.

Brian didn't answer.

Deep down, she knew that Angelo needed to protect her and her mother, of course she did. But at the time, it didn't make sense. Eddie's case wasn't a high-profile one. It was just one arrest among many two years ago, when a drug crime syndicate had been busted. From what she knew, Eddie wasn't even one of the kingpins. Just a loser with a modicum of charm. *Memo to self: never marry the handsome bouncer from the dodgiest club in town.*

Sometimes, at boarding school, Sally would dream of her real father coming to pick her up in a flash car, something a mob boss would drive – maybe a black Chrysler. The tinted window would glide down and Eddie, sitting in the back seat (because he had a driver), would say, 'Come for a ride, Sally,' and then she'd get in, and he would take her somewhere super fancy.

What a load of crap! She'd only ever seen him twice after he left: once when he'd come to the unit she shared with her mother, banging on the door, stoned and asking for money; the second time, when he'd turned up to her school unannounced and wearing boxer shorts, yelling through the iron fence that he had a present for her.

Her attention drifted back to her phone call. Brian was telling a joke about an Irishman and an Englishman. She'd heard it so many times, but she listened anyway. *Yeah, yeah, the same guy always loses out.* Finally, Brian assured her he'd call in a few days if he found out anything about Lyn's fraud case.

*

An hour later, Sally was sitting in a hairdressing salon in the city's east, watching as Brooke Arruda's friend, Mel, blow-dried the locks of a woman in a tight leopard-print dress. Mel was sorry that she couldn't stop for a break, but her client was a regular, desperate for a blow-dry. Would Sally mind talking while she worked? She only had a few minutes to go.

No, on the contrary, Sally was content to watch Mel do her thing while the pleasant buzz of female conversation filled the air. It was quite hypnotic.

'Sorry about Brooke's mum not wanting to talk to you.' Mel raised her voice over the hairdryer. 'Inez has really bad days, barely gets out of bed. Even before Brooke died, she got migraines, but after . . . Now she seems to get them every week. Poor Inez, she's been depressed for years. Sometimes when I go around there, she's that medicated she can hardly speak.'

It was a blow, not being able to talk to Brooke's mother, but when Mel had called to pass on the message, she had agreed to speak to Sally instead. She asked how Mel knew Brooke, then sat back and listened as the friendly stylist turned off the dryer and talked.

They'd been at hair and beauty school together, she said, before Brooke left to major in cosmetics. Brooke was funny, kind and generous. She loved animals and flowers and scented candles. She was a really good singer, she never forgot birthdays. Mel missed her every day.

'When was the last time you saw her?'

'Two weeks before? She'd been laying low, you know, with that business of the stalker.'

'Stalker?' Sally looked up in surprise.

'Yeah, celebrity stalker – they're so common. Brooke had been

146

on a really popular reality TV show, and ever since it finished, she thought someone was watching her.'

'In what way?' Sally shifted on her chair.

Mel stood back, studying her client's hair. 'She'd seen someone hiding outside her apartment block, and another time she came home after a night out and was convinced that someone had been in there.'

'Convinced?'

'Well, just a feeling, she said, that something was *off*. You know that feeling?'

'Yeah.' Sally nodded. Every woman knew *that feeling*, and probably quite a few blokes too. But *that feeling* wouldn't cut it in a police report.

'And then,' Mel said, 'after she went to the police, Brooke started receiving really threatening messages on her socials from fake accounts. *You think you're so good, bitch*, and *Ugly mole*, that sort of thing.'

'People are arseholes,' Mel's customer piped up.

The hairdresser nodded, and began spraying a perfumed mist all over her client's hair.

'You'd look so hot with a wispy fringe.' Mel was pointing at Sally with the hairspray can. 'No need to change your hair length, and it'd be perfect with the shape of your face.'

'Would it?' Sally asked, considering. She stroked the tight bun on the back of her head. Her hair was so long now. Yes, she needed a fringe.

Mel gave a final whoosh of spray all over the woman's head, and Sally breathed it in. One of the stylists walked past and asked if she'd like to try some hand cream; it was new and smelled heavenly. Sally held out her hand like a devotee and then rubbed in the pink cream. *God,* she thought, sniffing her hand dreamily then sinking back into her chair, *I could live here.* She saw herself as one of those cartoon characters, dazed and swooning with little birds flying in circles above her fringed head.

A young assistant sailed past them with takeaway coffees and then gave a shriek as she dropped one. The sudden crash made Sally sit up, and with a shock, she looked at the time.

'Well,' she said, 'thanks for answering my questions. I should get going.'

'No problem!' Mel smiled. 'And get a fringe!'

Sally listened to the radio and sang aloud to stay awake on the drive home. It seemed much longer than on the way there. Drab suburbs gave way to flat paddocks, then hills and then finally, as the landscape thickened and grew close, there was the long spine of the Great Dividing Range rising up in the east. As a child, Sally had, like most kids, drawn jagged points for mountains. But those were the mountains of Europe, imagined from fairy tales. Australian mountains weren't so dramatic or showy. The largest mountains usually had rounded, flattened tops, like an old man's head. On an information sign along the Razor trail, she'd read that was because Australian mountains were so much older than their European cousins, weathered down over hundreds of thousands of years.

She left a message on Pat's voicemail, then rang Jim, who said that he was just coming back down from the mountain and would see her later on. He'd had an interesting chat with a scientist from the Australian National University, who was carrying out a thirty-year study into dingoes in the High Country. She'd been up along the mountain, replacing the old cameras with new ones. The survey was going to be one of the biggest of its kind.

'There're video cameras up on the mountain?' Sally frowned. 'I didn't know that.'

'Yep – Parks Vic, universities and running fanatics wanting to document their times along the Razor to Alpine Road.'

'Right.' Sally's eyes flicked to the long line of mountains again. *Cameras in the bush?* 'Do you think they would have been there ten years ago?'

'I knew you'd ask me that,' Jim said. She could hear the smile in his voice. 'She told me the police requested any footage taken from cameras near the Precipice campsite at the time of the Mountain Murders.'

'And?' Sally held her breath.

'And . . . there were no cameras at that site. They don't put them where people camp – legal issues and all that.'

'Bloody hell!' Sally huffed, then told him about her day. How she'd driven all the way to Melbourne and back for apparently nothing. (Other than possibly getting a fringe.)

'When will you be home?'

'Under an hour.'

'We've got dinner at my parents', remember.'

'I remember.' She'd forgotten. 'My mum said she'd come too – don't know if she'll turn up, though.'

'Okay. Drive safe.'

She hung up and took the turn-off for the Alpine Road towards the mountains, into the shadows. Up there, dingoes roamed, as well as brumbies, pigs, deer and foxes. The cameras Jim had mentioned were interesting, and it reminded her of the photos Bill Durant used to take of campers, the ones that earned him the name 'The Creeper'. She remembered the images of the hikers on their last day, the ones by the pools; Brooke looking at her foot, Lyn and Russell chatting like old friends.

The images had made her feel queasy, because that same night all would be murdered . . . but it was more than that. There was something about the photos, *that feeling*. She'd need to look at them again.

She glanced at the clock: four forty. Her bum was sore from sitting down for so long. She was thinking about making a stop and stretching her legs when a Toyota Camry sped past, way too fast for this single-lane, country road. Automatically, Sally turned on the blue lights and drove after it along the straight stretch of road. Eventually the driver slowed and pulled over.

The Camry was battered and scraped along one side. She recognised the driver immediately. It was Blake Melus, who played footy with Jim and was a regular in the pub.

Thin and pale with a thick head of white hair, Blake was a cotton bud in human form. His crumpled brown T-shirt had 'Bundy's not a drink, it's a lifestyle' emblazoned across it. He was okay, she didn't mind him.

'Sorry, Blake, going to have to book you for speeding.'

'Aww, come on, Sally, you let me off last time.'

She had and regretted that now. When she'd been in Edenville less than a week, she'd let him off after they'd begun talking about her new job. 'Good to have a new cop in town,' he'd said. 'The last one was a prick, no one liked him.' And she'd succumbed, how stupid.

'Not this time, Blake,' she said, crisply. '117 k's in a 100 zone – it's pretty clear.'

'Well, fuck me,' he sneered with half a smile. 'The dancing queen's put her foot down.'

Her stomach lurched at the jab. 'Licence, please.'

'Geez, gone all serious all of a sudden, haven't you, Sal? Bit different when you've got a few wines under your belt.'

Sally jotted down his details, began writing up the report. She wasn't going to rise to it. 'If you have any further questions about the fine, call the number I've circled on this form.'

'I heard you fucked Disco at a party. Not so high and mighty then, were you, officer?'

Sally paused, then squinted down at the details she'd written. 'Hang on,' she said. 'I've made a mistake! I've written here that you were doing 117 k's in the 100 zone, but I've got it wrong, haven't I? You were doing 127. That's a $500 fine plus a loss of licence!'

Blake frowned. 'Hang on . . .'

Sally handed him the unchanged paper. 'You've got thirty days,' she said stiffly. 'And it's Senior Constable White.'

CHAPTER 21

Ten years earlier

To Kate's relief, the Precipice campsite came into view. Rarely used, it wasn't as well cleared as the others on the Razor, but its old hut and drop toilet were a welcome sight. It had been a hard afternoon's walk, and while Kate knew that the next day would bring relief as the hike ended, she could detect a vague sense of resentment from the group, as if it was her fault they'd had a rough afternoon.

And to be fair, it *was* her decision to make the shortcut, which meant the tiring few hours they'd just endured. Even though she was pleased that in a day's time she'd be back home with Ric, Kate couldn't help feeling a pang of guilt for the half-hearted way she'd handled this walk and the people on it. Even Brooke's blister – a few years ago, she would have spotted earlier that the young woman was struggling and asked about any soreness in her feet. She might even have taped up the girl's heels as a precaution.

Russell dropped his pack to use the toilet, and the rest of the group moved on. Kate picked up the man's pack and carried it the last two hundred metres to the campsite.

'Not bad.' Lyn gazed about her.

'You can look in the hut, but we won't be sleeping in it,' Kate said, throwing the two packs on the ground. 'They're usually full of rats.'

'I wouldn't want to sleep in that.' Brooke studied the old hut, with its broken window and crumbling chimney. 'It's got serial-killer vibes.'

Normally, Kate found the huts of the High Country charming remnants of days past, but in this fading light and coupled with her strange mood, she could see what Brooke meant.

'Let's check your foot,' Kate said to the younger woman, who nodded stiffly.

Russell wandered back into camp, and both he and Lyn began pulling tents out of their packs.

'How's it feeling?' Kate asked.

'Okay.' Brooke winced as she bent to unlace her boot.

The tape around the blister was brown with dirt. At Kate's urging, Brooke carefully removed it to reveal an oozing pink wound.

'I'll put some antiseptic on that.' Kate grimaced. 'Let it breathe a little.'

'What about our tent?' Brooke pointed to where Lyn was now laying it out, pegging the corners.

'I'll help her – you rest a bit.' Kate rummaged about in her pack for the medical kit, then carefully dabbed some antiseptic on the angry wound. 'Once I was walking in the Prom and saw a woman being winched up by a helicopter. I thought she must have broken a limb or something, but it was because of a terrible blister – she simply could not walk. Her husband was wild! They didn't have health insurance, and it was going to cost over five grand.'

'I'd love to have heard *that* conversation when they got back home,' Brooke grinned. 'But if she couldn't walk, she couldn't walk.'

'I feel for the poor bloke,' Russell chipped in, as he laid out the fly of his tent. 'You only get ten years for murder. Marriage is a life sentence.'

'What do you mean?' Kate had seen Russell's wife dropping him off at the start of the walk. 'You're married, aren't you?'

The fly was now over Russell's head, and he struggled within it like a ghost in a pantomime. 'Yes,' he said, hands flailing under the material. 'I'm afraid I am.' His head dodged this way and that as he thrashed under the nylon. 'Now, where's the front door in this thing?'

The women laughed uncertainly.

'Found it!' Russell's eyes peeked through a window.

'Well, you better get moving with it.' Lyn's eyes were on the sky. 'I just felt a drop of rain.'

CHAPTER 22

It was nearly dark when Sally turned into the main street of Edenville. Kyle, she knew, had already locked up for the day, so she was surprised to see a dusty red Mazda parked out the front of the station. For a brief second, she puzzled as to who it could be, before she remembered with a jolt of guilt. Her mother, Deb.

Sally got out her phone. Her mother answered just as she was about to give up.

'I'm at the supermarket, be there in a sec . . . hurrying now!'

Sally walked across the road and turned right to the IGA. It took her a moment to recognise her mother in the failing light, but then there was Deb, racing towards her, in a very clingy outfit.

'I've got the wine!' she called out from half a block away. 'It's local!'

They met and hugged, Deb holding on tightly. For the first time, Sally felt how fragile her mother was, how much thinner and smaller she was in comparison to her.

'It's great to see you, Mum,' she said, pulling away. 'I'm sorry I'm late.'

'My daughter, the policewoman.' Deb smiled, stepping back and studying her. 'I've told everyone about you being in the FBI.'

'That's American.'

'Well, that's what I say.' Deb grabbed her in for another quick hug. 'Country life suits you, Sally. Must be all the fresh air.'

Sally picked up two of the shopping bags, and they sauntered back to the station. Deb looked about her, bright and interested. 'Bet the tree-changers love it here.'

'They do.'

'And when they move here, it's to the *real* country, isn't it? Not like when my friends move to those cool towns a train trip from the city. I call those towns "HedgeYourBets".'

'Nothing wrong with that.'

'Oh, I know! I love those towns, but my friends shouldn't call themselves tree-changers. More like "suburb exchangers". But you, you've really moved . . .' She made her voice dramatic and low. 'To the *country*. Still, for all that, I couldn't live here.'

'Why not?'

'Too claustrophobic.' Deb tilted her head to the mountains. 'I like to know what's coming at me. Here you can't see a thing for the blasted trees.'

Later, after a dinner of roast chicken and then lemon cheesecake at the Brears' house, Deb joined Jim and his father in a game of cards, while Sally helped Marion load the dishwasher.

'Jim tells me you've been visiting Lex Durant?' Jim's mum said, as she rinsed off the roasting tray.

'Yes. It's the ten-year anniversary, and the Durants have been talking to the press. Harassment and stuff. Lex is even going around saying that Bill didn't kill those campers. That it was a corrupt investigation from the start.'

'Ahh, Bill – "The Creeper",' Marion said, using her fingers for quotation marks.

'Yeah, because he used to—'

'Creep around campsites,' Marion said dryly, 'and spy on the campers, yes – I've heard people say that.'

'You don't believe it?' Sally raised her eyebrows.

'No, it's not that I don't believe it – but honestly, have you heard the stories? It's as if every single camper on the mountain was spied on. Everyone has a tale about Bill Durant creeping up on them: lighting fires around their tent, pulling up tent pegs, taking photographs, appearing out of nowhere. Honestly, it must have been a full-time job for the man!'

The two women chuckled.

'I just think that he's become a bit of a myth,' Marion added. 'I'm not saying the stories are totally made up, but I do believe they are exaggerated.' She bent to load a tray beneath the oven. When she straightened again, her face was flushed pink. 'Menopause,' she said. 'It's the gift that keeps on giving.'

Sally poured her a glass of water, and then got one for herself. They stood leaning on the kitchen bench, drinking and listening to peals of laughter from the other room.

'My sister used to be a social worker around here,' Marion said after a while. 'I remember her telling me what her supervisors said about the Durant family, and what they found after the murders on the mountain.'

'What were they saying?' Sally took a sip of water. 'Lex is claiming there was some police harassment.'

'Oh, I have no doubt about that,' Marion said wryly. 'The police in the area – especially the ones who came back with tales of what they'd seen at the campsite – they were bursting with rage at Bill Durant, and they blamed it on the entire family, of course.'

'Do you know anything specific about that?'

'Sorry, not really. It's more hearsay – rocks through the windows, revving car engines late at night outside their home, pulling them up for no reason, that sort of thing. But remember, that was all happening *before* the murders too, after Robert Durant shot an officer back in the eighties.'

Sally looked through the window at the neat little garden outside, and the tidy stretch of road that ran directly through town. Big oak trees lined each side; the weatherboard houses were all glowing in soft light. *Such a lovely town,* she thought, *unless you're a Durant.*

'My sister – her name's June – she said that way back then, social services were more interested in the problems *within* the family.' Marion turned again to the sink, flicking on the hot water. 'She said that a school teacher had expressed concern over the two girls, I've forgotten their names . . .'

'Annie and Faith.'

'Yes.' Marion looked surprised that Sally answered so readily. 'Yes, that's right. Poor little things.'

'What happened to them?'

'After their mum died and their dad went to prison, the girls were looked after by their older brothers. Neil and Bill would have been in their early to mid-twenties, Lex probably seventeen or so? It didn't go so well.'

The laughter in the other room had died down, and a door slammed. Deb must have gone outside with Jim and his dad.

Sally picked up a tea towel and began drying the plates Marion was stacking in the dish rack. 'What do you mean?'

'There was a lot of drinking, probably drugs too. Fights, guns in the house – not a good environment.'

Sally thought about the old swing set she'd seen at the side of Lex's house. Warped and broken. Difficult to imagine the sisters playing on it. Impossible, even, to imagine children's voices within that house.

'Did they get taken away by social services?'

'Yes, apparently it was awful. The older brother, Neil, he was off his face on drugs – swearing and threatening the social workers and police. The girls were almost as afraid of him as they were of the people who were meant to rescue them.'

Sally had never been on such a call-out, but she could imagine it: the crying, the pleading, the screams.

'But you know,' Marion continued, 'the girls were placed in a nice home not too far away. I really do think they had a few happy years.'

'Faith died, though, didn't she?'

'Yes. Leukaemia. Poor little thing. She must have been only eight or nine. I swear, that family must have a gene for serious illness.'

Or tragedy.

'Jim has probably mentioned that I used to work at the pharmacy in town . . .' He hadn't. Sally nodded vaguely.

'Well,' Marion continued, 'Bill used to come in there regularly. I barely spoke to him, but it did make me think about genetics and illness. I should have studied science.'

Sally put down the dish she was drying. 'Why would Bill come into the pharmacy regularly?'

'Ondansetron,' Marion said.

Sally waited.

'It's a drug to help with nausea. For people undergoing chemotherapy.'

What?

'Hardly anyone knew it, but Bill Durant was a very ill man.'

The front door slammed again, and after a few seconds Jim poked his head into the kitchen. 'Just showed Deb the pizza oven. Now we're setting up the Monopoly board. Keen?'

'As mustard!' his mother declared.

'I know you can't stay much longer.' Jim looked at Sally. 'We'll just have a quick game.'

'Make Deb the banker then,' Sally grinned. 'We'll all go broke.'

Marion left to help them set up the board, while Sally slowly wiped the benchtops and folded the tea towel. Police probably didn't know about Bill's illness, she thought; there'd been no need for an autopsy, after all. Lex hadn't let on to her that he knew – but then, Sally remembered, Lex had left the Durant home to go and live on the coast. Perhaps not even his family was aware how sick Bill had been. And what did it really mean, that Bill had been having chemo before he died? Not much, she had to admit. It didn't change the facts as they stood, or that glaring DNA finding. It didn't change Bill's history of threatening to shoot people.

Yet how different it all was, Sally considered, to the case of Ric Barone, Kate's husband. The footy club had held a fundraiser for him when he was ill.

No fundraisers for Bill; not for a Durant.

It was only an hour later, when they were saying their farewells, that Sally remembered to ask Marion about the other sister, Annie.

'She fell off the radar,' Marion said, pausing to think. 'Although I did hear from someone that she'd had treatment for breast cancer.'

'That family must have had the worst luck in the whole world,' Sally said.

'Luck's got nothing to do with it,' Jim's father said.

Jim held Sally's hand tight as they crossed the front yard. 'Yeah. What goes around, comes around,' he said.

CHAPTER 23

Tuesday morning and Sally was up early. She went for a jog and came home to find her mother already packing to go. 'I've got a job interview!' she announced. 'At an old people's home, helping out with mealtimes and so forth.'

Deb would suit such a role, Sally thought. She was brisk and friendly and kind. But her mother rarely stuck at anything for long. She hoped this time it would be different.

'When are you renovating?'

'What?' Sally looked up, confused at the sudden change of topic. 'I'm not.'

'Why this then?' Deb was pointing to the envelope on the dining table, where Sally had written down the words she'd seen on the piece of paper in the alleyway. 'They're paint colours, aren't they? Warm and cool whites – I remember from my design course.'

'Really?'

'Whisper White, Snowy Mountains, Lexicon and Hog Bristle – they're all very popular.'

Sally picked up the envelope and stared at it in astonishment. 'Mum! You're amazing!'

'Yes, well,' her mother sniffed, pleased. 'I do know some things.'

'You sure do.' Paint colours. Now she thought about it, the four words weren't so interesting. The tantalising 'Lex' had hinted at darker things, but a cool white now looked more likely. A slim chance, ever so slim, that her attacker had reached for a tissue and then pulled out the note by accident, dropping it on the ground? She willed herself to remember the moments just before she'd fallen: a figure in her peripheral vision, quick footsteps as she lay stunned on the ground. *What else? Think!*

'Sally . . .' Deb hesitated as she zipped up her bag. 'I had a visitor last week, a not very pleasant one.'

'Who?' Sally was jolted from her thoughts.

'One of Eddie's friends, someone he knew from the nightclubs.'

A coil tightened in Sally's stomach. 'What did he want?'

'Nothing. In fact, he wanted to know if *he* could do anything for *me*.' Deb picked up her bag and began walking out to her car.

Following her, Sally realised she'd been holding her breath. 'Why are you telling me this? I don't care about Eddie.'

'Maybe, but he cares about you. He may not have always shown it, but he does.'

'Yeah, right.'

'He still calls you, doesn't he? Occasionally?'

'I never answer.' Whenever the number for the prison came up on her phone, she didn't pick up. In any case, it was rare that he called: two, maybe three times a year.

Deb opened the car door and threw her bag in. 'You should one of these days, Sally. It'd do you both good to talk.'

'He's still in jail, isn't he?' Sally closed her eyes, imagining Eddie rocking up to her station with his tatts and mullet. The town would have a field day. 'Please don't tell me he's out.'

'No, he's still in jail.' Deb pursed her lips. 'He's covering for someone, I just know it; I can't see him planning any of the big crimes he's accused of.'

He's not smart enough, for a start, Sally thought.

'Eddie may have been low on the crime gang's list,' Deb continued, 'but now that he's taking the hit for them, it seems his star is rising. I think his so-called friends on the outside want to let him know that they're looking after us in return.'

'I don't want anything from him or them,' Sally said in a rush. 'I don't want to hear anything about it – I'm a cop, remember? God! It's making me nervous even talking about this.' She looked around furtively, as if someone might be listening in.

'I know, I know.' Deb cleared her throat. 'Just watch yourself, okay? The guy said to call him if I needed anything, and I certainly won't be doing *that*.'

Sally leaned against the car bonnet, hunching her shoulders. 'Why did you ever, *ever* get involved with someone as dodgy as Eddie?'

Deb laughed. 'If I hadn't, you wouldn't be here.'

'I know *that*,' Sally said crossly. 'But you know what I mean.'

Her mother leaned forward on the bonnet beside her, looking down at her long thin legs. Sally's, in comparison, were short and strong, covered up by her sensible work pants.

'Eddie was a catch when I first saw him,' Deb admitted.

'Some catch.'

'I'm not talking money, more like charisma. He was so fun. Hilarious, really. You do have some of him in you, you know, the good bits. And he was a great dancer!'

Sally didn't say anything. Deb nudged her in the side with an elbow. 'Don't you like a man who can dance?'

Jim rarely danced. The few times she'd seen him break out the moves, it had been something cringey like the sprinkler.

'Anyway' – her mother wasn't finished – 'I just thought I should warn you. I'll tell Angelo too, just in case.'

'Right.' The father figures in her life! One lolling about in a cell, the other too busy fighting crime to contact her.

Deb caught her eye roll. 'Ange loves you, Sally.' She folded her long legs into the front seat of the car. 'I know we had a bad break-up, but he was so good for you. I mean, look at you now – an FBI agent!'

Deb blew her a kiss, and Sally stood on the road waving till she could no longer see her mother's old car.

There had never been any games of Monopoly or homemade cheesecake in her mother's childhood. Deb's single mother, Carla, had died of cervical cancer when Sally was three. To the young Sally, the words Cervical Cancer sounded kind of magical – like a brilliant constellation of stars. In fact, when she'd designed a huge poster in primary school of a starry night, complete with bursting Ovarian Cysts and Fertile Galaxies, and titled it 'A Night of Cervical Cancer!', her Grade Four teacher had had an earnest chat with her and rung up Deb. But now Sally remembered her mother loved that painting and had kept it above her bed for many years.

The day stretched ahead, warm but with a hint of rain. On her way to the station, Sally parked outside Therese's cafe and bought a takeaway coffee. Remembering that the owner always wrote a special note for Lex on the lid, she looked at hers, only to see a P on the top, which she guessed was for 'Police'.

'No note for you?'

Glen the school teacher was smiling at her as he lined up to order.

'None.' Sally grinned back. 'And I have to say, I'm devo.'

'Don't worry,' he said, feigning sadness. 'Therese once wrote "glasses" on my lid. It would have been quicker to write "Glen".'

'You can't win them all,' Sally said, smiling as she walked past him and out the door.

At the station, Sally reflected that she had only two more interviews to conduct: Russell Walker's wife, and his former colleague. Then, she was done.

Now, Sally sipped her coffee while she looked at the photos taken from Bill Durant's phone.

Why did he do this? The Creeper was a good name for someone who could move quietly through the bush without being observed.

Sally didn't know much about photography, but on second viewing she couldn't help noticing that the images, while disturbing, did not appear overly intimate. There was no lingering on faces, no close-ups, no focusing on one particular person. Rather, they were taken in a detached way, as if recording the numbers of a threatened species. Did that make them more or less scary?

The police and the media had jumped on the images as a sign that Bill Durant was stalking the hikers before he struck that evening. But now, in the weak morning light, Sally was looking at them through a new lens. *Bill was keeping a record*, she thought. *He's not fixated on the people themselves.* Only two photos, when looked at together, offered anything of real interest.

One was a shot of Kate, frowning in concentration, looking over her right shoulder. The other, taken a moment later, was of the back of her head as she leaned, peering or listening, into the bush. *Interesting.* At first, Sally thought perhaps Kate had heard Bill nearby – after all, the photos were taken at close range, perhaps from fifteen metres away. But then, Sally realised, Kate was looking in the *opposite* direction to where Bill must have been. She'd seen or heard something else out there in the bush.

What was it? Sally picked up the photos again: the first one with Kate's furrowed brow. The second of her looking into the trees. Was she imagining it, or did Kate appear fearful? The open mouth, the tension in her eyes.

Sally sat back, blowing air out of her cheeks. She stood up and stretched, took another look at the image, squared her shoulders.

She rang Pat.

'So, you think there were two people stalking the campers?' Her boss sounded incredulous. 'And based on what – a photo of the guide with her mouth half open?'

'Yeah, I mean, she looks as if she's seen something . . .' Sally's voice trailed off. Now that she studied the photos again, maybe she was imagining it. Maybe Kate had simply spotted an animal in the undergrowth. Or maybe she was just halfway through saying something. Maybe.

'Anything else to add, Sally?' Pat said, impatiently. 'I've got a meeting in two minutes.'

'Bill was taking medicine for chemotherapy.'

'Now *that's* interesting. How did you find out?'

Sally told him about Marion and the pharmacy.

'Still, doesn't change anything,' Pat said, echoing her earlier thoughts. 'If anything, it bolsters the whole case – Bill had nothing left to lose, so why not do the very thing you've been threatening to for years?'

'Bill was taking medication for cancer. He wanted to get better.'

'Right.' Pat sounded doubtful. 'What's next?'

'I'm about to visit the last of the relatives and friends – Russell Walker's. I didn't get to speak to Brooke's mother, and I haven't been able to get hold of Tom Evans' family in the UK.'

'Good, good, then after that maybe we can get back to normal. Any more word from Lex or Neil?'

'No.'

'Okay. Well, I'll be off. Remember, more facts like the chemo, and less of the guesswork.'

Sally hung up with that now all-too-familiar feeling of embarrassment, and looked out the window. Really, she didn't need to call Pat every time she had a hunch about something. Next time, she'd be more discerning, less excited by any random theory that occurred to her.

The door to the station opened and Kyle walked in, looking pleased with himself. 'I just got all ten right in the quiz on Mountain FM,' he said.

'Yeah?' Sally was impressed. She'd never scored ten. 'What was the last question?' It was always the most difficult.

'What was Madonna's first hit? I knew it because of my mum. It was "Holiday".'

'Good work. I would have said "Lucky Star".'

Kyle shrugged, modest. 'Yeah well, that would have been a fair guess too. So, anything you want me to do while you're gone?'

Sally considered what she needed. 'How are you going with those police harassment claims?'

Kyle looked down at his desk and spread out his hands. 'There's not that much, to be honest. The Durants claimed that the local

168

police stopped them loads of times, but there's no record of it. Looks like they were making a bunch of stuff up.'

Sally rummaged through her small backpack for her water bottle. 'Well, then maybe start looking into whether there were any other witnesses to the police treatment, like neighbours or whatever. If it's police harassment we're looking into, then we probably shouldn't just look at our own records.'

'Sure.' Kyle picked up a pen, scribbled something down.

If he was being sulky, Sally didn't have time to be annoyed. 'Also, a journalist by the name of Rob Gains may call. Give him nothing.'

'Yep.'

Kyle looked past Sally towards the photos of the victims she had placed on the pinboard above her desk. He pointed to Brooke. 'She was so good-looking, wasn't she? Mum remembers her from some reality show.'

'Yeah, Brooke was a bit of a celebrity.'

'Anyone'd die to be with someone like that,' Kyle murmured. 'What a loss.'

Only when she'd walked out of the station did Sally register that Kyle was thinking of her male fans and not Brooke, the murdered woman.

Heading down the Hume once again, Sally was stuck behind a caravan for what seemed like forever. It had one of those stickers of a family on it: a mother, a father and three children. *God*, Sally thought, *that looks like hell.*

One summer, during the time in between Eddie and Angelo, Sally and her mother had lived in a Jayco. Deb had played 'Walking on Sunshine' by Katrina and the Waves on loop, though the uplifting beat did little to hide the fact that they were in the back yard of one of Eddie's friends, and had to share a bathroom with three strange men who looked like the farmers in *Fantastic Mr Fox*.

Before she'd had the chance to knock, Sally saw the flick of a curtain and heard the heavy footsteps of someone hurrying to the door.

'I'm coming!' a voice said, excited. 'Just a sec!'

The door opened and Russell's widow, Donna Walker, stood there in the gloomy hallway, her face pale.

'Come in, come in,' she said. 'You must be Constable White. I've made cupcakes, do you like cupcakes? I didn't *make* them, I bought a packet – but you won't tell anyone, will you? Ha, ha, they're Betty Crocker, not White Wings.'

Sally followed Donna into a small living room. She was built like many middle-aged women: solid on top, thin legs, like a character from Mr Men.

'Have a seat! Have a seat!' Donna waved at her to sit down.

The Walker house was small and dark, with trinkets of cats, dogs and little shepherdess figurines holding staffs. A big television took up space below a print of a dewy English pastoral scene. A 'Bless this Mess' sign hung over a cabinet displaying plates and cups and saucers. It was designed to be cutesy and homely, but to Sally, the crowded room was overlaid with desperation born of loneliness.

'Sit here, sit here!' Thick gold bangles jangled on her wrist as the woman removed a cushion with three puppies embroidered on it. 'This is the comfy chair, a Jason Recliner. Do you want to recline in it? Russell used to practically live in this chair!'

Sally sat, and felt herself sink deep.

'It goes right back!' Donna exclaimed, and Sally was suddenly lying as flat as a board.

With another pull of the lever, Donna brought Sally back to a regular sitting position. 'We bought our chairs together from La-Z-Boy Furniture,' she said. 'He got this one, and I got that one.' She pointed to an identical chair on the opposite side of the room. 'They cost a fortune – but Russell always wanted us to be super comfy.'

'That must have been nice,' Sally said weakly.

After all the chatter, a heavy silence suddenly fell over the room. She felt all the eyes of the shepherd girls gazing down on them. 'Where did you and Russell meet?'

'Near here.' Donna's voice grew sad. 'We worked at the same cafe before he got his job in IT. It was just a little place, by the petrol station out of town. I didn't have a car, so he used to give me a lift. We were friends first.' Donna studied the puppy cushion. 'Then he asked me out, and it all went on from there. It was the happiest I'd ever been. We went to Niagara Falls and Disneyland Florida for our honeymoon.'

Donna's eyes rose to the mantelpiece, to a photo of the beaming new bride, standing beside a paddleboat wearing Minnie Mouse ears. 'Russell loved it there.'

'I can tell,' Sally said, although she couldn't really. In the photo, he was biting into a huge burger, his Mickey ears tipped to one side.

Donna's mouth opened, and for a moment Sally thought she might start crying. 'How could anyone do such a thing?' she asked quietly, still staring at the photo. 'Shoot someone while they slept. Russell never hurt anyone! Everyone liked Russ, everyone!'

'I'm so sorry, Donna.' Sally glanced down at the carpet. 'I know it must be difficult for you to talk about all of this, but we're just looking at a few things related to the investigation.'

'Why?' Donna gazed at her sadly. 'Is there anything new to add?'

'Not at this stage.'

'So why are you bothering? What good will it do?'

'We're looking into a few items of interest. There's some links we've discovered.'

'Links?'

'Nothing firm,' Sally hastily added. 'Just crossing all our Ts.'

Donna reached for a tissue on the mantelpiece and blew her nose long and hard. 'Well, whatever you're doing, I'm glad the man who murdered Russ killed himself. I know that's bad, but I am!'

Sally waited, till the other woman collected herself. 'You dropped Russell off for the walk, didn't you?' she asked, gently.

'Yes, I drove him all the way there, up that mountain. He was going to get a lift back home with the walking company.'

'And how did he seem then?'

'Excited – happy!' Donna said, shaking her head in confusion. 'He was looking forward to a few days away from . . .'

An uncomfortable beat followed.

'Away from what?'

'Just from his work and the city and, you know . . . it's so busy, and you hardly get time, and sometimes you need to clear your head and . . .'

'Donna.' Sally put it as delicately as she could. 'Was Russell maybe a little bit *unhappy* when he left?'

The widow's cheeks sucked in and out. 'I don't know.' She took one of the figurines and stared mournfully at it. 'He'd been moody in the weeks before the hike. I tried asking him about it, but he wouldn't tell me anything. I kept quiet, because you know how men like to go into their man cave sometimes.'

Sally nodded, while thinking, *No*.

'But then, as we were driving up that mountain, Russell said that maybe he'd like a bit of a break. Not a separation or anything, but a bit of a break. I've never told anyone this before, but you being here and so kind, and it's been ten years, and – yes. Russ mentioned a bit of a break.'

'Oh.' Sally didn't know what to say. She'd never read this anywhere.

'I didn't know what to do when he said that. I mean – it's Russell! I'd been with him since I was twenty-five! I just said, "Russ, speak to me, you can tell me anything," but he never said a word. And you know what? I think that maybe he was just stressed at work and the walk was going to do him good. When I got home that night after dropping him off, I was sure everything was going to be okay. I thought I might book us a cruise as a surprise for our anniversary. But I never did, of course.'

The heaviness in the air was alleviated somewhat by a soft whirring coming from the corner of the room. A black disc began humming its way towards Sally.

'Ahh!' Donna rallied. 'It's my robot vacuum. I program it to start like this every day.' The little thing buzzed underneath Sally's chair, and she lifted her feet to accommodate it.

'I got it two weeks ago.' Donna smiled fondly at the thing. 'It's the newest model, the Powervac, but I like to call it RoboCop as a joke. Isn't that funny?'

Sally watched as the disc barrelled dangerously towards the cord of a lamp. The disc hesitated for a moment before turning in another direction.

'Yes, very funny,' Sally said. 'I might have to get one.' She never would.

'I don't know if I made the right decision,' Donna said vaguely, sad again. 'Agreeing to go back to the Razor on the anniversary. But the other lady was so nice about it.'

'The other lady?' Sally felt a thud in her chest.

'Laura Wynter. The girl who was there that night, the one who survived it – she's asked for a representative from each family to go back there this weekend. But I don't know if I'll make it. I'm not as fit as I once was.'

Given Donna's elastic-waisted tracksuit pants, slippers and oversized jumper, Sally didn't doubt it. She'd spotted an asthma pump in between the shepherdess figurines. But then again, she reminded herself, you never could tell. She'd done the City2Surf run in Sydney three times and was always amazed at the people who finished. You could look out of shape, but that didn't mean you had no grit.

Sally stood and dusted off the crumbs from her cupcake.

'Would you like another one?' Donna jumped up too. 'I can't eat them all on my own!'

'No, thank you,' Sally said, moving to the door.

'I wondered . . .' the woman started, and then stopped. 'I thought that maybe before you left, you'd like to look at some photos of Russell? It might help with your investigation? I've kept them all, even the ones his mother gave me from when he was a baby. He was adorable! A real cheeky little mite.'

Sally hesitated. She had another interview and the long trip back. It wasn't particularly enjoyable to drive along country roads at night. And baby photos! How would they advance her case? But Donna's face . . .

'Sure,' she said, relenting. 'I'd love that.'

'Well, sit, sit! I'll bring out the albums.'

With a deep sigh, Sally sunk back into the Jason Recliner and waited.

It was a full hour before she finally managed to exit the house. She stood outside, took a deep breath and turned to wave to Donna, who was smiling at her from the front window. She wondered briefly at the firmness of the woman's love for her murdered husband, whose last words to her were about wanting a 'break'. Was Russell planning to leave Donna entirely? And if so, what exactly did that mean for her investigation?

She walked to her car and sat in it for a moment, thinking about the Walkers.

There was another thing bothering her. Donna had said that Russell had been shot in his sleep. Was that what the police had told her? Sally knew that Russell was bludgeoned first, then shot. At least, that's what she'd read in the report. Why tell the widow something different? She knew that there were conflicting reports about the murders, particularly in the days afterwards, when the press got hold of the story. So what was the truth?

She called Brian in Melbourne, asked him if he knew anyone in Forensics who'd be willing to shed some light on the Mountain Murders.

Her old mate cleared his throat. 'Leah Haigh might know about it. She was in Investigations a decade ago and was always interested in that case. She's in Forensics now.'

'Leah Haigh!'

'Yeah,' Brian said, swallowing his cough lozenge. 'The very same.'

Sally knew Leah as brusque, awkward in groups. Not many people were fans of her, sometimes calling her 'Loosen Up Leah' behind her back. But Sally found her nice enough, and the more experienced police officer had never minded answering Sally's many questions when she was brand new in the force.

'Can you give me her number?'

'Sending it through now. I'll give her a heads up you'll be calling – you know she doesn't like to be surprised.'

Sally thanked him and hung up, then drove the short distance to a decidedly unlovely park, where she got out and stretched her legs. Keeping her eye on a group of teenage boys who had taken over the playground and were joyously swearing, Sally drank the rest of her water and called the number Brian had sent through.

'Leah!' Sally said, warm. 'How are you?'

'Good.' Leah's voice was as flat as a pancake. She was never one for small talk.

'Fuck you!' one of the boys called in a sing-song voice.

'No, fuck *you*!' the other boy called back.

'Great, great.' Sally cupped her hand over the phone to block out their noise. 'So, did Brian tell you what I've been doing? I'm looking into the Mountain Murders, just double-checking things so the media can't jump on us for any reason come the weekend.'

'Right.' Leah wasn't buying it.

'Dick*head*!'

'Wank*er*!'

Sally got back into her car and shut the door. 'And because I think there's a few things that weren't looked into properly, details that could reflect poorly on the original investigation.'

'Yes?' Now Leah sounded interested. She was, not surprisingly, a stickler for the rules.

'I don't think we ever looked at anyone aside from Bill Durant. I'm not saying that he didn't do it, but due diligence and all. The victims and their families weren't even investigated properly.'

'That's because of the DNA.'

'Yes, but you know – *you know*, Leah, that we need more evidence than that to secure a conviction.'

'I do.' Leah sniffed. 'Of course. What questions did you have?' She wasn't giving anything away. 'I might know a few things.'

'Brian told me that. He said you knew a lot about the case.'

'So, what do you want to know?'

'Well, I'm sure I read that Russell was murdered more viciously than the others, that he was hit with a hammer as well as being shot. Is that true? If so, I'm wondering whether that's because he was the only male present at the campsite.'

'Besides Bill Durant, the accused.'

'Yes, besides him.'

'There was the student too, Tom.'

'But he was killed further up the track, wasn't he? He was separate from the hiking group.'

A short pause.

'Have you read much about the crime scene?' Leah's voice was calm, efficient.

'Only the report that everyone received.'

'Right. The forensic one contained more detail.'

'Can you tell me about it? Please, Leah?'

'I brought up the report and my old notes, when Brian told me you might call. You'll probably know most of it.'

'That's okay.'

Leah exhaled. 'So, according to the report, local police first found the bodies of Tom Evans and Brooke Arruda along the trail leading to the campsite. Both had been shot: one in the chest, one in the head. They were killed instantly.'

'Have you got the names of the officers there?'

In the background, Sally could hear a flipping of pages. Leah was back on the line. 'Senior Sergeant Patrick Kennedy from Wexton police station and Sergeant Paul Cornell.'

Patrick Kennedy? Sally's mouth fell open, and for a few seconds she was unable to speak. Her boss, Pat?

'Sally? Are you there?' Leah asked, impatient.

'Yeah, I'm here.' She put Leah on speaker and began jotting notes into her phone. The revelation about Pat would have to wait. 'What about the scene at the campsite, what can you tell me about that?'

'Lyn and Kate had both been shot: Lyn in her chest, Kate below the shoulder and on her right side. She bled to death and was found in a seated position, leaning against a gum just outside the circle of tents. Lyn was in her tent, half in her sleeping bag. Russell had been bludgeoned in the face with the butt of the rifle, not a hammer, and shot in the back of the head. He was half out of his tent.

'Next,' Leah continued, 'police located the body of Bill Durant, a 30-30 beside his right hand, shot in the side of the head. He was situated on the top of the small crest overlooking the campsite and the trail. He had a knife wound to his thigh, later found to be from Kate Barone's pocketknife that was discovered a few metres from her body.'

'I did not know that.' Sally shook her head.

'We always keep some details hidden. It was only since I started working in Forensics that I learned it all.'

Sally wrote down what she'd heard.

'The victims were all found to have been shot by a 30-30 rifle, which was then traced to Bill Durant's father, long since deceased. But interestingly, *Bill's* registered gun was never found.'

'Yes, Bill's brother Lex says that Bill favoured the 30-06.'

'It's more powerful, has a longer range. But what's also interesting is that a 30-30 is difficult to shoot on target when you're on the move, and when you're at any sort of distance. It's why police assumed that the victims were all killed at close range.'

'It that what you assume too?'

'I don't assume anything.'

Sally was quiet for a moment. 'And then there was the DNA. The report I read had very little detail on that.'

'Yes,' Leah said. 'Traces on Russell's cheek, near Kate Barone – presumably from the wound on Bill's leg – and on the pocketknife.'

'Leah,' Sally asked tentatively, 'do you think it is possible that someone else, other than Bill, did this? It's just that I've been talking with Lex Durant, and it doesn't seem to make sense. None of it. Everyone just jumped on Bill.'

'DNA evidence tends to make cops do that.'

'Yeah.'

'Sally.' Leah's voice was surprisingly gentle now. 'Some cases don't seem to make sense. Sometimes, you just have to let the evidence speak for itself.'

'I get that. But what did the crime scene *look* like? I'm trying to imagine it. I mean, from what you said, it sounds sort of chaotic.'

'Well,' Leah said. 'You tell me.'

Sally took a breath. 'The way Lyn and Kate were shot, that sounds like it was business, quick. And Brooke, she was killed because she was getting away, and Tom was just in the wrong place at the wrong time. But Russell – why bash him in the face then shoot him? That's strange.'

'I agree. Homicide looked into that. They were told that Bill Durant was often aggressive with males. He wasn't averse to fighting, no matter how large the opponent. And maybe Russell was threatening to put up a fight.'

'What, with a tent peg?'

'I'm just telling you what I've read.' She pictured Leah holding her palms up in protest.

'Thanks.' It sounded more gruff than she meant it to. 'You've been a real help, Leah.'

'No problem.' The older cop hung up before Sally could say any more.

'Loser!'

'Idiot!'

The two boys were back at it again, even more boisterous.

'Hey, boys!' Sally wound down her window. 'Cut out that language! And it is not nice to talk to your friends like that!'

'Friends!' The boys fell about laughing. 'We're not friends! We're brothers!'

CHAPTER 24

Focused Solutions IT was a small company based in Melbourne's CBD. A bored receptionist pointed Sally to a dark corner of the open-plan office, where a man named Ashley Peetz was shovelling down a chocolate bar while staring at a screen. Sally introduced herself and asked if it was a good time to talk.

'Yeah, it is,' he said. 'I'm on a break, so we can talk but, just so you know, I'm keeping an eye on this chess game. Pablo from Barcelona here's trying to pull a new one on me . . .'

Sally squinted at his screen, where a horse jumped across a chess board. 'Are you actually playing with a man from Spain?'

'Yeah, and he's . . . wait a sec . . .' Ashley ran his fingers over the keyboard, then gave a cheer. 'Classic error!' He shook his head with a grudging smile. 'He never learns.'

'Do you know him?' Sally screwed up her face.

'Nope.' Ashley sat back with a satisfied expression. 'Could be a twelve-year-old girl from Bacchus Marsh, who knows? But he *says* his name is Pablo, so that's what I call him.'

'Okay, well, as I explained on the phone, we're just going over the original investigation into the Mountain Murders.'

The man swivelled around in his swing chair and held his hands up in mock protest. 'It wasn't me, officer!' he said in a bad Cockney accent. 'I swear on me poor old mother's life!'

Cringe.

'So how would you describe your friendship with Russell – did you know him well?'

'Yes, I suppose.' The man shrugged. 'He was the sort who kept to himself. But we did play the occasional game of golf together, you know' – he grimaced – 'in a company-sanctioned outing.'

'Did he ever say anything that might indicate he had enemies?'

'Enemies? What – are we in Grade Three?' Ashley gave a brief laugh.

That's rich, Sally thought. *When you're playing computer games.*

'Well, was Russell on unpleasant terms with anyone, or say he was frightened at all?'

'No! From what I saw, he was just beginning to wake up and live. He was married, you know.'

There was something unpleasant about the man's smile.

'What do you mean by "just beginning to wake up"?'

'Marriage, it's a jail sentence.'

'So, you're married?'

'Nope. Never. I like my freedom.'

In other words, no one will have you.

Ashley shook his head at the screen and then typed at a furious pace, half smiling as he did so. After a minute, he sat back in his chair and clasped his hands behind his head. Sally immediately stepped away. His underarms were wet with sweat, and he reeked of BO.

'Russell showed me something before he left.' Ashley jiggled his eyebrows. 'And let's just say, the man was seriously punching above his weight. Gives hope to the rest of us: dreams can come true and all that.'

Sally looked around. There was only one other man in the room, headphones on and head down, typing steadily. 'What did Russell show you?'

'A photo on his phone. It had been sent to him – one of those Snapchat images which disappear in a few seconds, but he was smart enough to take a screenshot before it went. He sent it to me.'

'You didn't keep it, did you?' It was a long shot, but why not ask? Sally had photos on her phone from years ago. Maybe not ten years ago, but three at least.

'Not on my phone, I wouldn't,' he said. 'But my photos transfer to the cloud, and I've got a load of storage space, so yeah – I might have it.'

Sally tried to keep her voice casual. 'Okay. Well, it'd be great if you could have a quick look, just while I'm here.'

The man was already clicking at his laptop with the skill of a concert pianist.

'When Russell got killed, I went back and read all of his texts, all of his work emails, like I was trying to find a clue or something. I mean, who would want to murder Russ? He was about the most ordinary bloke in the long, bland history of ordinary blokes.' He gave a short laugh, clearly not placing himself in that category. 'After a few weeks, I couldn't even remember what Russell looked like, he was that ordinary. Ah, here we go!' The man was holding out his hands in a 'ta da!' gesture to the screen. 'Found it.'

Though Sally's contact lenses weren't the best, even she could tell that the woman on the screen was drop-dead gorgeous. Long brown hair thrown back, coy smile, mouth open slightly as if to say, *Hello, you.* She was clearly a model, or an aspiring one – the way she tilted her chin slightly forward, elongating her neck in a typical catalogue pose; the designer active wear; the soft lighting.

'I know, right?' Ashley was staring at the screen. 'Lucky man, eh?'

Sally was taken aback. He actually believed that *this woman* would be interested in Russell Walker?

'Who knew old Russ had it in him, eh? She probably thought he was loaded.'

'And was he?' Sally asked. Her dislike for Ashley Peetz was deepening by the second.

'Not on the wage here, he wasn't. And not judging by his golf clubs. Man must have had something though.'

Sally took a photo of the woman on the screen. The whole situation rankled. 'Did you share this image with anyone else?' she asked him before she left.

Ashley tapped the side of his nose with his stubby finger. 'What happens on the golf course stays on the golf course.'

'Right.' Sally looked at him with distaste.

The man turned back to his computer, flicking it onto another screen. In the reflected light, his face appeared eerily robotic.

'Ahh!' He brightened. 'Pablo's back!'

CHAPTER 25

An alert on her phone reminded her: it was the football/netball do tonight. *Bloody hell!* An evening on the couch was all she longed for, but the motto of the club was 'Never Tire, Never Die', and she must rally to the cause. Jim rang to let her know he'd meet her at the sports hall; he needed to check on some minor flood damage on a road out of town. She told him about Ashley and his creepy online behaviour, and about Donna and the little figurines that dotted her lounge room.

'. . . and she literally wanted to marry her Jason Recliner,' Sally said, as she unlocked her front door and hurried into her house.

'Maybe we should get a matching pair of them when I move in,' Jim suggested.

'Yeah, let's. We can eat dinner from trays every night while we watch TV,' Sally answered.

'Wish we were doing that tonight,' Jim grumbled. 'I sort of can't be bothered going out.'

'Never Tire, Never Die, Jim,' Sally said, scanning her wardrobe. 'See you there.'

*

Now, having shed her staid work clothes, Sally was done up in low heels, blue wide-leg pants, a tight blue top and, after a moment's deliberation, one of her favourite jackets, a glittery, silvery number that had cost her a fortune.

The club was already busy, the car park full. Edenville's finest poured into the clubrooms, greeting one another, chatting.

Sally found a spot on the deck, which overlooked the oval, now brightly lit as if it was the MCG.

'New lights,' said a voice behind her. 'Council paid for them. Flash, aren't they?'

Sally turned. It was Lorraine Caruthers, their netball team's long-time manager.

There was a plaque on the wall downstairs dedicated to Lorraine and her husband Neville for all the work they'd done for the football/netball club over the years. It was people like the Caruthers who helped to keep towns like Edenville alive. They ran committees, were volunteers in the Country Fire Authority; they sold tickets for prizes of trailers of wood outside the IGA; they visited old neighbours; they were serious about Tidy Towns.

The two women gazed over the hallowed ground of the oval to the Razor in the background, dark against the brilliant lights.

Lorraine looked up at the mountain. 'It always reminds me of those terrifying teachers who used to bend over to look at your work when you were in Prep.'

Sally gave a short laugh in recognition.

'Up in Western Queensland, where I worked years ago,' Lorraine mused, 'they'd muster cattle in aircraft. You could fly over thousands of acres up that way, everything laid out bare; the gullies, the river systems, the gorges. It's all visible. Took me a while to get used to it again down here, having the mountains all around, the chilly nights. I used to feel suffocated.' They stared into the night. In a certain light, with the moving clouds and the deepening skies, the mountain appeared as if it was pressing in.

Behind them, people were filing in and taking their seats around circular tables decorated with white tablecloths. A trophy sat in the centre of each one, depicting a player from earlier times. Sally checked her phone. 'How long do you think this'll go for, Lorraine? I've got to get a heap of stuff done for work.'

The woman cocked her head. 'Shouldn't take more than two hours, at least it better not. There's a *Jack Reacher* on the telly.' She fanned herself down, big mouth wide open. 'I love Tom Cruise, all his movies, every one, just love 'em.'

'Yeah?' Sally only knew *Top Gun*, and only because her step-father liked to quote from it so much.

'Oooh yeah.' Lorraine affected a swoon. 'When that man moves . . . I tell you, I could go home, turn on *Mission Impossible*, and watch Tom Cruise run till the end of days.'

'A true fan,' Sally managed, laughing hard.

Lorraine nodded, gave a wicked grin, then pointed to a figure walking below them towards the clubhouse. 'But seriously, once the awards are handed out and Her Grace there has finished speaking, we'll be allowed to go.'

'Her Grace', in this case, was Norma Kerns, the longstanding president of the football/netball club. A former champion of the netball team and winner of countless Best Player awards, she was someone to be respected. And feared. The old president, bent over and thin as a fishhook, moved across the oval at speed, her face grim with determination.

'Tough old bird,' Lorraine said, sucking on her Ventolin. 'Believe it or not, before her shoulder, she was the best Centre we ever had. She was known as "Stormin' Norma" back then.'

'How are you, Sal?' It was Cara, the current Centre and undisputed leader of their team, who'd sneaked up behind them. 'Excited to be at your first Edenville sports event?'

'Sure! And you'll win every award, Cara,' Sally said. 'They should just give them to you now.'

'Oh, I don't know.' Cara raised her eyebrows. 'Our new player had been pretty good this season.'

'That's true,' Lorraine agreed, and the two women smiled kindly at Sally. 'Best Wing Attack we've had for years.'

Norma had now made her way into the room, and the crowd parted for her as she approached the microphone. The stragglers began taking their seats.

'Is Jim coming?' Cara asked, searching around the room.

'He said he would, but you know Jim – he'll be busy dragging roadkill off some track somewhere.'

'Well, sit with us. Lorraine, there's a spot for you too.'

Sally followed them towards Cara's table. There sat Disco, looking up expectantly at Cara, and Sally felt the sharp embarrassment she suffered every time she saw him.

'I know you kissed him,' Cara whispered to her from side-on as they put their coats behind their chairs. 'Don't worry about it! We weren't together then.'

'I was with Jim though.'

'Barely. Come on, it's a small town. Everyone's kissed everyone at some stage.'

'Okay.'

'I kissed Jim once.'

'Did you?' The women sat down.

'Yeah – when we were sixteen. It's why I don't drink Southern Comfort any more. His breath, my god it was terrible!'

They both laughed.

'I'm getting a drink.' Disco stood, thankfully unaware of what they were saying. 'You girls want one?'

'I'll have a Savvy B please, love,' Lorraine said.

'Me too.' Cara turned to Sally. 'Sal, you? Or would you prefer a whiskey?'

'I'm fine with a wine.' She grinned. 'Thanks, Disco.'

He nodded pleasantly and turned to the bar. He wasn't one to feel shame.

'Anyway, he's kissed *everyone*!' Cara said fondly, watching him leave. 'Has Disco kissed you too, Lorraine?'

'Not as yet,' Lorraine answered. A screech from the speakers up front made them turn their heads. Norma was standing beside a lectern, tapping into the microphone, then cupping a hand behind her ear and nodding once she saw that people could hear.

'Here we go,' Lorraine whispered out of the side of her mouth.

A clearing of the throat and then, in a stern voice, Norma welcomed everyone to the evening. She read out a list of the wins and losses for the season and said, without any hint of warmth, that she hoped sincerely they'd all do better next year.

'Kill me!' Cara whispered. 'I feel like I'm in school again.'

Sally smothered a laugh and leaned back, happy. The evening was proving to be far more enjoyable than she'd imagined.

One man was given a lifetime award for dedication to the club, and the crowd hushed as he began talking. After ten minutes of thank yous, Norma told the old man that enough was enough, and snatched back the mic.

Lorraine sipped her drink and gestured towards the stage, where Norma was holding court. 'Looking at the two of you' – she shook her head – 'you couldn't be more different.'

It was an odd thing to say. Sally shrugged, and pulled a plate of chicken and vegetables towards her. 'Well, yeah. Norma's like seventy, and I'm twenty-four.'

'No, not that – as police officers, you couldn't be more different.'

Sally paused a second. 'Was Norma in the police force?'

'Ha, yes! Was she ever. One of those people who lived for the job.'

Norma *did* have the look of an old cop about her: slightly grizzled, a hard edge.

'She was shot actually,' Lorraine went on. 'That's why she left.'

'Oh!' Sally sat up straight, making the connection. 'By Bill Durant's father?'

'Yes, that's right. He got her in the shoulder – notice how she's kind of imbalanced on one side? Still fit as a fiddle though.'

They looked at the older woman. Rather than a fiddle, Sally thought that Norma was more like a rusty bit of wire you find in the yard, bent but lightweight and strong.

'She was the boss of the station back then,' Lorraine continued. 'Ruled the roost.'

'Who else did she work with?'

'Well, let's see . . . There would have been Paul Cornell – he's in a retirement home now, early onset dementia. And poor old Harry Pickett too.'

It took a moment to register. *Harry Pickett.* The old farmer who'd shot himself and left the note for his wife?

Lorraine caught the look on her face. 'Yep, Harry. He was a policeman there for a while, went back to farming after Norma left the force.'

Sally considered Lorraine for a moment. 'You must know everyone around here.'

The woman shrugged and ate a chip. 'Most. Not all.'

'Did you go to primary school with Bill Durant?'

'He was younger than me, but yes, I did. And Neil too.'

'What were they like?'

'I could hardly say! They were very rarely there.' Lorraine shook her head and shovelled some more chips into her mouth. 'When they did come, it'd be without shoes on half the time, poor kids. Mostly they didn't last a whole day before being asked to leave again for bad behaviour.'

In the background, Sally could see Disco weaving his way towards them with the drinks. Like a lot of people, he'd been trapped at the bar, too scared to move once Norma started speaking. Now, with the formalities over, a relaxed mood settled over the clubroom.

By the time Sally had finished her meal, the music was starting up, and a few people were beginning to dance. Cara was talking to a footballer named Kooka Gee. Kooka had a laugh like a kookaburra; it was kind of legendary. When he laughed, Kooka threw back his head, and his lips came together in a circle, beaklike.

The crowd was growing boisterous, and a few people called for her to do the Cossack – she hurriedly shut them down. 'Work,' she said vaguely. 'I have to get to work.' And she really did, despite the fact that Jim had not yet turned up. The talk about Neil and Bill Durant made her itch to look deeper.

Collecting her jacket and bag, she said some brief goodbyes and sneaked out of the hall.

At the top of the steps, Blake Melus was leaning against a wall. 'Paid that fine you gave me.'

'Good for you.' Sally pushed past him and started walking down the steps.

'Think you're a fucken star, don't you?'

'What was that?' She turned, narrowed her eyes.

'I *said*' – Blake ran a hand through his white hair – 'you think you're a *bloody star*.'

'Sally!' Out of the darkness, Jim appeared, and she hurried down the rest of the steps towards him.

'I'm just heading off,' she said, deciding to ignore Blake. 'I've got heaps of work to do.'

'Sorry, Sal, I got held up. Want me to come home with you?'

'No, you stay and have fun. The music's just started.'

In the background, Kooka set off one of his raucous laughs. Jim grinned and gave her a kiss on the top of her head. 'All right ... although you look so hot I'm thinking of coming with you anyway.'

'Yeah, yeah, right. Now *go*.' She pushed him towards the entrance.

At the door, he turned around. 'You right to drive?'

'Yep.' Sally didn't like how Jim looked at her closely when he asked that. 'I've only had two wines.'

'Okay.' He blew her a kiss, and walked inside and out of sight.

Sally climbed into the front seat of her car. The car park was still packed; no doubt responsible people would be getting lifts home. She hoped she wouldn't have to attend some accident in the night: an easy-to-miss turn on these dark roads after a couple of wines ... How many had she had? Two? It might have been three. *Yes,* she thought, *it was three. Come on, you knew it was three.*

As the resident policewoman, she knew she should not be driving, and it was only a short, twenty-minute walk home – five minutes on the main road, and then she could skip onto the side track that ran to the back of her house. She had her phone with the torch on it: easy. It wasn't even that cold.

Once on the dark lane she began a brisk walk, wishing that she'd brought her runners so she could have swapped. Lucky she wasn't wearing her blue suede high heels – she'd *nearly* worn them.

The night air was growing chilly now. She reached into her bag and put on her fancy jacket. The light from her phone bobbed about in front of her, uneven. From somewhere in the bush to the left, an owl barked, its low *woop-woop* making her jump. *God,* Sally thought, *what's to be afraid of out here? It's just a country road.* For a second, the image of Neil Durant holding up a pretend gun came to mind, and she banished it. *Woop-woop.* That bloody owl.

Ignoring a growing sense of unease, she took the dirt track option that cut off a quarter of an hour. She'd be home in no time.

She was soon regretting her decision. The track was narrow, full of potholes and puddles. The trees stood thickly on each side, touching in parts overhead, giving the impression that she was walking into a dark tunnel. Hurrying on, she was stopped in her tracks when a high rasping sound behind her made her turn sharply.

A torchlight shone directly at her, and she held a hand to her eyes. 'Who is it?' she asked, more wildly than she meant to. 'Who is it?!'

'It's me!' Lorraine Caruthers twisted her phone to show herself, her face looking big and ghostly in the torch's beam. 'I was driving home and saw a light bobbing along this track and thought it must be you, seeing as your car's back at the clubhouse. I was worried something was wrong. Thought you might need a lift. Come on, my car's just back there, didn't want to drive over the potholes.'

Sally relaxed. 'Thanks, Lorraine. I'm really okay, but you know what? A lift would be great.'

As they walked back towards Lorraine's car, the older woman started telling her about her time in the CFA. So absorbed was she in the story that when she first saw the headlights, Sally didn't feel afraid.

'That's odd . . .' Lorraine said, squinting, as the vehicle drove towards them. 'It's going very slow.'

They kept walking along the edge of the track, Lorraine speculating that it was probably someone who'd taken the wrong turn and was now looking for a way to get back to the main road. It happened all the time, she said.

Sally squinted. 'Has it stopped?'

The car, not one hundred metres in front of them, appeared to be just sitting in the middle of the track.

A lost tourist maybe, looking for the mountain road? Or someone who'd left it a bit late to find a camping spot?

The vehicle's engine revved, once, twice, then roared to life. And suddenly, the car was bearing straight down on them, blinding them.

'Jesus!' Lorraine shouted. 'Slow down!'

The car did not slow; if anything, it seemed to speed up.

'Jump!' Sally screamed over the din. 'Now!'

But Lorraine seemed frozen to the spot, and at the last moment, Sally hurled herself at her and pulled them both into a ditch at the edge of the bush.

The car sped on down the track at full speed.

In their muddy hollow, the two women collected themselves as best they could.

'You're bleeding,' Lorraine said, breathless, shining the light into Sally's face.

There was a cut on her cheek from where she'd hit the stones as they fell. She touched it and held out her bloody fingers under the torchlight.

'So are you,' Sally said after a pause, her heart still thumping.

Lorraine's forearm was dripping blood.

'What happened just then?' Lorraine fished a handkerchief out of her pocket to wipe her arm, as Sally stumbled back onto the main road and checked her phone signal. Faint but enough. She got through to Jim, asked him to meet them. His voice on the other end was tired, then anxious as she explained what had happened. He wanted her to stay on the line, but she hung up, suddenly exhausted.

'You'll miss the Tom Cruise movie,' Sally said vaguely, peering into the trees.

'I don't care.' Lorraine climbed back onto the road beside her. 'You saved me. Seriously. You can be my Wing Attack any time.'

'Bullshit, Lorraine.' She gave her best Cruise impression. 'You can be mine.'

CHAPTER 26

When Jim picked them up ten minutes later, they were standing beside Lorraine's car, checking out their cuts and grazes. 'You two okay? Jesus, it looks like you've been in a fight.'

'Yeah,' Lorraine answered, weary. 'With a Corolla and its dodgy muffler.'

Sally turned to her. 'You sure about the muffler? I didn't notice.'

'Pretty sure.' Lorraine moved her arm and winced. 'That rumbling sound. You didn't notice?'

Sally shook her head.

'Geez! You reckon the person was drunk, or what?' Jim was shaking his head.

Someone like Jim, Sally thought, would always find it difficult to imagine how anyone could intentionally cause a person harm. In that regard, he was an innocent.

Lorraine dabbed at her arm. 'Kids probably, drugs.'

'The driver saw us,' Sally said, flat. 'We were in the headlights for three full seconds at least. I bet when I come to check the tyre marks tomorrow, there'll be no evidence of swerving. They drove straight at us.'

'You're saying they wanted to kill us?' Lorraine asked, incredulous.

'I'm not sure I'd go that far,' Sally said slowly. 'We did have time to jump to the side. But at the very least, they meant to seriously give us a fright.'

Later, having seen Lorraine safely home, Sally took a long shower. Then Jim helped her to dab Betadine onto her grazes.

'It must have been an outsider,' he mused. 'I can't think of anyone in town who would do this.'

'Just because you've lived here all your life, doesn't mean you know everyone,' Sally said stiffly.

'I get that, but what idiot would do this?'

'Can you remember if anyone left the clubhouse shortly after me?'

'Well,' he said, frowning, 'people were coming and going. I was with Disco and Kooka – I know they didn't leave . . .'

'Yes? And?'

'Glen left as I was arriving,' Jim said slowly. 'He said he had schoolwork to do. Norma was gone; Lorraine had left too, obviously. And I think Cara had gone before you, and Blake . . .'

'Blake left just after me?'

'Yeah, but then he came back saying his girlfriend could get stuffed, he was staying out with the boys. He's a dickhead, but we could hardly tell him to piss off.'

Really? Why not? Sally thought.

Weary and sore, she let Jim fuss over her while she stared into space. Outside, the rain had started up again, washing away vital evidence, filling the creeks and rivers, causing more havoc on the road. She needed to call Pat, or someone at the Wexton station. What was the procedure now? She was so tired.

'You should go to bed,' Jim said, wiping up some spilt antiseptic.

'Sure. You go,' Sally said automatically. 'I'll be there in a sec.'

He hesitated at the door. 'You don't really think the person meant to run you over, do you?'

'I don't know,' she admitted. 'But the timing of it . . . it's weird that this happened on the week of the anniversary. Do you think it's connected? Every time I think about it, there are more questions. There's been . . .' She hovered around the subject of the kick to her back. Now might be the time to finally tell him.

'I know you're a cop, but you should try *not* to think about it,' Jim cut in. 'Going over and over things . . . It doesn't help.'

Sally looked up at her boyfriend, standing there in front of her. He'd been the first witness to the Mountain Murders, and yet she'd never fully ventured into that harrowing part of his past.

'Jim,' she said plainly. 'You need to tell me about the night of the massacre. I'm investigating the case, and you were there. Please, I need to hear your side of it.'

He didn't move, didn't respond.

'It could be really important. Come on, Jim.'

'Now, really?'

'Yeah. Now.'

He finally looked at her and exhaled slowly. He walked to the sink and got himself a glass of water. 'Okay,' he said in a low, almost croaky voice. 'I'll tell it one more time.'

He sat down beside her. 'Where do you want me to start? I'd bumped into Kate and her group earlier that day. We even talked about the gunshots we'd all been hearing. I told her I thought they were rogue hunters – they're not uncommon. That there was nothing to worry about.' He winced as he said that.

'Could it have been Bill Durant?'

'I guess so. He was always roaming the Razor.'

Sally nodded and gave him the space to continue.

'When I left her group and continued on, I met another hiker, who said he'd warned them about the weather. It was just starting to rain, so I thought I should go back and check – see if they'd made their minds up to return like he had. I thought maybe I could help them carry their packs or whatever. The older guy with Kate, he didn't look too fit.'

Russell.

'I thought that they might have made their way back to the Viking campsite – but when I got there, they weren't there. And that's when I remembered Kate had said something about maybe taking the Jagged Ridge trail. It was a slim possibility, the track was not well known – but Kate, she was an experienced hiker.'

'It must have been getting late then.'

'It was, and Jagged Ridge is tricky in parts. I kept wondering how that big man would cope with it, and the rain would make things worse. So I headed down towards that track, and then, in the distance, I heard gunshots.'

'Can you remember how many?'

'Two. I think. There'd been some thunder about, which could have masked more, but I definitely heard two.'

Brooke and Tom.

'I knew the sounds came from along the Jagged Ridge, so I kept going. I still thought it was a deer hunter . . . but then I came across the bodies. Two of them, shot.' Jim's face was pale as he recounted the story. 'I called the police, who said they'd already been contacted and were on their way. There was a sort of whimpering, and I looked down the side of the path, and there was Laura, huddled over. She was really distressed, saying that the girl who was shot had shouted that there were more dead and that someone was coming. She didn't want me to go. She begged me not to leave her, but I had to check.' Jim stopped, took a sip of water. 'I was so scared.'

Sally reached over and squeezed his arm. 'But you still went there, didn't you? What did you see?'

Jim took a deep breath. 'Up the path and in the campsite, they were all dead. I saw the big guy with his face smashed in. Kate, sitting by a tree, dead. I didn't see the other lady, Lyn. She was shot dead in one of the tents and I didn't see Bill's body at all.'

Sally waited while Jim picked up his glass, then put it down again without taking a sip.

'I didn't really know what to do. So I ran back to where Laura was and tried to get her to walk back to the start of the Razor with me. From there, we could call for help, or drive down the mountain. But she was crying and crying, and she wouldn't move. In the end, I had to carry her – not all the way, but most of it. She was so heavy,' he added, almost as an afterthought. 'When we eventually made it, Pat and the other police were already there. They took over.'

It felt cruel to press him further, but this might be her only chance. Sally leaned in. 'Jim, was there anything, anything at the scene that you might have forgotten to tell? I know you said one time that there was a fox near the bodies.'

'Yeah,' he said. 'Seems stupid now, but it was just standing there – looking at me like it owned the whole bloody scene. I told that to the papers, didn't I?'

'You did.' Sally rubbed his hand.

'But what I didn't tell them' – he was staring into her eyes now – 'was that when I was standing there, looking at the fox, I felt that someone was watching me.'

A knot of anxiety twisted in Sally's chest. 'Did you see anyone?'

'No. It was just a feeling. I've had it there, on the track, at times. Most bushwalkers have – it's like your instincts giving you a warning. It was probably another fox.'

'Probably.' Sally nodded slowly. *Probably.*

CHAPTER 27

'All right then,' Pat Kennedy said, not bothering to sit on one of the station's solid but notoriously uncomfortable chairs. 'Give us a rundown.'

Sally told Pat and Kyle what had happened the night before, filling them in on the event at the club, and then the car, possibly a Corolla, running at her and Lorraine. She included Lorraine's observation that the car had a dodgy muffler.

Pat nodded, filing it away in his head. 'You see any conflict at the presentations? Anyone got a problem with you or Lorraine?'

'Lorraine is very popular, from what I know. As for me . . . well, I'm a cop, aren't I?'

'Maybe it was random,' Kyle said, hopefully. 'Maybe it was just some idiot who did it on a whim.'

'Or the person didn't see the two of you? A local hoon, driving too fast?' Pat suggested. 'Wouldn't be the first time.'

'Oh, it was deliberate!' Sally was annoyed at how high her voice rose at the end.

'You're sure?'

'I'm sure.' She looked up. 'Believe me, the driver took their time to see that it was us. I'm not sure that they meant to *kill* us, but it felt like it at the time.'

'The real question is' – Pat looked at her closely – 'why target the two of you?'

'I don't think Lorraine was the intended target.' Sally shifted on her feet. 'I think I was.'

The senior police officer narrowed his eyes. 'Is there something else, Sally?'

'Yes,' she admitted. 'On Friday night, in the alley outside the pub. Someone kicked me really hard in the back.' It was a relief to finally say it out loud.

'What?' She was expecting Pat to be angry that she'd kept it from him, but it appeared there were no recriminations, at least not for now.

'I was taking in some fresh air. Someone kicked me and knocked me over. When I got up and turned, no one was there.'

Kyle went to say something, and Sally butted in, 'I'm *not* imagining this. I know I was pretty wasted, but I can remember it well. Besides . . .' She lifted up the back of her top and pulled down her pants a couple of inches. 'There's still a bit of a mark.'

The bruises were starting to fade, but from the horror on Kyle's face she knew they could still be seen. 'You should have reported it,' he said sharply.

'I know. And I will. I'll write it up, I promise.'

Pat looked at his watch and sighed. He stared at Sally but said nothing.

'Pat?' No reaction. 'Pat. What would you like me to do?'

'I'd like you to write up the report and then go home and have a rest. You've been up half the night.'

'I'm okay and I—'

'No!' her boss said, firmly. 'You should go home. Kyle and I will go out to the crime scene to check if there are any tyre tracks. Between the two of us, we can question the few houses along there to see if they heard anything. I know that there are at least two clearings along that track, where you could easily hide a car. We can check those too. Kyle, can you go and get my laptop from the car?' He threw his younger colleague his keys.

When it was just two of them, he resumed his staring match. 'Sally, you should have told me about what happened at the pub.'

'I know, but . . . I sort of felt, well, a bit of an idiot really.'

'You're not an idiot, Sal. You're a bloody good officer. Stop worrying about being judged all the time – you're up to this job. I wouldn't have approved you to be in the station on your own if I didn't think so.'

'I thought my stepdad approved that.' Sally sniffed.

'He might be the Assistant Commissioner, but *I'm* the boss in this area.' Pat grinned at her. 'Norma wanted me to put Kyle in charge, and I said no way, not when I've got this brilliant whipper-snapper coming up here. We're lucky to have you.'

Sally's smile wobbled. She blinked, trying to stave off tears.

'If something like that ever happens again – *tell me.*'

'Yeah, I will.' A beat followed. 'Pat?'

'Yeah?'

'How come you never told me you were one of the cops at the scene after the Mountain Murders?'

Her boss was silent for a moment. 'I'd been a cop in this area for six months then.' He straightened his shoulders. 'Everyone in this town will have a story about the Mountain Murders and the Durants.' He nodded towards Kyle, who had returned with the laptop. 'Even those who were young at the time.'

'My great-aunt is Norma Kerns.' Kyle looked at Sally. 'She was shot by Robert Durant. It ruined her career.'

That's why Norma wanted him in charge, Sally thought. *Talk about nepotism.*

Pat had pulled himself together. 'What happened to Norma was tragic, no denying it. She was a good cop. But she's done all right for herself.'

'Yeah,' Kyle added, keen to lighten the mood. 'She got a payout from the police; it was like three hundred—'

'Okay,' Pat cut the young man off. 'Let's get moving. Sally, I want you to go home. We'll call you later.'

She nodded, felt a wave of tiredness wash over her. God, she needed sleep.

When their colleague was out of earshot, Pat turned to her. 'Sally,' he said quietly. 'Me being at the Precipice in the aftermath of the murders was traumatising, I can't pretend it wasn't. And as for the Durants – that family was rotten before the killings. When Bill shot himself, it was probably the only good deed he'd ever done.'

Pat had said she should go home, not that she should go *directly* home.

Sally was passing the turn-off to the gun club when she remembered she hadn't been to visit the owner about the break-in. Maybe while there she could pick his brains about the murder weapon.

Inside a newly painted brick building, which had clearly once been a house, the man named Soupy – sometimes Soup Strainer, for his magnificent moustache – was counting boxes. 'It's the new constable!' he boomed like a circus master. 'What can I do you for?'

Sally reminded him about the break-in he'd reported a week ago.

'A mistake!' Soupy bellowed. 'Should have told you that. Sorry!'

'Not to worry.' She asked him about the two guns she was interested in: the 30-06, favoured by Bill, and the murder weapon, the 30-30.

'Well, let's see.' Soupy's moustache wiggled in joy. 'The 30-06 is, in my view, one of the best rifles around. Its power and accuracy make it a popular choice for many hunters here – it's great for our sambar deer. Does have a high recoil, but honestly, if it's deer you're wanting to hunt, then I always recommend the trusty 30-06.'

'What about a 30-30?'

'Now, your 30-30 is a medium-powered rifle. It's the one you often see in old cowboy movies. You know the sort?'

'I think so.'

'The 30-30 Winchester is a close-range lever action. Good for pigs and goats. It's legal to use for deer, but hardly anyone does. Good quality gun and you can take it apart, it fits nicely into a bag. If you're looking for a recreational gun, I'd suggest a 30-30. Can do you a good deal, if you like.'

'Not at the moment, but thanks.' The gun shop was relatively big for such a small town. 'You do a good business here?' she asked.

'Huge! This town's full of shooters, and of course we get the tourists. We hold competitions: long range, short range. Have done for years. I've got the old winners' board out the back. People here love their guns. They become part of their identity – they really do.' He nodded towards a shotgun with genuine affection. 'We've got people here who have guns that their great-grandfather owned. Still working! I do a bit of antique repairing too. Got a nice Lee–Enfield I'm doing up, was found in Vietnam.'

'Really?' Sally was ready to go home. But Soupy wasn't ready to let her leave. He took down a gun from the shelf behind him and leaned over the counter to pass it to her.

'Check out this rifle,' he said. 'The .308. Now, this beauty can engage a target at one thousand yards. But for your ethical shot placement, you'll need to be at more like five hundred.' Sally took the rifle from him, and after a moment's hesitation, rested it in the crook of her shoulder and peered through the scope.

'Go on!' Soupy encouraged her with a wave of his hand. 'Take a look around.'

Slowly, Sally turned, looking down the line of sight. Out the window, a magpie appeared startlingly close. She could see its feathers, its cold black eye . . .

'Nice, eh?'

Soupy's voice brought her back to the room. She thanked him, handing over the gun.

As she left the place, Sally reflected that *nice* wasn't exactly the right word to describe the feeling she'd had when she felt the weight of the .308 and peered down its length.

No, nice was not the right word. Creepy – now that would be more apt.

CHAPTER 28

Chewing liquorice, Sally scrolled through social media while she kicked a pair of shoes under her bed and threw clothes into a washing basket. Instagram was full of beautiful women with long wavy hair, either on the beach, in a van, or lounging beside a man. They reminded her of the image Russell had sent his colleague. She pulled it up on her phone while she carried dirty cups from her bedroom into the kitchen.

How glamorous his girlfriend was compared to poor Donna, with her Powervac and her easy chair! She stared at the woman, frowning. Why did she feel like she'd met her before?

She heard Jim opening the front door with his keys. 'Sal! You in?'

'In the kitchen!' she called back. 'Come in.'

On impulse, she sent the photo of the woman to Corina, Jac and Marni. **Know who this is?** she wrote.

'Who are you texting?' Jim's big frame was towering over her. She reached up, gave his forearm a squeeze.

'Just work,' she said. 'How are you?'

He shrugged. 'I got asked to go on that conference to Wagga

this weekend. Have to leave here tomorrow night. But more importantly, how are *you*?'

'You wanted to go on that conference, didn't you? Good work, Jim.' She patted him on the hand.

Her boyfriend nodded.

'And as for me, well, I'm fine.' And she was fine, Sally realised. Better than fine. It was the police work, the job which made her so. Angelo might have been right: that like him, she was made for the job.

She wondered how Pat and Kyle were going on the dirt track. 'I thought you were meant to be checking river levels or something?'

'I was doing that,' Jim replied. 'But while I was on the call about the conference, I stopped in town for a coffee and then saw Kyle, who said you'd gone home.'

'Yeah, Pat said I should have a rest.'

'Good. You deserve a break after last night.' He was hovering over her. 'And then something weird happened. When I came out of the coffee shop, there was a note on my windscreen. "Your girlfriend is cheating on you."'

He held out a battered piece of paper to her, and Sally squinted at it, feeling ill. The words were there, in blue writing and underlined twice.

'*What?* Who would do that?'

'I don't know.' Jim spoke slowly.

'That's crazy.'

'Yeah.' He still stood facing her. 'I mean, why would someone write such a thing?'

'I've got no idea.' Sally's mind was racing. Blake maybe, or . . .?' 'You didn't see Neil Durant, did you?'

'No, but anyway, I don't know if I'd recognise him.'

Sally pulled up the photo of Neil on her laptop. Jim peered at it, then shook his head.

'Is someone out to get me?' Sally said, more to herself. *The pub, the speeding car, and now this?*

'I don't know,' Jim said abruptly.

'Is everything all right?' She stood, facing him. 'I mean, is there something you want to ask me?'

He didn't believe it, surely.

'It's just that . . .' Jim picked up the one and only orange in her fruit bowl and threw it from hand to hand. 'Remember that thing you told me when we first got together? About your mum?'

She walked past him and turned to the dishwasher, began unloading it. Cutlery first, all gleaming and hot and clean. 'I am not my mother.'

'That's not what you said then.'

She raised her eyes to the ceiling and took a deep breath.

'Are you listening to me, Sally?'

'Yeah.' She regretted telling Jim so much about her mother. Deb wasn't all bad, definitely not: she was funny and generous a lot of the time. Her mother was also, Sally admitted, mostly loyal – just not when it came to men.

'Remember how you said you were nervous you'd end up like her? Like how she was always moving on from bloke to bloke, never settling down?' Jim ran a hand through his hair. 'You were worried that you had that in you, like you could never be satisfied with one thing.'

Sally stared at her reflection in the window. It was distorted; if she moved slightly to the side, it looked like there were two of her. 'I know what I said, Jim.' She'd been newly in love, drunk, and in a confessional mood. 'But really? You're using drunken nonsense to justify your suspicions? And now, at this time?'

'Well, you can't blame me, can you?'

'Jim, I am *not* like my mother.'

She didn't mention the Disco kiss.

The phone in her pocket buzzed. It was Corina. 'I have to get this,' she said coldly, turning away.

'Shouldn't we talk about this?' Jim asked. 'And are you sure there's nothing else you want to tell me?'

Sally swore softly. 'What are you, a priest?'

As she listened to Jim slam the front door and back his car out of her driveway (no heart-shaped hands this time), she took two deep breaths, then put her phone to her ear and asked: 'So do you know who that's a photo of?'

'Of course I do,' Corina said. 'Don't you *ever* watch TV?'

CHAPTER 29

Ten years earlier

'Look,' Russell said, feigning reluctance while staring into his phone. 'She doesn't like me sharing this – she's got an ex-boyfriend who is very possessive. But it's not as if you lot are going to tell. What happens on the mountain stays on the mountain, right?' He tapped the side of his nose. 'Here's a photo of her – her name's Yona. We've been together for six weeks.'

He turned his phone around, and Lyn and Kate leaned in, peering at the image.

'Wow.' Kate looked at the svelte woman lounging in tight lycra shorts and a crop top. 'She's gorgeous.'

'I'm catching up with her after this: we're getting married.' Russell couldn't hide his pride.

'But you're already married,' Lyn said.

'Sort of.' Russell sniffed. 'We've been separated for months. We haven't been happy for years. Donna knows about Yona, it's not some secret thing.'

'Well, that's nice.' Lyn appeared unconvinced.

Russell was still gazing at his phone. He held it up again for them to look at. 'She's a ripper, isn't she?'

The women tried to look impressed. But really, it *was* difficult to imagine him with someone like that. Lyn raised her eyebrows at Kate, and Kate returned the gesture. *Yeah, as if.*

Brooke wandered back to the group. She stood behind Russell and squinted at his phone. 'Oh, that's my friend!' she said. 'The one I told you about from *Love and Fortune*. How do you know Ruby?'

CHAPTER 30

'Holy shit!' Sally said. 'What does this even mean?'

'It means what I said. That it's a photo of Ruby Heath. She was on *a reality dating show*. Why?'

'I'll tell you later. Thanks, Corina. Bye.'

Sally stared out of the window, thinking. Her first instinct was to call Pat and tell him. But Pat was busy with the near hit-and-run, and her recent phone call about the photos of Kate looking frightened still lingered in her mind. So, Russell had been cheating on his wife. What did that really prove? People did it all the time. Except that Russell *hadn't* been cheating on his wife. His girlfriend didn't exist. He'd been faking it. Unless Ruby Heath herself was scamming him.

Sally googled the TV star. A quick search revealed a Facebook page on private settings. Instagram was private too. But another search linked her name to parkrun Huntly – and there, Sally saw a photo of the attractive woman among a group of athletes, post-run. Sally looked up the Facebook page for parkrun Huntly and there was Ruby Heath again, this time with her arms around a male runner.

Second in the over-30 category, local builder Adam Kaplan with his wife Ruby Heath.

In a Google search for 'Huntly builder', Adam Kaplan's name was first on the list, complete with phone number, email and website.

Sally sat back in her chair, shaking her head. It had taken less than three minutes to find Ruby Heath's contact details online.

CHAPTER 31

Ten years earlier

'No.' Russell's correction was mild but firm. 'This is Yona. She emigrated from Russia a few years ago, but now she lives in Sydney. She's a photographer.'

Brooke shook her head, undeterred. 'Nope.' She looked at the photo again. 'That is Ruby Heath. She lives in Huntly, near Bendigo. She got married last year, two-page spread in *That's Life*. Her husband's the spit of Ben Affleck, totally gorgeous.'

Russell looked confused. 'You're wrong. Her name is Yona. She's flying in this week, and she's meeting me at the end of the walk.'

Brooke put a hand on the man's shoulder. 'Russell. It's Ruby Heath.'

He continued speaking as if he hadn't heard her. 'We've got it all planned, after this walk. You can see her then. I've booked the hotel, and I've . . .'

'Paid for it already?' Lyn spoke plainly. 'Paid for most things to do with Yona, I'm guessing.'

'Lyn.' Brooke shot her a warning look. 'Stop.'

216

Russell sat staring into his phone, shoulders sagging. 'It's Yona,' he said, faintly.

'Russell.' Lyn was gentle now. 'Have you ever met Yona in person?'

The big man shook his head.

CHAPTER 32

For a former TV celebrity like Ruby Heath, Sally had imagined a modern home painted snow-white with a minimalist garden. Instead, she pulled up to an old wooden house, with two utes and a pile of weatherboard palings out the front. A loud saw whined from a shed close by.

By the time she'd located Ruby's home address and made the two-hour drive to Huntly, it was late afternoon. But this couldn't wait. Besides, it took her mind off her row with Jim.

An attractive woman in blue jeans, a flannel shirt and Blund- stone boots appeared from around the corner of the house. Another surprise. Sally had imagined white jeans and heels, for sure. The toddler clasped around Ruby's waist played with her glossy brown ponytail.

'Hello!' she cried over the sound of the saw. 'Come inside where it's quieter.'

The home had a messy charm – photos everywhere, children's drawings, an old stove, and glass jars with plant cuttings on the windowsill.

'Sorry, the place is literally a building site. We're getting a renovation done, and we're doing the bulk of it ourselves.'

Through the window, Sally could see the back of a tall man working on the saw.

'That's my husband, Adam,' Ruby said. 'He was a lawyer five years ago, can you believe it!' She held her hands up in the air. '"The self-sufficiency dream." And this is my daughter, Yael.'

Yael scrunched up her little nose and gave her mother's hair a good yank.

'Oww! That's enough, you ratbag.' Ruby gently sat her daughter down on a play mat filled with toys. Yael picked up a doll and began chewing on its arm.

Sally looked about her. *So, this is what it's like to be properly grown up*, she thought. Young kids, a husband, a cheerful mess. Ruby was probably only a decade older than her, but it felt like she was from another era.

Ruby smiled as if she'd heard Sally's thoughts. 'Ten years ago, I don't think anyone would have imagined this sort of life for me: in gumboots, no make-up, throwing stuff in skips, building compost. People thought I would have just continued on the reality TV circuit, become an influencer or something. No one ever considered my degree in horticulture.' Ruby nodded towards Sally. 'You know what I mean, don't you? It would be the same with you, I'd imagine. The young cop, blonde and pretty. *Don't take her too seriously.*'

'My colleagues are pretty good.' And they were pretty good, they were. But even as she was thinking fondly of the people she worked alongside, she remembered her old colleague Brian, who once said loudly that it was nice to finally have someone young and bubbly in the station. What did that even mean? And it was Brian too who, more than once, had looked over her head to address male colleagues when he was giving instructions. It wasn't overt – but it was surely there. *Well, stuff them*, she thought suddenly. *I won't put up with it now.*

On her play mat, Yael began to make grumbling noises. Ruby kneeled down and handed her a piece of carrot. Both women watched fondly as the little girl shoved it into her mouth.

'Thanks for seeing me,' Sally said, collecting herself. 'As I said on the phone, this is about the Mountain Murders, and Russell Walker in particular. Did you know him?' She held up the photo of Russell in his lopsided Mickey Mouse ears.

'No.' The woman leaned in, pushing a length of hair behind her ears. 'No, I'm sorry – as I said, I don't know anything about him. I mean, when you asked me, I looked him up and I did recognise him as being one of the people killed. But really, I'd never had anything to do with him! It's scary to think someone's stolen your identity.'

'Yeah, it's creepy.'

Outside, the saw stopped suddenly.

'But you know what is really weird about it all?' Ruby continued. 'I did have a connection to one of the victims.'

'What sort of connection?'

'Brooke Arruda and I were both on the same TV show. One of those ones where the girls compete for the guy's attention. She lasted longer than me, as I recall,' Ruby said dryly. 'Anyway, we became friends for a while. I liked something she did on Facebook; she did the same; et cetera, et cetera. I was so sorry when she died. She seemed really motivated, was talking about her online business and so forth. I bought some make-up from her – it was great quality. She was doing well.

'Except . . .' Ruby gave a dramatic pause. 'A few weeks before she was killed, I saw a friend from those old days in Melbourne.

220

Kitten, her name was. She's still doing the D-list celeb thing, trying to scratch a living. Anyway, she said that Brooke had told her I'd been a real friend to her recently, and she was grateful. But that's so weird, because I hadn't been in contact with her for ages. And even then, we were only friends—'

Sally knew instinctively what Ruby was going to say.

Lyn's older women's group . . . Brooke's stalker . . . Russell's girl-friend . . .

'You were only friends with her online,' Sally finished.

CHAPTER 33

Ten years earlier

Brooke sat down on a log beside Russell. 'It was Ruby who suggested I come on this walk! She gave me a gift voucher for it; how could I refuse? She said it would be good for me. She's really kind, always offering advice, or compliments or whatever.'

'How did she suggest it to you?' Lyn asked. 'Did she call you?'

'No. We always chatted on Messenger.'

There was a pause, charged.

'I thanked her for the idea,' Brooke went on, puzzled, 'and said that we should catch up.'

It was cold up there on the mountain. Kate wished she'd remembered her other gloves. She'd forgotten too many things. 'So,' she said, 'both Russell and Brooke booked this hike after someone suggested it to them online?'

'What about you, Lyn?' Russell asked hopefully. 'You chose it yourself, didn't you?'

Lyn grimaced. 'No. I'm in an online group for women. One of them told me about it. Said there was a special deal on. Wasn't there?'

'No,' Kate said. 'It was the same price as always.' As the wind cut through the trees, Kate wrapped her arms tight about herself.

'God,' Russell said in shock. 'What the hell have I been doing?'

The wind swirled again, higher now, like a child's wail.

'Someone's playing with us,' Lyn said.

'But why? And who?' Russell was bewildered. 'You?' he said wildly, looking at Kate. 'You got us all here for this walk!'

'I didn't contact you,' Kate pointed out. 'You all booked and paid online. I just didn't ask any questions.'

'I don't understand!' Brooke cried. 'What does this all mean?'

'It means' – Lyn stared hard into the night sky – 'we've all been catfished.'

CHAPTER 34

'*What did you say?*'

Sally had called Pat at home, and he wasn't happy. 'The Mountain Murders, I've found a link. The victims on the Razor. They were being catfished.'

'Explain,' Pat snapped, though Sally could barely hear him; there was a lot of noise in the background before a door slammed and it all went quiet. They were having a birthday party, he said. For his *mother-in-law*.

'Russell Walker was being lured online by someone who was pretending to be his new girlfriend. The photo the person posted was actually someone who knew Brooke Arruda.'

'And?' Pat sounded dubious.

'So I called Brooke's mum, Inez, just now. She says that Brooke went on the hike after she was given a gift voucher by a friend named Ruby, who she'd met on a TV show. But Ruby denies it, says she barely had any contact with Brooke around that time. She thought it was strange when a mutual friend said how kind she'd been to Brooke. I think someone used Ruby's identity to get to Russell *and* Brooke.'

'Right . . .'

'Brooke also had a stalker. She went to the police about it once, when she thought someone had been in her home. After that, she started to receive threatening messages online.'

There was a clearing of the throat. 'This is very interesting. Good work. But really, how is it connected to their murders? What have Lyn and Kate got to do with it? And the other hiker, Tom?'

'Lyn was scammed out of a lot of money, and she was on a site for older women. That's how she found out about the walk. Tom – I agree that he was in the wrong place at the wrong time. And Kate – well, I'm not sure. But the others . . . you've got to admit, it's strange, isn't it? I mean, this seriously needs checking out.'

'Okay, okay.' Pat's voice was slow, deliberate: he may have been taking notes. 'I agree, what you've found warrants further investigation, but what are you suggesting? That a catfisher murdered them?'

'Why not? It's happened before.' On the drive back from Ruby's house, she'd made a stop at a McDonald's Drive Thru and looked it up while waiting for her order. Online trolls had murdered their targets when they were close to having their real identities discovered, or when they grew desperate for more attention. Middle-aged blokes pretended to be teenage girls. Young women stole profiles of famous people to lure men on the net. A father believed it when a CIA operative told him to kill someone, only to find out that that CIA agent was actually his fifteen-year-old daughter. You could be anyone online.

'And what about the evidence against Durant?' Pat persisted. 'The DNA sample, the gun with his prints on it? And he was definitely there, at the scene.'

'He was murdered too.'

'What?!'

'Maybe there was a second Creeper in the mountains.'

Her boss made a dismissive sound.

'Pat,' Sally spoke plainly, 'I don't think Bill did this. It doesn't fit – there's too many other factors at play.'

'It fits all right. The law said it fit ten years ago. The police said it fit.'

'Maybe the police were wrong.'

'Sally, I mean – come on!'

'There's more to these murders than Bill Durant. I just know it. The victims may have been strangers, but they *were* linked.'

'Everyone is linked if you look hard enough, Sally. I met a bloke in Turkey who went out with my cousin Abby. He said he might have married her, only she was already engaged to a man who played for Fremantle.'

'Yeah, well—'

'And you know what? That player from Fremantle? I was at uni with him! It's a small world, Sally.'

'Pat, I mean it, I—'

'Go back through the evidence we got on Bill. Look at that family, then you'll see: it was Bill. It could only be Bill.'

'I could show you some of the stuff I've found? Some of the links. And maybe you could look through them, and—?'

'Yeah, yeah.' Pat sighed. 'Send them through. I'll look over them when I get to work in the morning. Why not? It's not as if I'm busy or anything. And I thought I'd told you to get some rest! What are you even doing? Take tomorrow off – that's an *order*. Kyle can hold the fort.'

Sally hung up the phone, dispirited. She was driving back through the Whipstick forest now, the thin trees close to the road.

She racked her brain to work out how it could all fit in. She *knew* there was something in her catfishing theory. It was like

Tetris, where you had to line up the blocks, moving and rotating them as they fell. And catfishing, what did it mean *exactly*?

She slowed and turned off the road into a sandy area under the trees. Switching on the car's interior light and digging out her glasses, she googled the term.

Catfishing: to lure someone online.

There was a heavy bang on her driver's window, and Sally gave a sharp scream. Through the glass a man's face was half lit up by the car interior, the blackness beyond giving him a ghostly appearance. She pressed the lock.

'Are you okay?' the man was saying. 'Need a hand?'

There were no cars on this stretch of road. She hadn't seen one for at least half an hour. And no lights either, save for the dim moon and the garish interior of the car.

She shook her head, then found her voice. 'I'm all right,' she said through the closed window. Then, after a pause: 'Thank you.'

The man nodded, his long, thin face unsmiling. When he stepped out of the light of the car, it was as though he'd vanished into thin air.

CHAPTER 35

Thursday brought less rain, more wind. Sally slept in and spent the morning in bed, shopping online and catching up on her socials. Under her handle @SalPal she agreed to go to a twenty-fifth birthday party for her friend Loz, bought two pairs of shoes at a bargain price, and perused a new line of eyeshadows. It was all so boring! She itched to get to work, longed to be at the station – anything but this waiting around.

She was just about to go for a walk when Jim rang and invited her to a late lunch at the pub. There was a conciliatory tone in his voice, and after the call, she grudgingly admitted that maybe she'd been a little harsh the day before. Plus, she sometimes harboured a secret fear that she was a bit like her flighty mum. Kissing Disco at the party – case in point. Maybe Jim had found out after all?

She dressed in jeans and a long-sleeve cashmere jumper with a navy blazer over the top. Low heels – no need to go overboard.

Jim, Sally thought, *he's such a catch.* She liked how he'd piggy-backed her over wet lawn when she was wearing suede shoes, how he'd cover her eyes when a scary bit was coming up in a horror film, and how he'd clapped along proudly when she'd first demonstrated her skill at the Cossack. He was good to his parents; he was kind. He read. She liked his friends. It was Jim who'd told her that his favourite trees, the snow gums, were known as White Sallys. He didn't know why, but when he'd first heard her name, Jim said it had made him like her all the more. Sally thought back to how he'd told her about what had happened on the mountain, how he'd admitted he'd been so scared when he'd seen the bodies. She could do a lot worse than Jim, and probably not much better.

As Sally entered the main street of Edenville, a cool breeze cut through the deep blue of the afternoon.

Her phone rang: Leah Haigh.

'Sally, hello. Am I interrupting you?'

'No, it's fine. How are you?'

'Good. Listen, about the Mountain Murders, you got me thinking about the case again – I went in and had another look at the reports. From what I can see, the initial investigation was fairly regular. It's just that . . . well, the DNA.'

Sally held her phone up close to her ear and kept walking. A car tooted and she waved absentmindedly.

'You are right: it was the DNA, in conjunction with the other evidence – the gun, the circumstances surrounding Durant's past threats and so forth – that really convinced the police and the media that he was the culprit. But . . .'

'But what?' Sally stood stock still.

'One of the DNA samples was only a partial match.'

'What's that mean?'

'Remember, the other two samples were definitely Bill Durant's.'

'Yes, but the partial one – what does it mean, Leah?'

'Now I haven't looked deeply into it – but the partial match does mean we cannot *definitively* state that the DNA is Bill Durant's.'

'But it's partial – doesn't that mean it has to be partially his?'

'Probably. It certainly could be that. But – and this is speculation, remember – we cannot discount a sibling.'

Sally felt an unfurling deep inside her chest. 'Were the other siblings tested?'

'It doesn't look like it. With all the evidence and the history . . . the police would have seen no need.'

'Can we do it now?' Sally asked. 'There's two Durant brothers in town at the moment.'

'Talk to your supervisor, Sally.' There was a hint of warning in Leah's voice. 'You need to do this properly.'

'Don't worry. I will.' Sally's mind was racing. She closed her eyes. 'Leah, thanks. Thanks a lot.'

A sibling? An idea struck her, so incredulous she had to gasp. Looking at her watch, she began walking quickly, and then, after a minute, threw off her heels and ran with them in her hands along the neat footpath. By the time she pushed open the doors of Edenville Gun Club, she was panting and sweaty.

'What in the blazes?!' Soup Strainer looked up in astonishment. 'I was just shutting up!'

'That winners' board for the rifle-shooting contests from years ago – you still have it, don't you?'

'We do. But as I said, we put it out back. Too much of Bill Durant on it – year after year. You could say that seeing his name *triggered* people.' The man beamed at his own joke.

'But not every year?'

'Eh?'

'Bill didn't win *every* year?'

Soupy looked at her in a new light. 'Well, yes, there were other winners . . . Those Durants were good, I told you that.'

He hoisted his big body up from his barstool and led her to a storeroom.

Sally waited while he found the keys and unlocked the door, flicking on the light to reveal a room piled high with shooting memorabilia, trophies, framed images of guns and, in the back corner, the winners' board. It was a huge square of dark wood lined with gold.

Bill Durant's name shone out in silver block writing: 1985, 1986, 1987, 1988, 1991, 1993: champion of the long-distance shoot.

And there again! B. Durant: 1995 and 1996.

No wonder they'd had to take the board down.

Then Sally's eyes were drawn to the years 1990 and 1992. The long-range rifle shooting award had been won by a different person.

'As you can see, it wasn't only Bill who was a shooter in the family.'

'Yeah,' Sally breathed.

L. Durant had won it in 1990 and 1992.

When Sally got to the pub, she found Jim in the bar with Disco, standing next to an empty fireplace. The relaxed looks on their faces was enough to allay her initial fear that this was all some set-up to confront her about her indiscreet pash.

'I'd given up on you,' Jim said mildly. 'What's up?'

'Nothing.' She resisted the urge to rub her hands against invisible flames. 'But look, I'm so sorry, I have to get back to work. Is it okay if we skip lunch?'

His face fell. 'I thought Pat said you didn't have to work today?'

'It's important, I promise.'

When Jim didn't respond, Disco jumped in. 'How are you, Sal? Jim told me someone tried to run you over. What a prick.'

'Yeah, it wasn't fun,' Sally said with a quick smile, not taking her eyes off her boyfriend.

'Jim said the car might have a dodgy muffler,' Disco went on, 'so I spoke to a mate at the mechanic's in Wexton. He's the sort who knows everyone's cars around here. He's getting back to me.'

'That's great. Thanks, Disco.' Sally paused, then: 'Actually, can you also ask if Lex Durant owns any other cars?' From what she'd seen, Lex only had his ute, but you never knew.

'Yeah.' Disco frowned. 'Wait, you're saying that Lex might be—'

'I'm not saying anything,' Sally said. 'Just thinking about a few things.'

'If it's those Durants—'

'Disco, mate,' Jim cut in. 'She didn't say that.'

'Let me know if you hear anything more about the car, Disco,' Sally said, then turned to her boyfriend. 'I'll see you later, Jim.'

He shrugged. 'I'm leaving for Wagga tonight.'

'Oh.' She stood there, feeling the presence of Disco between them. She'd forgotten about the conference. 'Well, have fun.'

Disco cleared his throat and looked deep into his beer.

'I hear Wagga goes off,' she trailed awkwardly. 'So yeah, you'll probably have a good time.'

Jim nodded, and after a short pause, she turned on her heel, giving a backward wave goodbye.

Outside, her rising annoyance towards Jim was further exacerbated by Glen waving at her from across the street. He made the hand sign for coffee and then pointed at Therese's cafe. She shook her head and tapped her watch.

What is it with the men of this town, she thought as she hurried home. *It's either kiss me or kick me; I can't keep up.*

CHAPTER 36

Lex still wasn't answering his phone. Sally sat in her car outside the Durant house, waiting for Pat to arrive. Her boss had been firm: wait for him before she went in. While his response to the partial DNA revelation had been ominously muted, his response to her request to take swabs from the brothers had not. 'Wait outside, Sally,' he'd said, crisply. '*I'm not asking.*'

There was an old Toyota parked on the front yard, muffler intact. Sally raised her phone, took a photo of it. She couldn't hear the dogs. Hesitantly, she stepped out of her vehicle. 'Hello!' she called. 'Lex!'

Nothing.

Listening out for the menacing growl of the dogs, she took a few steps towards the porch. 'Hello?'

In the stillness of the moment, Sally was reminded of how isolated the Durant place was. The dirt road that led to the house stopped abruptly fifty metres past it, and from there the bush began. You could climb to the top of the Razor from the back of the house, through the bush, over gullies and rivers and cliffs. It was only a fifteen-minute drive into town, but out here, among the thick mountain ash and undergrowth, you could be forgiven for thinking that you'd been dropped in the middle of nowhere.

There was the sound of an engine, and through the trees, Sally could make out Pat's HiLux, easily negotiating the potholes of the rough road.

He pulled up and wound down his window, looking at her accusingly. 'You're not even supposed to be working today.'

'I know.'

'You haven't been inside, have you?'

'No,' Sally replied, annoyed. 'But I don't think anyone's home. I can't hear the dogs.'

'Ahh, the dogs.' Her boss stared at the dilapidated weatherboard. 'I remember them.'

'You were here a lot after the Mountain Murders, weren't you?' Sally couldn't hide the faint censorious tone.

'Yeah.' Pat gazed at the house. 'I was.' He indicated for them to go forward, and she followed him towards the rickety porch steps. 'I was still new in the job, eager to be one of the team. From my wife's family, I heard all the stories of the Durants – and the police hated them, especially as Norma had been shot by Bill's father.' Pat waved a hand over the facade. 'It's not easy to admit now, but the whole town despised them.'

The poor family, the dirty kids, the cars on the verge, the bad language, the lank hair, the fags, the tatts, the takeaway food. It was the looseness of things that rattled people, Sally knew. Not for the first time since meeting Lex, she felt a strange sensation, as if she were somehow split in two: if not for a chance meeting between her mother and Angelo outside a cocktail bar in Adelaide years ago, her life may have taken a different route. It made her alert to the chaos of uncertain lives.

'So, you hassled them, yeah?' Sally stood on the porch beside her tall boss, leaning on the wall, while he knocked loudly.

'Not proud of it, Sal. Not something I'd admit at performance reviews, but yeah – there was a bit of carry-on. Nothing physical, just a constant presence.'

'Pat.' Sally had wanted to ask this since she'd heard from Leah. 'Did you know that one of the DNA matches for Bill was only partial?'

'I did not.' Pat looked down at her, grim. 'And it would be an understatement to say that I'm not happy about it. The findings were firm, that's what we were always told: Forensics, the gun, Bill's background as a stalker. All those stories Norma and the old cops told about him – it just made sense to all of us that it could only be Bill.'

'The partial finding may not mean anything.'

'You're right, it may not.' Pat rapped again, harder, on the door. 'But I'll be asking questions now, believe me.'

No one answered, so Pat turned the handle and nudged the door open with his boot. 'Lex? Neil?'

No sign of the brothers, but in the distance, the sound of dogs, their barks growing closer.

The police officers walked down the porch steps to the side of the house, where a Furphy tank lay, weeds growing out of it like whiskers. Now they could just make out a figure walking behind the pack of dogs.

'What's he holding?' Sally asked in horror, as Neil Durant came into view.

'Git back here,' Neil called to his dogs. 'Git back!'

Pat didn't answer, instead shouting out to the eldest of the Durant siblings: 'Been hunting, Neil?'

She finally recognised what Neil was carrying. The body of a dead pig.

'Just a little piggy,' Neil called in reply, a cigarette hanging from the side of his mouth. 'This is what happens when pigs come onto my property.'

Pat drew himself up to his full height. 'We just need to talk, Neil.'

Neil came closer, his mottled face the same pink as the dead animal he held. 'I know you – you're the cop who used to pull me up every time I left the house.'

Pat didn't deny it. 'Just for a few weeks, Neil.'

'Whole family hates pigs.'

'You seem to like the one you're holding.'

'Yeah, I like it. It's *dead*.'

Sally fought the instinct to step closer to her boss.

'Can you tell us where you were last Friday night?' Pat asked. Sally looked up at her boss in surprise. She hadn't realised he was going to bring up her assault in the alleyway.

'Pub.' Neil spat out the flat cigarette. 'Just for a few.' He turned to her, grinning. 'Saw *you* there. Pissed as a newt, funny as.'

'You said something to me, didn't you?' she ventured. 'Something about cops being arseholes?'

'Probably.' The man was still grinning. 'It's what I usually say to pigs.'

'Did you attack me?'

For a brief second, Neil's face fell. Sally thought she detected a moment of confusion.

'She asked' – Pat moved closer to the man – 'if you attacked her.'

'No.' Neil held up the dead creature, waved it in front of their faces. 'But only because I didn't think of it.'

'Are you threatening a police officer?' Pat's voice was low and insistent. Without warning, he grabbed Neil's arm and pressed his face in close.

'No,' Neil spat.

Pat released him, and the man grabbed at his arm where the sergeant's fingers had dug in. The pig swung wildly on its hook, droplets of blood splattering the path.

'Did you see anyone go out of the pub after me?' Sally asked. 'People saw you speak to me just before I left.'

Neil sniffed, looked at the dead animal. 'The owner went out behind you. Taking rubbish. I went back to the bar.'

Sally's mind reeled. The owner, Steve? That affable bloke with the monobrow?

'We're revisiting the Mountain Murders.' Pat's voice was back to normal. 'Need you to think about your statement again, let us know where you were on that day ten years ago.'

Neil walked over to a tap at the side of the house, put the pig on the ground and turned the water on, washing his hands.

'My statement's the same. Only Bill was living here then. I was in Shepparton and then Melbourne. Got alibis, you know that.'

'And Lex?'

'Lex was living in some town down on the coast. Blue blood, blue balls, fuckin' cold bitches that way. It's not only the water what gives you the shivers.'

Same story as the original statements, Sally realised. Nothing new.

'We'll need a DNA sample from you,' Pat said, curtly. 'To exclude you conclusively from any involvement in the murders.'

'You allowed to do that? Take my DNA?'

'Yeah. If you refuse, we can get a court order.'

Sally watched as the man sniffed, thinking. No doubt he was imagining more cops, more paperwork and litigation.

'Yeah, do it then. Fuck it.'

Sally put her gloves on and moved towards Neil. She unpacked the swab and wiped it inside his mouth, a dark tunnel of rotting teeth.

'If this palaver is going to keep up,' he snapped, 'I'll need to ring my lawyer.'

'He's a mean bloke, that one,' Pat said, as they walked to their cars.

'I saw a mean side to you too,' Sally admitted. 'The way you grabbed him? Bloody hell, it was like something from *The Sopranos*.'

'Go right when you pull out of here,' Pat said, pointing, ignoring her jibe. 'The track leads back onto the main road.'

'Does it?' Sally always thought it was a dead end.

'Yep. Decades ago, the old school bus used to go this way. Gina used to catch it.'

'I never knew.' She retrieved her car keys from her pocket and clicked open the lock.

'So, we've got the DNA from Neil,' Pat said, looking behind him at the Durant house. 'Now we just need Lex's.'

'I'll find him,' Sally said.

'Good, and do it properly,' her boss warned. 'I want this wrapped up neat and tidy before the weekend.'

Sally handed him the DNA kit. 'There's still the sister, you know.'

Pat's face, at first confused, lightened. 'Right, the Durant girls. There's only one left, isn't there?'

Sally nodded. 'Annie.'

'Annie . . .' he said with a frown. 'I don't remember hearing about an Annie – but there were apparently always loads of people at the house.'

'Lex told me about her. Plus, Neil mentioned her in that crazy statement he made – remember? The one with the food and the black sunglasses?'

'Hard to forget that one: the police in suits, getting the kids to shoot cans. Cops cooking a full roast dinner!'

'Crazy, eh?'

'That's one way of putting it. Right, I need to head back to Wexton. I'll send off this sample today; tell Forensics that the one from Lex will be coming soon. I'll ask around about this Annie.'

'Great.'

Pat opened the door to his car. 'Keep me updated if you find anything more. And, Sally, don't do anything stupid.'

'I will if you say stuff like that.'

Pat turned to her. 'What was that?'

'You heard.'

She climbed into her own car, strangely satisfied. If her boss said anything back, she didn't stop to hear it.

CHAPTER 37

There were plenty of ways to find out the names of members in a family, but as Sally passed the rows of crosses and headstones in a neat area back from the road, she thought that a cemetery was as good a place as any. She'd been there once, for the funeral of Harry Pickett, the man whose death at his own hand had rocked the whole community. Now, she pulled into the iron gates a second time.

The Edenville cemetery, dating as far back as the 1840s and the Gold Rush, was separated neatly into denominations: the Protestants at the top of the hill; the Catholics – with their tombstones and Virgin Marys and angels – below. There was a Chinese section, off to the side, out of sight. Towards the very back was the lonely 'Strangers' section, named for those whose religion was unknown.

Remembering the photograph in the Durant house of the little girl in communion dress, Sally headed down to the Catholic section. The area was quiet, with overgrown paths and simple headstones. She read the inscriptions: the Mulligans had seen eight children die; Brigid Murphy was named for a saint;

Pat O'Connell was killed in the war. And what was that? Sally stopped short. A medium-sized headstone engraved with an old Victorian police badge – the five-pointed star with a crown on top – and the words 'Tenez le Droit' at the bottom. *Interesting*. The headstone commemorated a husband and wife, both members of the police force here, buried in 1992 and 1994: *Beloved parents: Francis and Bernadette Kerns*. So Norma – injured cop, president of the football club, and Kyle's great-aunt – came from a long line of coppers?

Three graves on – and probably much too close for Norma's liking – Sally found the Durant grave: a black headstone with a humble Jesus on the front, looking down.

Marlene Durant 1932–1981
Robert Durant 1933–1985
Faith Durant 1978–1987
Lovingly remembered by their family, Neil, Bill, Lex and Louanne.
'They walk beside us every day'

Sally knew that Bill was buried in the section closest to the crematorium. No one had insisted that he should be laid to rest alongside his family after he was accused of murder.

But what of the name Louanne? This could only be Annie, the sister who had 'got cancer', according to Lex. The sister who, along with Faith, was fostered out of the Durant family shortly after her father shot and injured Norma Kerns. Jim's mother had said the girls were treated poorly by the older brothers. Where was Annie now?

*

The coffee shop was still open, Sally noticed, as she drove back through town. Therese walked out and stood for a moment with her face to the sun, then adjusted a sign on the door.

It gave Sally an idea. She needed Lex's DNA. And Lex wasn't around. But what was the betting he was here this morning?

She parked and walked quickly to the bin outside the cafe, where, using a glove she'd retrieved from her glovebox, she poked her hand into the rubbish. She was in luck: not much there. The old rubbish must have been collected the day before.

Thank you, Edenville Council, she mouthed, before retrieving two coffee cups.

Sally rejected the cup with pink lipstick on the lid. The other one – with *Lex* and a smiley face drawn on the lid – she put carefully into an evidence bag and, ignoring the strange looks of a passer-by, jogged back to her car.

CHAPTER 38

Ten years earlier

Kate lay in her tent, alert and uneasy. It wasn't quite dark yet, but after the strange revelations about how and why they'd come on the walk, the hikers had drifted to their tents, stunned.

There was a strange foreboding, a heaviness in the air. Once, she'd been hiking on a remote track between Mount Despair and Barry Saddle and she'd sensed something, a shift in the atmosphere. She'd called out, thrown a rock into the bush, but there was nothing. Eventually, a wild dog appeared on the track in front of her, snarling. She must have smelled it.

Kate sniffed the air now. Nothing, save the dampness of the tent and her own socks. She checked the medical kit, then her day pack, feeling the reassuring shape of the satellite phone. If she really needed to, she could call someone, or even 000.

She listened again. All quiet. *Calm down, Kate. Get a grip.*

It was too early to sleep. But Kate lay back, unable to shake the nub of anxiety lingering in her mind. She tried to picture Ric, resting now, after his meal. Hopefully Nerissa had found him in good spirits.

The thought made her sit up: hang the cost, she *would* call now, just for one minute. It would make her feel more settled, and – even better – she could let Nerissa know they'd taken the Jagged Ridge shortcut and would be home a day earlier.

Retrieving the phone, she was heartened to hear the low chatting coming from Brooke and Lyn's tent. Despite their differences, the two women seemed to be getting along well.

Then, a sound outside the tent: a footstep, footsteps.

'Russell?' she called. 'Is that you?'

A shift in the atmosphere.

'Russell?'

Trust your instincts.

Now a rasping noise, thick and heavy like an animal. Except the growing shadow on her tent was undeniably human.

'Who's there?'

Trust. Your. Instincts.

Kate punched 000 into the sat phone and stared at the screen. *No signal. No signal!*

Just as she was about to crawl out of her tent, the quiet of the evening was shattered by a gunshot, and a penetrating scream.

CHAPTER 39

Rather than send the evidence via internal mail, Sally drove all the way to Wexton to deliver the DNA sample to Forensics. Pat walked out of his office just as she was leaving. 'Lex okay with giving his sample?'

Sally hesitated. 'Yup.'

'Good.' Her boss looked at a file he was holding, then back at her, curiously.

'So what's next, boss?' *Please don't ask any more questions about Lex.*

'What's next is that we take over. You've done a great job. It doesn't mean much yet, but we've put the feelers out on the victims. Any unusual connections. Time for you to focus on other things.'

'Aww, come on, Pat!' Sally's childish tone resurfaced. 'That's not fair.'

'It is fair, Sally.' Pat looked at her hard. 'This weekend you'll be busy with the hoo-ha around the anniversary and Laura Wynter coming back with a film crew.'

Sally rolled her eyes. That was the last thing she wanted to deal with. Laura Wynter.

'I'm told she wants to take family members up the Razor, spend a night there, *healing*.'

'What?' Sally's voice rose up in annoyance. 'That is the stupidest thing I've ever heard. I knew she wanted to take them to the start of the walk – but actually spend the night? I mean – bloody hell. And who will even lead them up there? They'll need a guide.'

Her boss gave her a long stare.

'What? You're not suggesting . . .'

'You've been up there plenty of times, haven't you? Hiked the Razor? Camped there?'

'Yes, I have, but—'

Pat blew air out of his mouth, checked his watch. 'You can do it, Sally. Do you good to get away for a night. You'll take the sat phone – give us a call if there's anything we need to know. We'll take care of the investigation down here.'

'While I'm babysitting the bereaved.'

'It's just one night.'

Sally pouted. 'I'm not appearing in her stupid documentary.'

'We wouldn't want you to. Just get them out there, one night, and back again. You never know, we could have it all sorted by then.'

On her way out of the station, muttering under her breath about Pat, Sally was distracted by a phone call from Jim's mother, Marion. Marion's sister had found an address for the house where the Durant girls, Annie and Faith, lived after they were removed from the family home in Edenville. It was in Wexton! Foster services mostly liked to place children in familiar surrounds. The woman who'd fostered the two girls was named Sandra Tuvey.

Marion didn't have anything else from her sister as yet. She'd keep trying.

Sally shook her head in admiration at Marion's persistence. Menopause did not slow that woman down.

The address for Sandra Tuvey was an eight-minute drive away. Well, why not? Sally turned on some Silver Sun Pickups and drove, considerably happier than she was five minutes before. When she arrived at the destination, however, it wasn't to a house but a shop named 'Tiles 'n' Tools'. Her mood dampened once more.

A man in the front office named Des said he didn't know a Sandra Tuvey, but his friend Shambles, who worked out the back, might. Des called for Shambles. A young man arrived whistling at the front desk and, noting Sally's police badge, paled.

'I swear it, we didn't know,' he said, holding up his hands in surrender. 'It was only after Chelsea and me set them off that we found out. I swear if we knew we wouldn't of done it.'

'Done what?' Sally asked. Shambles was seriously concerned.

The man frowned. 'You're not here about the gender reveal?'

'No.' Sally shook her head, confused. 'Why, what happened?'

'Chelsea and me set off a heap of helium balloons for the party. They all came out of this massive box, and just went off straight up – had no idea it was illegal.'

Neither did she. 'Oh, right. Well, it's a relatively minor thing and—'

'. . . just that after that time when I was caught with those two joints, I know I'm not supposed to get into any trouble and now with the baby on the way—'

'I'm actually here because I wanted to speak to anyone who might have known Sandra Tuvey,' Sally cut in. 'If she's still in the area, or maybe there's a family member around?'

'Oh.' The relief on the young man's face was palpable. He sat down on an esky by the door. 'Oh, thank Christ.'

'Sandra passed away,' Des answered. 'She was single, no kids of her own. I bought her house years ago, knocked it down and built up the business.'

'My mum used to live near here,' Shambles piped up, almost recovered and eager to be of assistance. 'I can ask her if you like.'

'Please.' Sally waited while Shambles made a call.

'Want a coffee or something?' Des asked.

'I'm good, thanks,' Sally said.

'Cops always been good to me.'

'We try.' Sally smiled at him.

'Sandra was a nice lady. Looked after hundreds of kids round here.'

Shambles snapped his phone shut. 'Mum's on her way, she's out taking the dogs for a walk. She'll be here in five.'

Sally thanked him. She and Shambles were probably around the same age, but their lives at this point in time were a universe apart. A gender reveal party?

'So, what are you having?' Sally asked. 'Boy or girl?'

'Girl,' Shambles declared with unadorned pride.

'Congratulations.'

'Should have just told everyone that,' Des said, shaking his head. 'No need to let off two hundred illegal pink bloody balloons.'

Shambles' mother arrived ten minutes later, two energetic Jack Russells making her work. 'I've been out looking for balloons!' she said, untangling the dogs' leads. 'They're probably in Gippsland by now.'

Hopefully, Sally thought. *Let the Bairnsdale cops work out the legalities of that one.*

'I'm Kerry Dickson, Sam's mother. Everyone calls him Shambles but me.'

'Senior Constable Sally White, from Edenville.'

'Ahh, Edenville!' The woman gave a wry smile. 'Well, it's a wonder you didn't know Sam already.' Sally said she didn't.

'A while back, Sam got caught up in some trouble. You know Blake Melus?'

Blake? Sally hadn't expected that. She gave a grim nod. 'I do.'

'Sam was mucking around with Blake, being a general sort of idiot. He got caught in possession of drugs recently, very minor. The sergeant here, Pat Kennedy, was firm – no more of it. Good advice, better for Sam to hear it from the police, he didn't listen to me. And now that he's got a baby on the way, Sam's determined to be on the straight and narrow.' Kerry shook her head, smiling. 'I'm rambling! You're not here about Blake and Sam, are you?'

As keen as she was to find out more about Blake Melus's vices, Sally explained that she was looking into the Durant girls, Annie and Faith, who were fostered by Sandra Tuvey. With the anniversary of the murders coming up, Sally added, police were just going over the old investigation.

Kerry seemed happy to talk no matter what the reason was. 'I used to live up the road, and played with all of Sandra Tuvey's foster kids at one point or another. Sandra loved the children to pieces. Didn't have a bad word to say about any of them, no matter where they had come from or whose kids they were.'

'Do you remember Faith and Annie?' Sally asked.

'Yes! I used to play with them too,' Kerry said, her curly hair bouncing up and down. 'Of course, I didn't know anything about their family then – and it was only later, when I read about the murders that I found out what their older brother Bill had done.'

Shambles and the business owner wandered inside. Sally sat on a bench seat and patted the dogs. Kerry sat down next to her. There was a saucer with butted out cigarettes between them. Sally picked it up and put it under the bench, far enough so the dogs couldn't get at it.

'The girls were all right,' Kerry continued. 'Faith was a cutie, but it's Annie I was with the most. She was a year or so older than me, and for a few weeks in one of the summer holidays we became really friendly.'

Sally was beginning to regret the time this was taking. It was getting late, and she didn't want to drive home during the sunset hours, when kangaroos regularly jumped out on the roads.

'We had fun together,' Kerry continued. 'But Annie could be a bit weird too.'

'Like how?' Sally asked.

'Well, we were friends, right? That holiday we'd have sleepovers, go to the pool, ring each other up. It was kind of intense. One time, we were watching a movie at my house, and Annie went to get something from my bedroom. When she came back, she was fully dressed in my clothes.'

'What?' Sally crinkled up her nose.

'Yeah, like, shoes, jeans, a top – everything. When I asked her about it she just said, "What do you mean? These are my clothes."'

'That's . . .'

'. . . creepy, yeah. And awkward. After a while, she said she was joking and she took them off. But she used to do stuff like that every now and then, play tricks. My mum didn't like her much, and I was kind of relieved when they moved on.'

'Do you know where Annie is now?'

'No, I'm sorry. I haven't seen her since she left that time. I did read that Faith died – so sad.'

Sally nodded, and gave each of the Jack Russells a pat. 'Thanks, Kerry,' she said. 'You've been a big help.'

Kerry looked pleased. She had the same pleasant smile as her son, Shambles. 'The thing I remember most about Annie was the way she talked about her family. She missed them so much.'

Family. Sally thought of Lex, alone in that rundown house. All the fights, the drugs, the trouble, the poverty. But even so: *Family.*

'One time Bill came to see her,' Kerry said, standing up to go. 'That's how I remember all of this so clearly. Bill came to see her once when I was there. He was only there very briefly. But you know what? Annie was thrilled to see him, *thrilled.*'

On the way home, fading light flicking through the tall trees, Sally caught the sight of an errant balloon caught up high in the branches of a lemon gum. Shambles' gender reveal party had potentially uncovered so much more than the sex of a child, Sally thought as she sped past.

CHAPTER 40

Ten years earlier

More gunshots as Kate hurried out of her sleeping bag. With shaking hands she grabbed the sat phone and crawled to the front of her tent.

Lyn and Brooke's tent had collapsed. The blood-spattered canvas was clinging to a shape within, struggling to get out.

Russell was slumped on the ground, his face a plate of raw meat. The man was dead; she knew it in a split second.

'Lyn!' Kate screamed in horror. 'Brooke!'

And suddenly, Brooke was beside her, breathing hard, shock written across her face. 'Lyn's been shot!' she gasped.

Was that the sound of a gun reloading? God. Someone was shooting at them from within the trees.

Another shot rang out, and Kate felt a burning sensation in her upper arm.

Searing pain.

She looked at her limb in disbelief. It was as if a hot knife was being speared into her arm, twisting into the flesh.

She couldn't breathe.

'What do I do? What do I do?' Brooke cried, her eyes darting from Russell's body to Kate.

'Run,' Kate panted. 'Go now, back along the track. Take the sat phone. Call for help.' With her good hand, she passed the phone to Brooke.

The young woman stared back at her, uncomprehending.

'Go, Brooke! Now!'

The girl turned and fled.

Kate felt her shattered bone, saw the blood leaking out.

With supreme effort, she stumbled out into the open space. 'Hey!' she roared in the general direction of the shots. 'Here!'

Her legs collapsed; she fell beside a tree. 'Over here!' she called, more weakly. 'Here!'

Sliding down to the base of the tree, Kate watched through half-closed eyes as a man approached.

She pulled out the pocketknife her husband had given her all those years ago. And as the world turned purple, then black, she flipped out the blade, and threw.

CHAPTER 41

The sky was ash-grey when Laura Wynter's crew arrived in town that Saturday, just as the school fete was opening up. Although everyone was hyper-aware of the anniversary, there was a festive mood. If anything, the commemoration gave the weekend a dangerous edge: half excitement, half dread.

Sally had spent the previous day moping about, looking in vain for more information on Annie, fielding calls from her mother, and half-heartedly cleaning her house. She'd told her boss about Kerry Dickson and her interactions with the Durants. It wasn't much. Pat, however, was interested in the fact that Kerry was the mother of Shambles.

'Nice enough young bloke,' Pat had said. 'Glad to hear he's keen on staying on the straight and narrow. Tell him not to let off any more bloody helium balloons.'

At one point in the day, Sally called Kyle to see what progress he'd made on the police interviews, but she was given a deliberately vague response. Maybe Pat had told him not to talk to her. And no word from Jim in Wagga Wagga.

With Brooke in mind, she'd googled 'stalkers', and then spent a couple of hours reading articles and case studies on what motivated a person to relentlessly follow someone else. It was generally believed, she read, that stalking was primarily driven by obsession and the need to possess. Interestingly, there were thought to be four different types of stalkers: the resentful stalker, the intimacy-seeking stalker, the incompetent suitor and the predatory stalker. Brooke's stalker surely fell into the 'intimacy seeker' – those who tended to focus on celebrities.

There were a frightening number of high-profile cases to read about, and a plethora of Netflix documentaries. Telling herself it was for work, Sally watched four episodes of a true crime show, where the stalker targeted not only his victim but also her sister, work colleagues and fiancé. That was another thing she learned: when stalkers become obsessed, their targets were not only the main focus of interest, but also those around them. One in five women were estimated to be stalked in their lifetime. One in freaking five! Knowing she wouldn't see him till after the walk, Sally sent Pat a text with the link to the main articles she'd read. **Brooke's stalker may be an obsessed fan?** she wrote. She didn't send him the Netflix documentary. That would be pushing it.

As for today, the school had set up a jumping castle, an apple-dunking station and dodgem cars, stinking of oil. Many of the kids attending probably wouldn't be aware that the murders had occurred a decade ago on this very weekend. Sally didn't know whether that was a good thing or a bad thing. *Good thing*, she decided after a moment. No point in dwelling on the past.

She stood among it all, looking at a makeshift stage. On the front of it, a sign read 'Miss Edenville' in childish letters.

'Don't tell me you're actually holding a beauty contest, Glen.'

Sally shook her head at the teacher, who was standing beside her. 'Bloody hell, I may have to arrest you for that.'

'Watch.' Glen pointed to the side of the stage.

As parents, grandparents and curious tourists gathered, a little girl in shorts and T-shirt climbed the steps to the stage with a proud smile. In her arms, she clutched a tiny rabbit, which she held out to the crowd. 'His name is Beyoncé,' she said to general laughter. The next child brought a noisy Dachshund, the next one a ferret named Troy. In the end, a Shetland pony was crowned Miss Edenville. She celebrated her win by taking a dump on the stage.

'Classy,' Glen said, to fits of laughter.

'And to think, I pooh-poohed the idea.' Sally grinned.

A small boy pulled on Glen's arm. 'Hello, Mr Downing.' Glen looked at him blankly for a moment, before turning back to Sally. 'There's a juggler and fireworks later on – will you be hanging around?'

'Glen!' A young mother had turned up and taken hold of her son. 'Sorry, Glen, he just really wanted to say hello to his favourite teacher.'

Sally took the opportunity to back away, smiling and mouthing her thanks. Glen started to say something, but the young mother had launched into a conversation about reading levels, and Sally was able to melt into the crowd.

The only visible sign, in fact, that the town was preparing for the anniversary of the Mountain Murders was a small caravan set to the side of the fete, with a table and chairs out the front. A sign, 'Wynter Productions', had been discreetly placed adjacent to the door.

Laura Wynter, slender, with glossy brunette locks, sat on one of the chairs, talking closely with a woman Sally didn't recognise.

With reluctance, she wandered over just as the other lady was leaving. Despite her reservations about the young woman Jim had rescued, Sally greeted Laura warmly enough. They chatted about Laura's trip up, Sally's role as guide on the walk tomorrow, and the town in general.

'I love your caravan!' she said, though she didn't really. 'It's great!' *Friendly, friendly.*

Laura showed her a video camera, said that she'd been trying to talk with people who remembered what it was like in Edenville in the days following the murders. 'It's important to get a local perspective, hear from the community, make it really place-based,' she said, sounding just like the city person she was. 'We want to know what it felt like to be here afterwards.'

Sally looked around. Though the fete was teeming with people, maybe three hundred of them, no one was showing much interest in Laura or the caravan, not even the little bowl of M&M'S on a side table.

'Spoken to many people?' Sally asked.

'Two.' Laura groaned. 'And one of them wasn't even here at the time. She just wanted to get her face on camera. I got the feeling the other one was simply after someone to chat to, so I sort of made an excuse and hurried them along.'

Sally studied Laura's face as she spoke. The woman was undeniably beautiful: angled features, strong jawline and perfect skin. Sophisticated. Confident. Laura probably wouldn't laugh so hard she got hiccups, Sally thought. She wouldn't do the Cossack at a pub.

'You're Jim's girlfriend, aren't you?' Laura said.

'Yes. Yes, I am.' Why did she have to repeat it as if she was trying to convince herself?

'He sent me a picture of you one time. You're even prettier in real life.'

'Thanks.' Sally wasn't sure how to take that.

'Jim is such a great person,' Laura continued, half in wonder. 'I'll never forget what he did for me. People use the word "hero" for all sorts of stupid things, but Jim, he really is one.'

Sally made a vague noise in agreement. The earlier warmth of their conversation was fading. A slight awkwardness crept in.

Laura started pushing buttons on the camera, adjusting the lens. The silence became pronounced.

'The lady who came to see me, who wasn't even here when the murders occurred,' Laura muttered eventually, 'was talking on behalf of her old neighbour, she said, who died two years ago.'

'Right.'

'She said that her neighbour knew the Durants. Said they were all troublemakers, Neil especially. And Bill was known for stalking campers and taking their photos. Did you know they used to call him The Creeper as well as Deer Man?' she asked with authority.

Sally was instantly annoyed. *Yes, I did know.*

'The woman said that on the afternoon before the murders, her neighbour saw Bill and one of his siblings out the front of their house and she knew, she just *knew* that something bad was going to happen.'

'What was that?' Sally frowned, alert.

Laura repeated herself. 'The woman said her neighbour knew something bad was going to happen. Ridiculous, right?'

'No, before that. What did she say about Bill? Her neighbour saw Bill and *who*?'

'Bill and one of his siblings out the front of their house . . .' Laura spoke slowly.

'Right, right.' Sally slumped into the deckchair, deep in thought. She'd always been led to believe that Bill was the only Durant at home that weekend.

If what Laura said was true, it changed things: not one Durant, but two.

CHAPTER 42

With Laura's help, Sally tracked down the woman whose neigh-bour claimed to have seen Bill with his sibling. Pauline had looked shocked, then delighted when the two young women swooped upon her as she was about to leave the fete.

The official statement she gave could hardly be called evidence. It was second-hand and little more than gossip. But, taken with Sally's earlier hunch that Kate had seen someone other than Bill in the bush, and that one of the DNA samples was only a partial match . . . well, it was worth at least a prickle of excitement.

Not one Durant, but two.

She wouldn't tell Pat. Not yet. She wasn't ready for another one of his infuriating putdowns.

Now back at home, Sally did a few dishes, then wandered about her living room, vaguely tidying and wondering what to do next. Tomorrow she'd leave on the memorial hike, or the vigil, or whatever it was. The night stretched out before her. What was Jim doing? she wondered. He'd be at his conference in Wagga Wagga. Despite the awkward moment at the pub, she messaged him, asking how it was going. A famous quote came to mind:

'No matter what happens in life, be kind to people.' She couldn't remember whether it was Gandhi who'd said it, or Taylor Swift, but she felt better as she moved about the room, folding clothes and picking up empty cups.

Next, she scrolled online and bought a pair of pink tights, then sold a Gorman dress on eBay for $40. *Thanks @SalPal!* came the message back. Sally felt a small thrill when she recognised that it was a regular buyer. She had a few of them online. They weren't friends exactly; more like second cousins you heard about, but never saw.

Her phone rang. 'Sally!' Laura Wynter trilled. 'It was so good to finally meet you! I'm really glad you're coming on the walk tomorrow.'

'Yes.' Sally wasn't sure how to respond – were they friends now?

'Jim says you'll do a great job of it.'

Does he now?

'He gave me your number, I hope you don't mind,' Laura continued smoothly. 'I wanted to know what I should take.'

Sally began listing the items, all the while thinking: *When did you speak to my boyfriend? Isn't he supposed to be in back-to-back seminars?*

'I'm actually excited about the walk,' Laura cut in. 'When we met up in Melbourne, Jim said that if it rains a lot, the mountains look amazing. It'll be great on camera.'

'You met up with Jim?'

'Yeah. At a bar a couple of months ago, just for a drink or two.'

'Right.' Sally's voice was tight. 'Good. Okay. So, I'll see you tomorrow then.' She hung up abruptly. Why hadn't he told her he'd seen Laura recently? And why had Laura brought it up just now?

Sally took a chocolate Freddo frog from a jar on the bench, tore the wrapping and chewed off its head.

She could forgive Jim for staying in touch with a woman he'd shared such a nightmare experience with. She could forgive him for having a drink with her now and again.

But what she couldn't understand was why he'd kept it a secret. She sat on the couch, knees up to her chest, brooding. Laura and Jim had probably gone to some fancy bar with dim lighting. Maybe they'd held hands over the table before walking back to Jim's hotel room . . .

Stuff it, she thought suddenly. *Who am I, Bridget Jones?* Picking up the phone, Sally called Jim and waited. When he answered, she asked about the drinks with Laura straight away. *No point beating around the bush.*

'It was just a drink.' Jim sounded annoyed.

'So why not tell me?' She kept her voice mild, aiming for an air of detached amusement.

There was loud music in the background, a burst of laughter. So much for butchers' paper and whiteboards; the Wagga conference was going off.

'Sorry,' Jim said. 'We've been at the pub since the last seminar.'

'I'm annoyed you didn't tell me about meeting up with Laura.' The detached air was slipping. 'Why didn't you?'

'You're always so weird about Laura.' His voice was suddenly clear. 'It's like you're jealous.'

'Well, that's because you never talk about her.'

'Why should I? In any case, you're one to talk about secrets . . .'

A moment's silence. Sally picked at a hole in her jeans. 'What do you mean?'

'You know. Disco. I got another note on my car before I left.'

Sally opened her mouth in surprise. 'Another note?'

'Yeah. *Your girlfriend fucked Disco.*'

What?!

'It was nothing.' Sally felt herself faltering. 'Just a drunken moment months and months ago. Just a kiss at a party. We never met up.'

'You can't blame drinking on everything, even if it was just a stupid pash.'

'I don't know what to say.' Sally shook her head, miserable and confused. 'I moved here and got this job, and I was maybe, I don't know – kind of panicking about suddenly being in the country with you and the commitment stuff and . . . I'm sorry, Jim. It was so long ago.'

Jim was silent for a moment. 'Sometimes you act like you're so much younger than you are.'

Sally snorted, not liking his pious tone. She'd just apologised, for Chrissake, she'd tried to *explain*. 'And sometimes,' she retorted, 'you act like you're older than you are. Like, fifty years older.'

Jim let out a long, exaggerated sigh which only further increased Sally's frustration.

'What, would you prefer it if I was more like Laura? Read heaps of books and be all arty?' She knew it was petulant; she cringed as she spoke, hating herself.

Jim cleared his throat, and when he spoke, his voice sounded very far away. 'Now you mention it, yeah. It wouldn't hurt.'

She didn't know who hung up first.

Taking a broom from the kitchen, Sally began swiping at spider webs in the corners of the room, all the time cursing Jim under her breath. And why, why didn't she say something clever and biting during their argument? She could never think of anything good to say when it mattered. Everything was crap.

There was a violent banging sound outside, and in her distracted state, it took her a moment to realise that someone was knocking at the door. 'Hello? Anyone home?'

She walked to the door and listened. It wasn't a voice she recognised.

'Hello?' the voice said again. 'Is Sally White in?'

Sally opened the door a crack. 'Yes?'

A thin, middle-aged man with a sallow face was on her doorstep. 'Sally!' He grinned. 'Finally!'

She felt a hot sickness in the pit of her stomach and gripped the side of the door, not letting him in. 'Who are you?' she asked, though she'd already guessed.

'A friend of a friend of a friend.' The man grinned again, whipping his head around, left to right, then left to right again. 'How come you never answer your dad's calls?'

'Go away. I don't want anything to do with Eddie.' She went to slam the door, but the skinny man shoved his foot inside the frame, granting him a small space into which he could stick his long, beaky face. If she screamed now, maybe Don might hear?

'Look, I'm just delivering a message from Eddie's friends. There's a lot of us, you know. Thanks to your old dad, we're free to go about our business in peace.'

Sally gritted her teeth. 'Piss off.'

'The message is, we look after the families of those who help us, even ones who've got cops in their ranks. We're a family, all of us.' He was enjoying this, she could tell.

'*No, thanks.*' She pushed against the door, but he wasn't budging.

'If you need anything, Sally, you just call me. We're here for you.' He passed her a small piece of paper. 'Anything you need.'

She grabbed at it, and he took a step back, placing his hand over his heart.

'Family,' he said.

CHAPTER 43

At 5.30 am, Sally was doing stretches on her yoga mat, trying to relieve the tightness that seemed to have overtaken her whole body. She lay on the mat, looking up at the ceiling. She'd barely slept all night, rattled rather than scared by the man at the door. *Typical!* she thought, as she studied the cracked paintwork on the ceiling. She'd been hanging out for a call from her stepdad, and instead received word from her biological father. Or rather, her biological father's criminal friend.

It was still dark outside, but a greyness was creeping into the sky.

She wondered if Eddie knew that his dodgy mates were promising favours to his ex-wife and daughter in exchange for him taking the rap.

She sat up and bent as far as she could over her straight legs, feeling the burn, but enjoying it too. And what favours would she ask for, anyway – she was a cop!

No run today; she had the walk over the Razor and back to do. Pat was coming to look after the station with Kyle while she was up on the mountain.

And out of the way, she thought, moving into a plank.

She showered and ate breakfast while alternately flicking through her phone and gazing absentmindedly out of the window. Relatively good weather for the walk, at least. They were lucky in that. And maybe it would do her some good to get out of Edenville, if only for two days. Fresh air, the mountains – it would give her time to think: about the Durants, about the police harassment. About Jim.

She went into the bedroom to gather up her hiking equipment – not top-of-the-range stuff, but good quality even so. She was pulling her tent and sleeping bag from the back of the cupboard when Disco rang.

'Hi, Disco.' After last night's argument with Jim, Sally was guarded. 'How are you?'

'I'm great, just here with Cara, having a chat. Hey, Cara, say hi to Sally.' Sally heard Cara shout hi. In relief, she shouted hi back.

'So what's up?' She found her Trangia and began pulling the pack apart, making sure all the tin parts were in place.

'I spoke to my mechanic mate again. He reckons that Kyle Roberts' Corolla might have a dodgy muffler. But he couldn't recall a rattle.'

Kyle Roberts. Her colleague?

'So, I swung by his house—'

'Disco!' Sally exploded. 'Leave this to us.'

'. . . and his mate said he was at his aunt's, helping her paint her house or something.'

His great-aunt, Norma Kerns.

'So yeah, I drove around there and gave him what for.'

'Please tell me you are joking, Disco.'

'Nah, I didn't do that. But I'd like to give him a beating.'

'It doesn't mean it's definitely Kyle's car.'

'Right.' Disco didn't sound convinced. 'I'll ask around, try to find out if he ever lends it to anyone.'

'Or if there's anyone else with a dodgy muffler on their Corolla!'

'Yeah, that's what I meant.'

'Well, thanks.' Sally looked at the pots. There was one missing . . . ahh! There it was, locked inside another. She pulled them apart.

'You'd think Norma would pay someone to get her house painted, wouldn't you?' Disco chatted on. 'The pub's doing well – but no, she gets Kyle and Blake to do it. Slave driver. Apparently, she wants it all finished before she goes up north in that massive caravan she loves so much, her pride and joy. Kooka says it's got a washing machine!'

'Blake was painting too?'

'Yeah – Blake and Kyle are her nephews.'

She pondered that for a moment. *Relatives, what they do for one another.*

'Disco,' she said after a pause. 'What do you mean about the pub doing so well? What's Norma got to do with it?'

'Norma's the owner.'

'I thought Steve was the owner?'

'Steve tends the bar.'

'He's not the owner?' Sally was sure she'd heard him refer to the Snow Lights as his pub.

'He's the *part* owner. He owns thirty per cent, Norma seventy.'

Sally thought back to what Neil Durant had said. That the owner had gone outside just after her on the night she was kicked in the back.

Blake and Kyle were Norma's grand-nephews.

269

Kyle's car might have a dodgy muffler.

Another thought: 'Disco, what colour are they painting Norma's house?' She picked up the Trangia pots while she waited on his answer, fitting them into each other, making them neat.

Disco wasn't fazed by the question. 'Same as every new house in this town. White.'

Sally clicked the little belt that looped around the Trangia and tightened the pots.

Whisper White, Snowy Mountains, Lexicon, Hog Bristle.

'Brilliant,' she said. 'Just brilliant.'

CHAPTER 44

She'd expected a full film crew, maybe a man in a *Peaky Blinders* cap sitting in a director's chair. But no: when Sally got to the start of the Razor, it was just Laura standing there in what looked like brand-new hiking gear, chatting to a skinny guy with orange hair. He introduced himself as Warren. He worked with Laura at their new production company.

'But aren't you making a documentary?' Sally asked, looking around. 'Where is everybody?'

Warren laughed, bouncing up and down to keep himself warm. 'This is everybody! It's a skeleton crew.'

You look a bit like a skeleton, Sally thought. One of those plastic ones that hang from a string and dangle about humorously.

'Warren isn't coming on the walk,' Laura added. 'He'll just take a few stills and get footage of us all together, setting off. From then on, it's just me with the audio and my camera. It's more authentic that way.'

'And a lot cheaper too.' Warren winked at Laura. 'I'll keep working from here, wait till you get back tomorrow.'

From where they stood on the Razor, Sally could see the road winding all the way down the mountain. Edenville was hidden among the thick trees in the valley. Two cars were steadily making their way up towards them, slowing around the bends, then accelerating.

Within minutes, the first car, a Prado, pulled up, and Martin Howlett wound down his window. He managed to ask where he should park without even looking at them, then drove to a grassy spot further up the road.

'Friendly bloke,' Warren commented.

'Oh yeah,' Sally said. 'He's a barrel of laughs.'

The second car, a new Mazda, came to a halt beside the Prado, and Donna Walker clambered out, waving energetically.

Warren nodded and smiled. 'She seems a bit warmer.'

'You could say that.'

Martin was decked out from head to toe in designer gear. *Thank god it's only two days*, Sally thought. Between him and Laura, and their brand-new boots, it was going to be a blister-fest.

Donna was wearing old runners and a daggy rain jacket. She carried a heavy pack on her back as she half ran to where they stood. 'I didn't think my new car would make it up the hill!' she said. 'But it did! Ha, ha! I had it in the wrong gear. I thought I was going to be late!' She threw her pack down and began rummaging at the top. 'Now, camera, camera. Got to get my camera out . . .'

'Here,' Warren said, 'I'll get a shot of all of you now. Anything I take, I can send to you.'

Laura, Martin and Donna walked across the road and huddled together at the sign welcoming hikers to the Razor. As the guide, Sally stood back.

'Where's Brooke's friend?' she asked. She'd been told that Inez Arruda had pulled out days before and suggested Kitten as her replacement.

'Kitten was a no,' Laura explained. 'She said commemorating Brooke in this way was *ghoulish.*'

The word had an immediate effect on Martin and Donna – both appeared startled, as if they'd only just realised why they'd come. But there was no escaping the reality of the massacre when Warren led them over to the memorial plaque. He directed them to read out the names, while he circled them, clicking his camera.

'I'm not sure about this,' Martin said stiffly when they were done. 'Will you be taking photos and filming the entire time?'

'No, no,' Laura assured him. 'This is a chance for you to just walk and think about your mum. I'll be talking to you on camera only when you feel comfortable. If you feel like venting, just let me know.'

There was horror in Martin's eyes at the very thought.

'Being here now,' Donna said earnestly, 'it makes me think of how I dropped Russell off, just over there!' Sally eyed Laura hurriedly turning on her camera. 'And he was so happy! If I ever thought for the slightest . . . that . . . you know, that would be the last time I'd ever see him, then I'd . . . then I'd . . .'

Sally was surprised to see Martin place a gentle hand on Donna's shoulder.

'Come on, now. You can't think like that,' he said. 'What happened to them up here, no one could have predicted it.'

It was just after 10 am. They needed to get moving. Neither Donna nor Martin looked fit, so Sally expected the pace would be slow, particularly as Laura would take up time with her filming. She reminded them to fill their water bottles if need be, and of the fact that on the Razor there'd be no reception for phones.

273

'I've got the sat phone in case of emergencies.' She patted her little day pack, which was connected to her larger hiking pack. 'But you'll be out of range till we get back here tomorrow.'

'When will that be?' Martin held his hand up to his forehead, looking along the track.

'Should be just before lunch, if we leave straight after breakfast and don't muck around.'

While everyone was talking and texting and fussing over last-minute pack arrangements, Sally took a moment to check her emails.

Most of it was spam, but there were two work-related messages: the first from Leah Haigh.

> *Been doing some more work on the Mountain Murders. Checked with Fraud about Lyn Howlett. Lyn had been agitating for answers on her online scamming case. Fraud had found one of the IP addresses the scammer used and was close to finding the other. They're going to send what they've got over to me. Lyn was on the right path to discover who her catfisher was, but the investigation pretty much died with her. I'm looking into some other aspects of the case too. Will call when I have news.*
> *Leah.*

Sally raised her eyebrows. Leah was now making enquiries of her own – *Good.* The more heads looking into it, the quicker they'd find answers. And Lyn, it seemed, had been close to unmasking her scammer. *Legend.*

She looked up. Warren was helping Laura to put her pack on; Martin was staring pointedly at his watch. Off to the side,

Donna zipped up her pack before bending down and, in a single movement, hauling it onto her knee and then swinging it around to fit on her shoulders. Sally felt like clapping.

The second email was from Jim's mother, Marion:

Hope you're well, Sally!! I asked my sister again about Annie and Faith. She can't find the report on them. ☹ She did say that she remembered the girls were very poorly treated by their older brothers, especially Neil, who was violent too. Faith, as you know, died from leukaemia, and Annie moved away, maybe to Melbourne?? She wasn't sure. Later, the poor woman got cancer and a fundraiser by a local charity raised over $5000 for her treatment. After that little is known. What a family!! Tragedy at every turn.

Sally forwarded the emails to Pat and Kyle, then turned off her phone.

Annie/Louanne was a mystery. How old would she be now – fifty?

Ignoring a loud sigh from Martin, she turned on her phone again and sent a quick email to Kyle:

Important!! Can you try to find out where Annie (or Louanne) Durant is now? We need a DNA test.

Her concerns about Kyle, the house painting, Norma, and the dodgy muffler could wait. She would be out of range for two days. She needed her colleague's help.

Hesitating for a second, she texted Jim:

Hey. I'm off on the memorial walk. See you tomorrow maybe, if you're free. Have fun at the conference.

She deleted it immediately and wrote:

Hi Jim. Have a good day, see you tomorrow.

No love heart emojis, not now. 'More like Laura,' he'd said.
In your dreams.

Her finger hovered over the send button, then moved to delete it.

Jim could get stuffed.

Just as she was about to turn off her phone for good, she received a message from Pat: the DNA results were back for Lex. A weak partial match. *Shit!*

Immediately, she rang her boss back. 'What's this mean?' she asked.

'It means what it says,' her boss answered. 'There's a partial match for Lex and the blood found on the mountain. We're about to bring him in.'

'Good work,' she said, after a pause.

'Well, you're the one who got us onto this, Sally,' Pat said.

'What about Neil?' No time for pride right now.

'I asked that: it takes longer for Forensics to match DNA than it does to discount it. Given that we've already heard back about Lex, it probably means that he's a match too.'

'Maybe even a stronger match,' Sally said aloud.

'We can't speculate on that – but we're bringing Neil in after we talk to Lex.'

'Have you seen either of them yet?'

'No, but I'm not in Edenville at the moment. I've told Kyle not to go to the Durant house till I get there.'

Sally looked up to see that Martin, Laura and Donna were lined up nearby, looking at her expectantly.

'Got to go, Pat,' she said. 'I've sent you some more info on Annie Durant – check it out.'

'Will do. I haven't forgotten her.'

'Also, Norma is part owner of the Edenville pub.'

'Eh?'

Sally hurriedly reminded him of what Neil said at the Durant house, that the owner went into the alleyway after her on the night she was kicked.

'Right.' Pat sounded doubtful. 'We'll check it out.'

The hikers were now staring at her with frustration.

She shoved her phone in her pocket.

'Okay, gang,' she said. 'Let's get moving.'

CHAPTER 45

'What got you into it? Bushwalking,' Donna asked.

Sally stepped over a fallen log, took a while to answer. 'It was my stepfather. Or rather, ex-stepfather,' she admitted. 'When my mum first got together with him, he used to take us out walking in the Adelaide Hills, and further along, to picnics on the Coorong. We'd take a thermos with Milo in it, some sandwiches and stuff.'

They'd been walking for almost two hours in pleasant conditions; a slight breeze, low cloud.

'Sounds nice.' Donna smiled.

Martin was trailing behind, and the women stopped to wait.

'Yeah,' Sally answered slowly. 'It was. After a while, my mum gave up joining us – she hated having to wee in the bush.'

'I get that!' Laura muttered, and Donna gave a barking laugh.

'So yeah, for a year or so, it was just me and Angelo.'

'You call your father "Angelo"?' Laura asked.

'I used to call him Dad,' Sally said, 'when I was a kid. But now I call him by his first name. Angelo or Ange.'

Donna picked up a stick and drew circles on the ground. 'I wasn't close with my father,' she said. 'But I always called him Pa.'

There was the sound of a click. Donna and Sally looked up to see that Laura was fiddling with a recorder.

'Please tell me you weren't taping that,' Sally snapped, shaking her head. 'You have to let us know when we're being recorded, Laura.'

Laura frowned at the small audio device. 'It wasn't taping, I don't think . . . I just can't work out why the record button keeps lighting up. God, I wish Warren was here, he'd show me. I'm such a lightweight. Wait a sec . . .'

Sally watched in surprise as Donna took the device from Laura and studied it intently. Leaving the two women to sort out the recorder, Sally wandered over to the path and then beyond it, to where the mountain sloped down to a valley filled with mountain ash. It was mid-afternoon, but they had plenty of time to make it to camp and set up before it got dark. She stood for a moment, watching as the sun's rays slid like ribbons of gold down the sharp descent. Someone much smarter than her could write a poem about that view, she mused. Or at least paint a picture of it. *I'd buy a painting of that,* Sally thought. *I'd stick it up in the lounge room where I could look at it every single day.*

Stepping forward, she peered towards the right, down a steep ravine. In the distance, huge boulders gave the impression of some ancient castle. That area was the Precipice.

What she'd said to the others had been true. Angelo had introduced her to hiking. In fact, they had walked this very path and camped along this way when she was young. It was Angelo who'd bought her first tent and shown her how to put it up. Angelo who'd demonstrated how to use a Trangia stove, and told her about dry bags and sleeping liners. The blow-up pillow she still used had once been his.

Angelo. Ange. *Dad.*

Martin rounded a bend, walking slowly, eyes on the path. 'I think I've got to turn back,' he said. It was his calf, he explained. He'd played tennis the night before and felt a twinge when he went for a volley. He could feel it now – not a tear just yet, but it was a 'distinct possibility'. He'd done it before; he knew 'the signs'.

'Want me to take a look at it?' Sally didn't really want to examine Martin's chicken leg, but she was the guide.

'No, no, it's all right. I know what it is. I'll turn back now. It's only, what? Two, two and a half hours?'

'You're going back?' Laura walked towards them, frowning. 'Why?'

'Sore calf.'

'We're *all* going back,' Sally said, her voice flat. 'We can't leave Martin on his own.'

'Of course you can!' He seemed almost angry. 'I'm perfectly fine, it'll just take me a bit longer.'

'Don't you want to carry on?' Donna joined their triangle. 'For . . . your mother?'

Martin's face flushed an angry red. 'I don't think this is doing anything at all for my mother. She's dead. She was murdered here ten years ago. Being on television isn't going to bring her back, is it?'

There was a short, uncomfortable silence.

'In fact,' Martin continued, 'this walk is unlikely to help anyone except Laura and her production company. God knows why I agreed to this!'

'What?' Laura sounded hurt. 'I invited you here to help you heal. Plus, I was part of it – I was here on the mountain too.'

Martin made a dismissive scoff. 'So how do you explain the camera crew who arrived in Edenville this afternoon? My wife

280

says they told her you were suggesting a joint deal. You'd let them come up here and film too.'

'No!' Donna gasped. 'Laura, you said it would be just us, just the families and you.'

Laura ducked her chin and shook her head. 'That's not true, Martin. I promise. Channel 11 got wind of what we're doing and wanted a piece of it, but I said no.'

'Did Warren stay behind because he was going to meet the other film crew at the start of the walk, bring them out to us?' Martin stared at her, his mouth a firm line.

The others turned to Laura. 'No!' she protested. 'Absolutely not.'

'In any case, I'm going.' Martin squared his shoulders and looked at Sally. 'I've had it.'

'Do we have to leave?' Donna asked, hesitant. 'I didn't think I would, but I'm enjoying the walk – and aside from all the documentary stuff, it's nice to think about Russ and how he must have enjoyed it up here.'

'And we've only just begun!' Laura burst out.

Sally hesitated. Guiding protocol meant that they should all either go back or, if deemed safe, escort the injured person to safety. But Martin was hardly injured: he had a sore calf muscle, and in fine weather it was only two hours back to his car.

'I know what.' She made a decision. 'I'll walk back with you halfway along the Saddle to the other side of Bald Hill, then make a call to Warren on the sat phone to come and meet you. I'll expect you to ring us once you're at your car.'

Martin nodded.

'Laura, can you give me Warren's number? You and Donna can walk on a bit – just half an hour or so – and then wait for me. Do some filming or whatever. As soon as I've heard from Warren and seen Martin walk off safely, I'll hurry back.'

Laura shrugged, while Donna gave a tiny nod and a smile.

After a few minutes on the track, Martin stopped. 'You really didn't need to come, you know.'

Sally rolled her eyes. 'I did, Martin. I'm the guide – get over it.'

He considered her for a moment, before continuing on. His walk, Sally noticed, was markedly improved.

There were some dark clouds now, looming in the west. Not dark enough to be ominous, but even so. She checked her watch. Plenty of time to make it to the Viking campsite, though she'd have to hurry back to the others once she'd seen Martin off.

The man's back was hunched, as if he was facing a head wind and had to push himself forward, ignoring all sight and sound. A strap had come loose on his pack and was trailing in the dirt. He looked like a dejected child. She felt a pang of sympathy for him. A man whose father had died relatively young. Then his mother had been murdered in the most horrific way on this very mountain range. What the hell was Laura doing, raking up the past? *Best to forget it*, Sally thought. Best to bury it under the ground. What use was the past anyway? It was a hyped-up party you didn't enjoy. Best to begin again, organise better music.

'Ahhh!' Martin tripped over the loose strap and Sally ran to him, helping him stand straight, then fixing up the offending tie.

'Why did you even come on this walk?' Sally couldn't help asking. 'When I saw you in the city, you said you weren't interested.'

'Laura mentioned it being made into a documentary. She hinted that there could be some money involved. We could do with some extra right now, with the school fees and whatnot.'

Right.

'But then, when I saw there was one other bloke and just Laura with that camera . . .'

'Yeah,' Sally said. 'Not exactly Paramount, is it?'

Martin gave a quiet laugh. He stood still for a moment, squinting into the weak sun. 'I haven't been able to think about Mum up here,' he said. 'Not at all.'

Sally wasn't sure what to say.

'I think it's because I don't want to imagine her in this place, where she died.'

'No.'

'She was a good mother,' Martin said stiffly. 'And despite what you think, I loved her very much.'

Sally felt a lump in her throat. For some reason, she pictured him as a child; little boy legs, vulnerable and thin. She patted the dodgy strap on his pack, made sure the side zip was done up properly.

Martin began walking for a few minutes more before stopping again. 'In fact, the person I *have* been thinking about up here is my father.'

Sally negotiated a cluster of pointy rocks. 'He passed away five years before your mum, is that right?'

'Yes. She was completely devastated, even though Dad wasn't always easy to live with.' Martin looked at a small patch of snow daisies clinging to the edge of the path. 'He loved it up here.'

'Your mum's friend told me that he was a deer hunter.'

'Yeah, although he wasn't only that.' Martin's gaze moved down the sweeping mountainside to the valley. 'He loved camping, fishing and walking. Before he met Mum, he used to spend all his holidays in this area – he had friends here, a girlfriend even! It was always like that – people loved Dad.'

'It's a wonder he didn't move to Edenville,' Sally said with a smile.

'Well, he met Mum, didn't he? Love of his life, he used to say. Spent most of his time in Melbourne then. Only came up here with her for weekends, or with Kevin.'

'What happened to the girlfriend?'

'Don't know, never asked. I don't think it was serious. But whatever, it didn't stop Dad talking about these mountains.'

'And did you like it up here too?' Sally asked.

Martin shrugged. 'I was never really an outdoors type. I liked to stay at home, and read or draw or whatnot.' He scratched at his thin arm. 'Sometimes I wonder where I came from.'

I get it. 'Maybe you're more like them than you think.'

Martin nodded slowly. 'That's true. I've got a wife and two healthy kids. Life's been pretty good. And as for Mum's money problems, it was frustrating – but mainly because she was so distracted during that time. I knew there was something going on, but she wouldn't discuss it at all with us. I used to get so angry with her.'

'Yeah, but I'm sure Lyn knew you loved her.'

'Yeah.' He nodded again. 'I think she did. I mean, families fight, don't they? It doesn't mean they don't care about each other.'

They began walking. In the far distance, Sally could make out the small hut that marked the beginning of the Razor walk. She took out the sat phone and called Warren on the number Laura had given her. The cameraman was more than happy to walk out and meet Martin, and yes – he'd give two rings on the phone once they got back to Martin's car.

'Warren,' Sally asked. 'You haven't organised another film crew to come up here, have you?'

Warren assured her he hadn't.

'And Laura? Did she arrange anyone else to come?'

This time, there was a pause before Warren said no.

There wasn't much more she could do. Thinking of the cost of satellite calls, Sally hung up and turned to Martin. 'Okay, you're right to go,' she said. 'Warren will meet you along the track.'

'This wasn't necessary, you know.' Martin sighed, but this time with a hint of a smile.

'Hey, Martin.' A vague thought was hovering somewhere in the back of Sally's mind. 'Do you know the name of your dad's girlfriend? The one he had up here before he met your mum?'

'No.' Martin frowned in thought. 'I don't think so. I know that once he said he felt a bit bad about how he'd treated her, because after he met Mum, he never contacted her again.'

'He ghosted her,' Sally murmured, sorry for the woman.

'I guess.' Martin smiled sadly. 'When Dad paid attention to you, it was like you had the sun shining on you. But then he could flick it off, just like that.' Martin clicked his fingers. 'And then, you were in the dark again.'

'Yeah?' Sally was still thinking about the old girlfriend. 'So, he didn't mention her again to you?'

'No. Only when he used to tease Mum sometimes, sing a song about her. Mum didn't care. What was it?' Martin cocked his head in thought. 'One of those old-time tunes, from the fifties or sixties . . .' He pointed his finger in the air like a maestro and softly sung: 'Da da daa daa – da, da, da, da . . . Sorry, I can't remember the rest. I'm getting old!'

They said goodbye, and he walked off down the last part of the Razor trail – long and narrow mostly, with a straight drop on either side. Suddenly Martin turned, cupping his hands around his mouth and calling back, 'The Kingsmen! That's it.

I remember now! That song was by the Kingsmen.'

Sally smiled and gave him the thumbs up. She'd never heard of them. The only old music she knew was stuff her mother liked, like INXS, U2 and Duran Duran. That music was okay, she admitted, and their fashion was wild, but she preferred the newer stuff. Taking a long drink from her water bottle, she hummed an INXS song while she watched the grieving man become first a dim figure, and then just a speck in the distance.

CHAPTER 46

When she saw the two women – Laura pacing and Donna sitting on a log – Sally was immediately struck by how much more comfortable Donna appeared in her surroundings than she would have expected. The older woman was chewing on a gum leaf, eyes drooping, ready for a nap. Laura, on the other hand, was behaving like a caged lion.

'Here you are!' Laura's false brightness smacked of irritation rather than joy, but Sally was too tired to care. She'd run twenty minutes, hard, and she needed a rest.

Besides, something odd had just happened, something that had made her run a little faster than normal. Back there on the track, just as she'd turned around and could no longer see the long stretch of the Razor, she thought she'd seen someone standing on the top of the rocky mound, less than three hundred metres away. No doubt just another hiker. But when she'd rubbed her eyes and looked again, no one was there.

If only she'd worn glasses, and not the stupid green lenses. Even her normal lenses would do, the ones that showed her boring pale blue eyes. She'd thought the green lenses would look better on film – what a vain idiot. They really were useless.

'We did some filming,' Donna said. 'But it didn't go very well.'

'It went *fine*.' Laura rolled her eyes. 'Donna told me all about how much she loved Russell, and they liked to do things together, go on trips, watch television together in their chairs. So she was surprised when he suddenly decided to come on this walk, just out of the blue.'

'Yes, that's what I said, didn't I?' Donna agreed. 'I said all that.'

Sally looked at Donna out of the corner of her eye. So far, the woman had fared much better than she'd thought, but now Donna looked tired, and all this filming wouldn't help. It was draining having to discuss feelings, feelings, feelings.

Laura was snapping at the straps on her pack and still pacing about. No doubt she wished Brooke's friend, Kitten, was here. Kitten would have had commercial appeal, looked attractive on camera. Not like Donna, with her red cheeks and woolly jumper with smiling sheep on the front.

'Let's go,' Sally said. 'Three hours' walk till the Viking.'

'Three hours!' Donna got to her feet. 'Is it really three more hours?'

Not for the first time, Sally noticed Donna's annoying tendency to parrot the subject of conversation and then turn it into a question. 'It is.'

Laura sighed and widened her eyes. 'That's what she said.'

As they walked over the next rise, Sally took a few minutes to climb to the top and look back at where they'd come from. Now, the starting point was barely visible.

But there it was again: the long shadow pointing east; someone walking in the distance, towards them.

'Tell you what,' she called down to Laura. 'See the next rise in front of us? Go to the left of it rather than the right. It's a bit narrower, but it cuts off at least twenty minutes.'

'Yay!' Donna raised a cheer.

When Laura reached the fork ahead, she hesitated, but Sally urged her on. The left path *was* far less well trodden, and the downward slope was definitely steeper, but it gave her some reassurance to know that the person behind them was unlikely to go this way.

'Be careful!' Sally watched as the other two women tentatively made their way along. If she were American, she might yell out, 'You're doing great!' but the truth was, they weren't doing great. Neither of them. Laura was striding out too fast for the path, and Donna was struggling to negotiate the rocks.

Sally felt a growing anxiety mixed with a simmering annoyance at her companions. *This time tomorrow, I'll be rid of them both*, she thought. *It can't come soon enough.*

'There's a little clearing about twenty minutes along – we can have a break there,' she called out, and Donna reached behind her to give a thumbs up.

The group struggled on.

The promised clearing was a small area of flattened grass, where kangaroos and wallabies slept. A copse of snow gums offered little shade, and the women sat on the edges of their packs, not willing to risk an ant attack.

Laura asked Donna about her years after Russell, when the media onslaught had died down.

'It was hard,' Donna said, not looking into the camera. 'It was as if everything ended when Russ died. I had to – I don't know – become someone else, just to survive.'

Sally looked away. It was too much. She hated shows like this, where people in pain were forced to reveal every part of themselves. *Bloody Laura*, she thought. *You're a leech.*

Donna quietly rubbed at her eyes and didn't continue.

'Why don't we talk about you for a change?' Sally stared at Laura, who was now hurriedly checking her camera. 'You were here too. What's your story about the Mountain Murders?'

'Yeah,' Donna said, sniffing. 'Tell us about Tom.'

Laura hesitated before reluctantly handing the camera to Donna, who clicked a button and held it up.

'Quick learner,' Laura smiled. 'You should be in film.'

Donna sniffed noisily. 'Ha, ha. No, thank you!'

'Okay.' Laura waited for Donna to give her the nod. 'Tom. Let's see.' She jutted her chin forward, looked up at the late afternoon sky. 'Yes, Tom was my boyfriend at the time of the murders, but I was planning to break up with him. As much as I hate to admit it now, I thought he was boring. He liked playing board games, watching nature shows, going bushwalking.' She smiled. 'The weird thing is, I like all of those things now. I was only young when it happened. We both were. Truth is, I had no idea how lucky I was.'

She stayed in her thoughts for a moment, then continued.

'We got lost on this walk. Took some path we weren't supposed to. Tom was meant to be navigating, but I didn't help at all. He did everything. Anyway, we were lost, began arguing. It was getting dark, hard to see, and it had started to rain. I had a sore foot. Then we heard a scream, or a shriek. It was poor Brooke, running up to us, screaming and screaming and screaming.'

Donna looked up from the camera, horrified. Sally wondered whether she should ask her to stop. A wind blew, cold.

'Laura?' she asked.

'Tom told me to get down – he really yelled at me, *Get down!* And I did. I slithered down the mountainside and stayed there. There was screaming and some shouting, and then there were gunshots. Two. Tom and Brooke, dead. Just one shot each.' Her voice was barely a whisper now.

Donna put the camera down and stared into the evening. No doubt she was thinking of what had happened to Russell minutes before.

'After a while, maybe twenty minutes, I heard something,' Laura said, her eyes wide. 'Like an animal, heavy breathing. It was the killer, I knew it. Coming back to check on them. There was this awful panting, and a dragging sound, and then – a stillness. I was terrified they were looking over the path right at me.'

'Could you see them?' Donna asked, transfixed.

'No. I was lying as flat as I could, partially hidden by a rock. It was pretty dark by then. And I didn't breathe, I *couldn't* breathe. Then I realised they were looking for the satellite phone. Brooke had one in her hand and must have dropped it. It had fallen just below the path. I didn't dare reach up to grab it.'

Though her face was blank and her voice was devoid of emotion, there were tears in Laura's eyes. 'I don't know how long I lay there in the rain and cold. The killer left, and then I waited and waited and waited. Eventually I crawled up to get the phone, called triple zero. I don't know how long after that Jim came. I was still in the same spot, huddled below the path.'

The biting wind blew through the open area, and a heavy mood settled over the group.

'Maybe this wasn't a good idea after all,' Laura admitted finally, shoulders slumped. 'I want to make films, but all my other ideas have been crap. Everyone says to mine your own experiences, so I thought – why not? I'm such a fucking loser.'

'Maybe we should go back?' Donna said to Sally in a small voice.

Sally shook her head. 'It'll be dark in under two hours. Quicker to make it to camp – it's not that far from here.'

The snow gums shivered; a large cloud passed overhead.

While the other two put their packs on, Sally once again walked to a high point above the clearing. It was harder to see now – she needed binoculars. She pulled them from her pack, then took her time scanning the mountain track, from the small rises on the Saddle to the canopy of snow gums and the rocky plain, to where they were now. Nothing. She wiped the binocular lenses and scanned again, this time more slowly. The wind whistled, thin and high. Nothing.

More clouds, like an army joining forces from the east.

And there, *there*, the lone figure making its way to the fork in the path.

She held her breath, watched.

The stranger took the left fork, on the same path they had come.

CHAPTER 47

The others were slowly making their way forward. No point hiding it any longer. 'I think someone's following us,' Sally called out.

'What?' Donna looked back, startled. 'Someone's *following* us? What do you mean?'

'I mean' – Sally tried to temper her irritation at the woman – 'that someone is following us. They've been tracking us for the last few hours. I first noticed it when I dropped off Martin. Since then, they've twice come the same way we have, even though we've avoided the regular route. There's definitely someone coming this way.'

Laura looked at her – was that fear in her eyes? – before reaching over to grab the binoculars. She ran up to the crest of the hill and held them to her eyes. 'I can't see a thing!' she called down after a few moments.

Donna looked relieved. 'Maybe you saw an animal,' she said to Sally. 'The light's deceiving at this time.'

'Hang on,' Laura called again, without looking around. 'There *is* someone coming!' Her voice wavered as she lowered the binoculars. 'And they're moving fast.'

'What? Oh my god!' Donna's voice twisted up in fear. '*Why?*'

Sally quickly walked up to Laura and grabbed the binoculars, training them on the Razor's ridge. There, in the distance, in the dark purple of evening, was a figure running along the track. Not that fast, really, but certainly steady. Yes, Laura was right – their follower was closing in.

'Perhaps it's a hiker?' Laura asked, her voice rising.

'They don't have a pack.' Sally tried to calm her thoughts. 'Could it be the press, Laura? Have you arranged something we don't know about? Another journalist?'

'No.' Laura was emphatic. 'I told you, I'd never do that.'

Sally narrowed her eyes, unconvinced.

'Maybe it's someone who just needs to tell us something?' Donna said, her voice rising with hope.

Sally nodded, thinking it through. 'Yes, but if it was something urgent, they'd have called us on the sat phone. I didn't receive any messages an hour back when we were on Bald Hill. I checked. The only time it has rung was when Warren gave us the signal to say that Martin was safe. And whoever it was, they were already following us by then.'

The three women stood silent, except for their quickening breaths.

Far below in the valley, a thick fog spun itself around the mountains, rising as the night grew cold.

'I know where we can lose whoever it is,' Sally announced finally. 'Not far ahead, we'll reach the Jagged Ridge track. We can take that track, wait till whoever it is passes, then loop back and keep going. Why not?'

'But what if the person follows us there!' There was an air of panic in Donna's voice.

'He won't know where we've gone. The track isn't signposted, and in this light, he won't see the turn-off. We'll move quickly now, so that he won't spot us turn there.'

Laura chewed her cheek, nodding. 'So, you know exactly where to go?'

'I'm a cop from here. I have to know where all the trails start and end.'

The group was quiet for a moment.

'If we're really worried,' Sally added, 'I can make a call on the sat phone when we next have a break. Come on, let's lose this creep!'

CHAPTER 48

The Jagged Ridge trail was rocky, and its exposed nature meant that the wind, growing in intensity, bit into them with menace.

Donna was struggling. 'One moment,' the woman said, holding up her hand. 'Just need to get my breath.'

There was a strained quality to her breathing that alarmed Sally. 'Are you asthmatic, Donna?' She remembered, now, the inhaler in Donna's lounge.

The woman was bent double, her hands on her knees. 'I forgot my Ventolin.'

'Christ!' Laura swore.

'Here. I've got one in the medical kit.' Sally put down her pack and kneeled, opening the day pack and rummaging about. 'You'll be okay. Just take nice, deep breaths.'

Donna bent over. 'I'm a bit dizzy,' she said. 'A bit . . .' Then suddenly Donna was falling forward, slipping down the slope.

Sally looked on in shock as the older woman tried to find purchase, fell on her stomach and slid down some more, snatching at the pack, pulling on it, trying to haul herself up.

Too late, Sally grabbed for the pack, but it was already rolling too fast, past Donna, who tried to catch it, and then down the mountain, bumping and flying through the air.

'Help!' Donna cried, as her feet slipped on rock and she scrambled further down.

Sally leaped into action, calling for Laura to hold out her hand, and then, with one hand in Laura's, she stretched down and grabbed onto Donna's wrist. The action halted Donna's slide and allowed her a moment to find a rock to wedge her feet in. With Sally's help, she climbed the short distance back up to the path.

'Are you all right?'

Donna nodded, tears in her eyes. 'The pack!' she gasped.

'It's okay.' Sally tried to sound reassuring. It wasn't her fault, after all. Laura, though, looked seriously pissed off.

'I could have died,' Donna whimpered.

'There's a ledge down there,' Laura pointed out. 'You would have been hurt – but not dead.'

'Come on,' Sally urged them, 'let's move to a more sheltered place. Not much we can do about the pack now.'

They began walking in strained silence till they reached a small clearing where they could all sit.

'Should we start going back to the other track now?' Laura asked. 'Whoever it was will have passed by now.'

'What, back up that track again?' Donna looked dismayed.

'We'll take it easy,' Sally soothed, though in reality, the track was more difficult than she'd remembered.

Donna gave a little cry. 'What if he's still there, or if he's waiting for us!'

'Why would he do that?' Laura's voice faded as she looked about uncertainly.

'I don't want to go back there!' Donna wailed. 'He'll be there! It's reminding me of what happened to Russell! Someone's out there!'

Sally studied the woman with a growing sense of unease. *Please*, she thought, *don't have a panic attack on me now. Just don't. Not out here, with no sat phone.*

'Calm down, Donna,' Laura said, sharp.

'I'm not going back up there!'

Sally sniffed, ran through options in her head. Ran through them again. 'We could keep going,' she said eventually. 'Push on to the next campsite. It's pretty straight from now on, more of a slight incline. It'll be a few more hours, but then tomorrow we could make our way straight to Alpine Road.'

'So it means we miss the Ladies Baths,' Donna said thinking aloud, 'but it would be quicker tomorrow.'

'And there's phone reception sooner this way,' Sally added. 'We can call Warren and get him to pick us up.'

Donna nodded. 'Let's do that. I'd rather do that.'

There was a pause, heavy in atmosphere. Sally could almost hear Laura's brain ticking. No doubt the idea of filming at the next site was terrifying, but intoxicating to the documentary maker. Footage from the actual site of the murders. Filming the same route she'd taken ten years before.

'Okay,' Laura said grimly, hauling her pack back on. 'Let's do it.'

'If only we had some snacks,' Donna said. 'I'm getting really hungry.'

'It's quite cold too,' Laura said. 'I didn't bring an extra thermal.'

Behind them, Sally gritted her teeth in frustration. The pack that was lost down the mountain had in it a first aid kid, her pocketknife, the sat phone, an extra top and some jelly snakes. Seriously, could anything else go wrong?

A stinging wind blew up the valley and the Precipice came into view, jutting out of the trees.

'It's so lonely out here,' Laura declared to no one in particular. 'I'm not sure why, but it is.'

'I'm glad you two are with me,' Donna peered at the rocky crag. 'I'd seriously hate to be here on my own.'

CHAPTER 49

Shit, it was cold. Sally watched as Laura fumbled with the video recorder, taking her time to slowly move around 360 degrees, aiming to capture the early evening in all its glory.

Since they'd reached the hidden campsite, their nerves had calmed somewhat.

If someone saw them now – Donna in her stupid jumper looking at photos of Russell on her phone, Laura videoing her surroundings, and Sally drying the Trangia after their meal – they'd assume they were simply three close friends on a bushwalk.

Nothing could be further from the truth.

But we were brought here, to this mountain, for the same reason, she thought. To try to make sense of a tragedy, and for the others perhaps to find some comfort, arrive at a form of closure.

Sally could never understand why grieving family members would visit the horrific sites where loved ones had died. Why put yourself through that?

But that's the thing, she thought. You *wanted* to feel every bit of it: you wanted to understand what it was they were feeling in their very last moments. You wanted to take some of their pain and put it on yourself.

In the far distance, a howling in the night made her jump.

'God! What was that?' Laura clutched at Donna's arm. 'I swear I heard a werewolf.'

'Wild dogs,' Donna said, matter of fact. 'Poor things have gone feral. It happens up here.'

It was dark now, and it was freezing.

'How do you know?' Laura asked, frowning.

'Well, I know it wasn't a *werewolf*.'

There was an extended pause while they all listened as, once again, the dogs howled in unison, then stopped abruptly.

'I'm going to bed,' Sally announced suddenly, tired of it all, and unable to shake a general sense of unease.

'But it's only 7 pm!' Laura sounded surprised.

'It's not like we can have toasted marshmallows on the fire,' Sally pointed out.

'Oh, come on,' Laura said. 'We haven't even had a proper chat. What about you? We don't know anything about you.'

'There's not much to tell.'

'Jim says you're amazing at your job.'

Sally wished there was a campfire: anything to stare at, so she wouldn't have to look at Laura's face right now. 'Does he?'

'Yeah. Last time I spoke to him, he said that you two are planning a trip together, to do that walk in Spain.' Laura sounded a little sad as she poked the ground with her finger. 'He said he's saving up for it.'

'He said that?' Sally replied in wonder. She and Jim occasionally talked about doing the Camino walk in a year's time, maybe even take six months off and work in Europe. It was Sally who'd enthused about it; Jim mainly listened.

'You're really lucky,' Laura said.

Sally didn't answer.

'When he was carrying me along the track, I kept rambling about this book I was reading, *Jekyll and Hyde*. I don't know why – I was in shock, I guess. I just kept talking about an assignment I had, and all the time he listened and said things like, "That sounds good," and "When's it due?" and he kept me from going crazy. He never got mad, or forced me to walk, although I must have weighed a ton.'

There was a short silence.

'He was reading that book the other day,' Sally finally said. 'He said it was a bit boring.'

'Did he?' Laura smiled. 'Fair enough. Warren says he's enjoying it, but with Waz, you never know. I think he likes sports autobiographies, but he's too afraid to admit it to me.'

The warmth in Laura's voice when she mentioned her colleague made Sally relax a little. She untied the elastic on her hair and redid her messy bun. 'It's weird, but I had this feeling . . . I thought that maybe Jim had been cheating on me with you.' She felt stupid saying it out loud now.

'What?!' Laura was shocked. 'No! Not ever, I promise.'

There was a loud exhale. 'I can't stand men who cheat!' Donna burst out, making Sally jump. She'd almost forgotten that there was another person among them; the woman had been sitting so quietly in the dark.

'Had experience in that area, have you, Donna?' Laura's dry voice, by contrast, was mildly amused.

'You could say that.' The woman turned her face away.

An awkward beat followed. Laura raised her eyebrows and looked at the ground.

'Hey.' Sally attempted to steer the conversation away from

Donna's pain. 'I've been trying to think. Do you two know what songs the Kingsmen played? They're an old-school band.'

Donna shrugged. 'Never heard of them. Why?'

'Just something funny Martin mentioned.'

'I've heard of them!' Laura brightened. 'They sang that song "Louie". You know' – her voice rose in song – 'Louie, Louie . . .'

'I don't know it,' Donna said, flat.

Louie, Sally thought. A song Lyn Howlett's charismatic husband sang to an old flame in the mountains. Louie, Louie.

Louanne.

CHAPTER 50

Jim Brear drove into Edenville with a growing sense of regret. All day, he'd been thinking about Sally and what a fool he'd been. He'd brought up the Disco thing the day after she'd almost been run over by some dickhead. What was that all about? His poor little ego.

And then, if that wasn't enough, he'd patronised – no, *insulted* – Sally before throwing Laura in her face.

Jim couldn't deny that there was something between him and Laura: how could there not be, after what they'd been through? All that time, carrying her back along the Razor's saddle, feeling her get heavier and heavier in his arms. That knife edge they'd been on. Their one purpose: to survive. He'd never have that with anyone else.

But those feelings would never go anywhere in real life. They both knew that.

And Laura wasn't Sally. His Sal.

He drove home, the mountains to the east, the river flashing silver at every turn. *Sally,* he thought, *now she's the real deal.* She certainly wasn't her mother, Jim knew that. Of course she wasn't.

Deb was funny and warm and entertaining. Sally was all that too – but she was also hardworking and loyal and independent. In a way, Sally was more like her stepfather Angelo than her mother Deb.

As he passed the first houses of Edenville, Jim decided, on impulse, to stop at the police station. See if she was still there; she often worked late. They could go for dinner. He would make amends.

Kyle Roberts was at the front desk, scribbling something with a look of pure concentration on his face.

'Kyle! Sally in?' Jim glanced briefly at the constable's notepad, where he'd written a number of lines and random words.

The young officer glanced up, puzzled. 'What? Oh. She's on the Razor with the film crew – didn't you know? She's guiding that memorial walk for the victims' families.'

'Shit, I forgot!' There he was again, so wrapped up in himself he'd forgotten about her night on the mountain.

Kyle sniffed, looked disapproving. Had Sally told him about their fight?

'Do you know when she'll be back?'

'Tomorrow.'

'Of course. Right.' Jim turned to go.

'How's her bruise looking now?' Kyle asked.

'Bruise?'

'On Sally's back – from the kicking she got last Friday night. I couldn't believe it!'

A sick feeling crept up Jim's throat.

'What with the hit-and-run as well, I think Pat was glad to get her out of town for a bit.'

'Right.'

'And now she's got me digging into the Durants. Dunno where any of them are. Lex isn't answering his phone.'

'Does Sally think it was Neil who kicked her?' Jim suddenly remembered Sally asking if he'd seen Lex's brother when he found the note on his car windscreen.

'I can't say. Pat wants me to track down Neil and Annie in particular. But that Annie, look, it's wild! I've got no clue where she is, but I've just found out that she got $5000 from a community group for cancer treatment, when she didn't even have cancer!' Kyle sounded quite excited by his discovery. 'And when people found out about it, she vanished! There is no trace of an Annie Durant at all.'

'Yeah?'

Kyle hesitated. 'Yeah.'

'Neil will be at Lex's, won't he?' Jim said, trying for a neutral tone.

Kyle shrugged. 'I've been ringing and ringing him, but he's not answering. I'd pay him a visit, but I have to wait until Pat gets here. He said not to go out there on my own.'

'Do you want me to pop up there?' Jim offered. If Neil was responsible for the hit-and-run, and the attack on Sally last Friday night, he'd like a word with the eldest Durant too.

Kyle opened his mouth to say something.

Jim didn't wait for his reply.

CHAPTER 51

Sally's eyes snapped open. She wasn't sure what had woken her, but guessed it was the numbing cold. She lay there wrapped in her sleeping bag, listening, straining her ears.

Nothing. Nothing, save the wind pulling at the fly.

She closed her eyes. Tried to get back to sleep. It had been difficult enough in the first place after she'd lain awake thinking of the possibility that Terry Howlett knew Louanne Durant. Now, she tried in vain to rest her mind. Something was off, she knew it. *What is it?* The feeling continued to nag.

A sound. This time, undeniable. The crunch of leaves beside her head and to the left.

Sally sat bolt upright as another crunch told her that someone or something was pacing around her tent.

A possum, most likely. She tried to remember if they'd packed away their food properly. Possums were smart; they could chew through material, reach in with their little paws and take whole bags of food.

The pacing continued: too far apart for a small animal.

'Donna?' she called, low but firm. 'Laura?'

Nothing but the crackle of leaves and twigs.

Peering through narrowed eyes, she felt about for her lens case. God, she couldn't see a thing. Why hadn't she brought her glasses?

She patted around the sides of her sleeping mat and at the foot of her bed.

A dark shape moved further to the front of the tent; large, undefined. She gasped, searching desperately now for her stupid lenses. She couldn't see. She couldn't see! Only shapes, some darker than others.

As she rose onto her knees, she was horrified to hear a slick wrenching sound and felt one of the pegs of her tent being lifted out.

'Who's out there?' she called. 'Stop it!'

Another peg, and now one side of her tent caved in.

Wriggling out of her sleeping bag, and blindly feeling her way, Sally crawled to the front door, patting her hands down it to find the zip. Opening it, and then the fly, she climbed out of her sagging tent to complete darkness. 'Who's there?' she called again, unable to hide a telltale quiver of fear.

She blinked, her sight blurry and confused. There were a few stabs of starlight in the black. In the darkness, not three metres away, was a figure, just standing there.

'Oh,' she said, finally recognising who it was. 'It's you. What the hell do you think you're doing?'

And then a shot rang out.

CHAPTER 52

Jim pulled up to the Durant house and fought against the instinctive fear in his gut. He knew all the stories about the Durants; he'd grown up hearing them. They were folklore in the playground. His own father had gone to school with Lex, and said he'd always kept a clear eye on him whenever money was handed in for the lunch orders.

The dogs were barking madly, but they hadn't turned on him, which meant they must be tied up. Edging to the side of the house, he could see the three dogs straining at their chains, growling at him, trying to race forward, their paws gouging the dirt with their effort.

Jim took two tentative steps towards them. An old four-litre milk container had been cut in half and was being used as the dogs' drinking bowls. Except the two halves were tipped over and empty.

He found a tap on the side of the building and, using a broken paling from the fence, edged the plastic halves over to him then filled them up. The dogs, silent now, were panting, a desperate pleading in their eyes. He pushed the bowls towards them and instantly they were upon them, sloshing, slurping up the water.

Strange. Lex loved his dogs. Where was he?

A grimy window above him let in just enough light to illuminate a made-up bed and a cupboard. Lex's bedroom, he guessed. The cover pulled up neatly to the pillow.

Where was Lex? Where was Neil?

'Anybody home?' Jim called, leaping up onto the porch. 'Lex!'

The thirsty dogs were a worry, but the stillness as Jim pushed open the front door was even more so.

With growing unease, Jim moved through the hall.

'Lex!' No one in the front room.

Down the long hallway: no photos, no prints on the wall. A strange, cloying smell filled the air. His heart was nearly beating out of his chest.

'Sally!' he now called, for no rational reason. '*Sal!*'

A bedroom to the left, the one he'd seen through the window. Nothing there.

A bedroom to his right, but altogether different: dishevelled quilt; clothes thrown about; one boot in the doorway, like a statement. And there was something on the bed – a small shape, moving, heaving.

With his heart pounding, Jim reached over, one hand still covering his nose, and pulled back the cover.

A black cat snarled at him. Teeth bared and mouth open. He reared away, throwing the bedclothes over it, and raced out into the hallway. The smell was almost unbearable now.

'*Lex!*'

The last door, at the end of the hallway, was jammed. He pushed at it. No movement: something was lodged behind it.

Feeling ill, Jim threw his whole weight against it, ramming the door hard. It opened.

His eyes circled the room in horror. Later, he would remember vividly only one clear thing. It was not the spread of dark blood, congealed and splattered all over the walls of the room. Nor was it the sight of Neil Durant, lying on his front, an axe wedged between his shoulder blades, head to the side, a stunned expression on his face.

No: the image that stayed with him, with startling clarity, was the arrangement of figurines all about the room. Twenty, maybe thirty of them, all looking to the centre, staring at the dead man lying in his pool of blood.

He focused on one little statue now. A shepherdess in blue, standing in the blood, and smiling triumphantly at the grotesque scene.

Racing outside, Jim grabbed his phone to call the police. Heart beating wildly, he saw that a message had come through from his mother titled 'Durants'.

Jim, I haven't heard from Sally. Here's the information she was asking for on the Durant kids. Can you pass it on?

Barely registering what he was doing, Jim opened the link and scanned through the reports she'd sent, picking out key words, a horrible realisation dawning . . .

Fuck.

And the figurines . . .

The Razor was half in darkness, looming over him, bearing down.

311

Through the bush, Jim could see a thin trail, snaking its way up. The Durants had trails all through the mountains, everyone knew that.

Breaking into a run, he called Pat. 'It's Jim. Neil Durant's dead. He's in the family home. But get a team up to the Razor *now*. Sally's in trouble!'

'Jim, for god's sake, man, where are you?' Pat's voice was sharp.

Jim ignored the branches smashing into his face. 'On the mountain.'

Then he turned his phone off, ran through a shallow creek, and began to climb.

CHAPTER 53

The figure had gone.

More crashing sounds.

Another shot?

For a moment, Sally thought she must be still dreaming. There was no denying the hysterical sobbing coming from the tent next to hers.

Shaking herself, she scrambled to the entrance of the second tent. 'Laura? Laura, it's me.'

Laura was crouched at the opening. 'It's happening again. Oh my god, it's happening again!'

'Shh. Keep calm,' Sally said, low, at the same time, coaxing her back into the cover of the trees. 'Where's Donna?'

'I think she's dead,' Laura wailed, pointing behind Sally to what appeared to be a pair of boots lying beside a bush in front of them. 'She got up to fix one of the ropes that was flapping. She was taking ages, and . . . and there was the shot . . . and there she is, and . . .'

Sally raced to the edge of the clearing to where a body lay. She ran her hand over it, feeling for a pulse in the neck.

But no, that wasn't right. She looked closely at the clothes, turned the body over. Felt a sharp pang of sorrow as she leaned down, towards the face.

She raced back to Laura, who was still weeping.

'We have to get out of here,' Sally hissed.

'Where? That trail is so exposed, you said so yourself. He'll just get us there, he'll shoot us. He'll shoot us!'

Sally ran her hands over her face, forcing herself to think. 'Oh no, the sat phone!' Their only means of communication, lost down the mountain.

'I have it,' Laura said through her sobs.

Sally turned to Laura, confused.

'I took the phone from the bag while we were having our break. Before Donna's fall. I was planning to call the journalists in Edenville and tell them to meet us along the track tomorrow, on our way back.'

'Christ, Laura, where is it?'

Laura scrabbled back into the tent. There was a fumbling and a rustling, and she reappeared.

With shaking hands, Sally took the phone and held it close to her useless eyes. Pressed 000.

Nothing.

She tried again.

'What's going on?' Laura's voice was panicked, high-pitched, her breathing rapid.

'No signal. It's too overcast, no satellite passing, *I don't know.*'

The dark, looming Precipice soared above them, offering both a shelter and a trap.

Sally jabbed in the numbers again, knowing they wouldn't work. *Come on!*

'What do we do?' Laura wailed.

'There's another way.' Sally looked up, feeling ill. 'It's less exposed.'

'Up there?' Laura followed her gaze. 'How?'

'I know the way.' Sally desperately tried to remember what Kate had written in her book.

'Wait!' Laura stared through the dark at the fallen body. 'Donna's legs are moving. She's moving! We need to help her!'

'No!' Sally grabbed Laura by the shoulders. 'Help me get to the rock. We need to go. *Now.*'

'But Donna—'

'*It's not Donna.*' Sally pulled Laura up and, hauling her along, began to run.

CHAPTER 54

Halfway up the climb, Jim stopped, hands on his knees, taking deep breaths. There was a cut on his forehead where he'd crashed into an overhanging branch, and blood was running into his eyes. He swiped at it distractedly. Where was the path? Where was the bloody path? Not even a path really; a thin, winding trail straight up from the back of the Durant property to the top of the Razor. He'd only taken it once when he was a kid – it was a shortcut to the Ladies Baths. He and his school friends had scared themselves stupid at the time with tales of the evil family who lived nearby.

Christ. Where was the path? Frantically, he stepped over blackberry bushes, ignoring the pain of the thorns and trying to push the memory of Neil's murdered body from his mind.

Phrases from the reports he'd read spurred him on, made him search harder:

Louanne and Faith removed from their home after
cruelty from older brother Neil
Louanne, isolated and lonely – too eager to please

There it was! The path, thin and pale, winding up the mountain. Without pausing, Jim began running.

Louanne's warning from police over fraud, for spying on neighbours
Unsettling behaviour, shifting personality
In the process of changing her name

Sally, he thought, his breathing already ragged as he forced himself up a steep incline. *Where are you?*
I'm sorry. Please be okay. I'm sorry.

Louanne cannot be found.

CHAPTER 55

It pained Sally to think of Lex Durant lying there, gravely injured. But she had to leave him. 'Annie shot me,' he'd managed to whisper, as she'd leaned over his injured body. 'Hide.'

With a cold dread, Sally realised that the man who'd been following them had wanted to keep them safe.

'You mean it's *Donna* shooting at us?' Laura's voice rose in horror.

'Yes.'

It was all falling into place. Donna losing the pack down the cliff. Donna knowing the area better than she'd admitted previously. Donna eager to get away from the person following them. Donna calling the Plunge Pools the Ladies Baths when only true locals called them that. She knew something was off about the woman, she knew! Lex had just confirmed it.

'Donna is Bill Durant's sister, Annie.'

'No!' Laura shook her head, uncomprehending. 'That's not right. It's Donna, Russell's wife.'

Breathe.

'That body?' Sally said, fast. 'It's Lex, Annie's brother. Annie — or rather Donna — shot him.'

At the rock, it was so dark, Sally had to press her face close to the other woman to make out her features. 'Now, listen,' she spoke deliberately. 'I'm going to climb up the Precipice to get reception. You stay, try to keep Lex conscious, put pressure on his wound. Keep to the trees, stay down low.'

'Wait!' Laura grabbed Sally's arm as she turned to leave. 'So, where's Donna – or whatever she's called?'

'She's been shot or injured. I don't know. I don't know!'

'Okay. Go,' Laura nodded. 'Go!'

'Lex has a gun beside him,' Sally instructed. 'If you need to, take it.'

Laura's face was a blur in the dark. 'And what will I do if Donna comes back?'

'Run.' Sally didn't turn around. 'Or shoot.'

CHAPTER 56

In the dim moonlight, Sally could just make out a thin, rocky track hugging the cliff. She took it now, as fast as she could. With her arms spread wide, and cheek to the rock, she felt along the path, aware of the sheer drop below. Wind screamed through the valley; her heart beat loud. A gap in the rock face, and she felt it – the chimney Kate had described in her book.

Move, Sally told herself. *Move!* She reached about for the promised rope, deliberately at first, and then wildly, till finally she found the thick twine, lodged into a crack on the side.

Giving it a sharp tug to test its reliability, she shoved the satellite phone in the inside pocket of her jacket and zipped it up. *Move.* She hauled herself up, using cracks in the rock as purchase. Now, the only sound was a faint dripping and the thin whistle of wind making its way down the narrow space. One metre more and silence: no sound yet of anyone approaching.

Reaching the top, Sally scrambled up a short ledge and then onto the flat rock of the Precipice, just as she detected a heavy thump in the space below.

Panicking, she leaned down and grabbed hold of the rope again to pull it up. But, horrified, she felt the thick twine grow taut. And in the blackness, Sally could just make out the top of someone's head, beginning to make the climb.

She looked around wildly for something to cut the rope with. But there was nothing – nothing! She scrambled backwards, feeling along the surface, trying to get away. There was nowhere to hide.

Just make the call, make the call.

She rang 000. Waited.

No dial tone.

'Come on!' she raged aloud to the night sky. '*Come on!*'

She tried again, and this time – a signal.

'Police, ambulance or fire?'

'Police!' she screamed. 'And ambulance. It's Senior Constable Sally White, I'm at the top of the Precipice, on the Razor. One person has been shot and I'm being chased!'

'Are you in a safe place?'

'No, I am fucking not!'

After shouting out her location again, she hung up and waited a few seconds, her mind wild with fear. She pressed her back against the rock again, facing the chimney, all the while trying to work out what to do.

Think. Think!

She could try to push Donna down the tunnel, prevent her from getting back up. But she was much smaller than Donna, and she couldn't see properly without her damn glasses.

Think!

Maybe find a rock to throw at her? But feeling around, there was nothing save the flat granite surface and a few little stones.

Could she wait till her stalker got to the top, and then try to dodge her? Fight her? God, she couldn't see!

In a rush, Kate's blog came to her: an alternative way down. What had she written?

Jump across a crevice on the east side.

Sally lay down flat, and pulled herself along the rock in that direction, ignoring the sharp stones which cut into her skin. *The gap must be so close!*

A sound at the chimney behind her, and heavy breathing. Like something from a horror movie, Sally turned to see the top of a head emerge.

Grabbing a handful of stones, Sally turned back to the rock, continuing to edge slowly along – terrified of falling down the ravine, and terrified of not finding it at all.

Where was it? She rolled a pebble in front of her, listening. Nothing. Another one, straining to hear. Rising panic. One more, and this time she rolled it away from her at a forty-five-degree angle. She heard it roll, and then the sound of it falling into an abyss, clanking all the way down.

'Sally!'

Ignoring the triumphant voice, Sally edged her way towards the crevice, conscious of the flatness of the space, the lack of places to hide. Help was hours away.

With a final grunt, Donna was up on the ledge.

Sally couldn't see – she couldn't see! But she could hear the older woman, hear her shuffling and trying to stand.

Sally turned her head to the crevice again. She stretched out a hand, and the rock ledge dropped away. Here it was. She reached down: the sharp drop, the rush of air. Should she lower herself down?

If she fell, she'd crash onto the rocks far below.

There was nothing she could do.

Or.

Maybe there was.

'Annie!' she called across the space, making it clear she knew who the woman was. 'I'm here.'

'Oh, Sally.' The breathy voice was so different from back there at the campsite. 'There you are. It's taken me a bit longer – my brother tackled me, and it took me ages to catch my breath. Asthma.'

'We can get you help,' Sally said, thinking quickly. 'I've called the emergency services. Someone will be here soon.'

'No, they won't.' The dark shape was moving slowly towards her. 'It takes hours and hours to get here. Last time, it took your boyfriend nearly four hours to walk across the Razor. I was watching when he found them.'

Annie had been there, watching, like a fox.

'You killed them all, didn't you, Annie – or is it Louanne?'

'Louanne.' The name came out slowly from the shadows. 'It's been ages since anyone called me that.'

Sally slipped one arm over the edge of the crevice again. Felt the angle of it veer straight down. Her head reeled. 'Why call yourself Donna?'

'I'm called lots of things: Louanne, Annie, Donna, Yona.'

Yona, of course.

'Just like you, Sally. You're SalPal, aren't you? We've all got other names.'

'We don't all go around killing people.' Maybe she should play for time?

'Russell was a bad husband. He said he was unhappy with me. I tested him, and he failed.'

'You tested him with Yona, or *Ruby*.'

'That's right. You're a smart one.' Annie gave a short chuckle. 'Where are you?'

'And Lyn?' Sally asked, still biding for time. 'You knew Terry, didn't you? Is that why you killed her?'

She sensed the woman stepping closer. 'Terry was my boyfriend. I was going to marry him. Then he left me for that *bitch*!'

'And the others?'

'I did Kate a favour. Her life was going nowhere.' Annie stopped. 'Where are you, Sally?'

Sally squeezed herself closer to the gap, felt again over the edge. She wondered if it was possible to survive such a fall. 'What about Brooke?'

'I gave her so much,' Annie snarled. 'The letters, the emails, the gifts, the visits, all that friendship. She had everything – and what does she do? Reports me!'

'And what did Tom ever do to you?'

'I didn't – I don't know . . . He was in the wrong place.' Sally could hear Annie's breath becoming laboured.

'So you shot them.'

'Not those two. Not Brooke and the Brit.'

'You killed your brother. You shot Bill.'

'Don't say that. Not Billy.' The woman sounded upset. 'I'm not a total monster.'

'You are. You shot all those people.' The whole time they'd been talking, Sally was running her hands over the edge of the crevice, trying to find some purchase. If she could lower herself down, just a metre or two . . .

'They were all getting closer to finding out who I was. Lyn was speaking to Fraud, Brooke went to the police; even Russell would have cottoned on when Yona didn't meet him at the end of the walk. They had to go.' Annie's breathy voice grew near. 'And now Laura with her documentary, and *you*, Sally, you've brought it all up again. Things are unravelling . . . I need to end this and become someone new.'

Sally held her arm out into the void, straightened it as far as she could. All she could feel was a cold rush of air. How far was it to the other side? One metre, or was it three? She couldn't remember.

A shuffling, and suddenly she saw Annie's looming figure silhouetted against the clouds. 'Online, I can be anyone I want,' Annie said. 'I could even be you.'

Seconds, seconds was all she had.

Think!

Trust your instincts.

'The police will be here soon.' Sally tried to shuffle further along, her face scraping the rock.

'Come on, Sally, I know you're here,' Annie said, almost gently. She was getting closer.

A large hand swiped out into the air.

Trust your instincts.

'Where are you?' Annie's voice had taken on a reedy quality, like a child's.

Sally raised herself up and crouched in a runner's pose. She could do it. She *had* to do it. Taking a deep breath, she leaped across the crevice, propelling herself as far as she could, arms reaching out, chest straining, wind rushing, the space too far . . .

She landed hard on the other side, knees scraping the edge, pulling herself along, then scrambling over sharp rock. She was crying, snot streaming from her nose, blood on her hands.

'Sally, where'd you go?' Over on the other side of the crevice, the little-girl voice grew closer still. Wheedling, pitiful. It was so dark now. Could Annie see what was right in front of her?

'I'm here!' Sally half sat up, sobbing.

There was heavy breathing, footsteps . . .

Come on, Sally willed. *Come closer.*

One step . . . two . . . Annie was getting nearer. Stalking. The air between them squeezed, became thin.

'Sally?' There was a scuffling, the sound of sliding stone.

And then an ear-piercing scream, as Annie Durant slipped into the jagged void.

CHAPTER 57

Sally lay on her back, looking up at the carpet of stars.

The mountain was very still now. The wind had quietened, but if she strained her ears, she could hear the rushing of it through the snow gums below, and its faint whistle through the deadly crevice.

She knew she should get up. Get back to Laura, check on Lex. But for now, all she could do was lie there and breathe.

Suddenly there was a shout. Her name. Sally forced herself to sit up, pay attention. It was definitely her name, being called again. Too early for the rescue services to arrive, but yes – she could hear a voice. In the growing light, she made out a boulder nearby and started to climb it, its smooth surface a comfort after the biting rocks below. Now, she was very high up, and when she narrowed her eyes, she could just make out the dark circle of the Precipice ledge – and was that the campsite far below?

'*Sally!*'

She saw, through the weak rays of a torchlight, that a figure was climbing up towards her. She felt no fear, but rather a strange calm.

'Sal?'

She opened her mouth, unable to speak. But there he was. There was Jim, climbing up to her. He was panting, sweaty, his hair a wild mess.

'Are you all right?' he asked, gasping for breath. 'Are you hurt?'

There was a strange ringing in her ears, as though all of this was very far away.

'You ran here,' she said simply.

'Yes.'

He'd run all the way up the mountain, and then climbed the Precipice and jumped over the crevice to reach her.

'Are you okay?' he asked again, urgent. 'Are you hurt?'

She felt a sob rise up in her throat. 'I'm not hurt.' And then: 'I think I'm going to be sick.'

Jim was beside her now; she could see a long cut above his eye. He held her hair back from her face as she retched, then wiped her mouth with the sleeve of his shirt.

'Christ,' he muttered, grabbing hold of her hand. 'Thank fuck you're all right. I've never been so scared in my life.'

Too tired to say anything, Sally nodded. She rested her sore and bloodied hand on his thigh, let him wrap his fingers around hers.

CHAPTER 58

Lex was propped against a tree when Sally and Jim made it back to the campsite. He was pale but conscious. Annie had shot him below the knee, but the bleeding had stopped and there was now a tatty bandage wrapped around the wound.

Laura sat beside him, her face red from crying. She jumped up when she saw them and embraced Sally, hard.

'He found you,' she said. 'Thank god.'

'Annie's gone,' Jim announced, not sugar-coating it. 'Help's on the way.'

They sat. Took a moment to catch their breaths and take stock.

'Lex' – Sally turned to the old man – 'I know it was you following us out there on the track.'

'You ran too bloody quickly for me,' Lex said, gruffly. 'Couldn't stop Annie in time.'

'How did you know to find us?'

'She called me, said she was at our home.' Lex rubbed at his arm. 'I was on my way back from the coast, heading over the mountain. Hadn't seen her in almost twenty years . . . but she said she was going to finish off Neil, before walking on the

Razor one last time. She said he deserved it, and that after this, I wouldn't see or hear from her again.'

'So you followed us.'

'Annie said she was going to do you in too. Said she needed to get rid of the cop and the others who were after her. And yeah, Therese had told me about your walk.'

'You saved us, Lex.'

'Almost lost you at one point. Had to retrace, then retrace again.' Lex gazed into the distance. 'When I found your camp, I shot into the air when I saw her near your tent. Tackled her down, and she damn well shot me.'

She didn't kill you though, Sally thought. *She could have, but she didn't . . .*

The sky became light grey, and a faint, shimmering pink appeared over the horizon.

'So,' Laura said after a while. 'Donna – or Annie – killed them all back then, shot them from up there on that hill?'

'She insisted she didn't shoot Tom or Brooke,' Sally replied. 'And then she got upset when I suggested she'd killed her brother. It was so weird.' She leaned into Jim, feeling his warmth.

A low thwacking sound filled the air, and from the west they could make out a chopper flying towards them, its metal surface glinting in the morning sun.

'But that's ridiculous. If she didn't shoot them, then who did?' Laura looked as if she might cry again. 'It had to be her! Weren't they all shot with the same gun?'

'I don't reckon she did shoot them. Not everyone, I mean.' Lex said it so quietly that they had to lean in to hear. 'Now that you've told me' – he nodded towards Laura – 'exactly where the two bodies were found on the track . . . I always thought they were shot closer to the camp. That's what I'd heard.'

The early reports, misleading in their errors; the gossip around town, Sally thought.

'And my brother . . . he was found up there?' Lex looked up to the nearby crest, where police had discovered Bill Durant's body, the 30-30 murder weapon beside him.

Sally nodded. 'That's right.'

Lex coughed into his hand, then wiped it on the ground. 'I'm not saying Annie didn't kill the ones down here in the campsite. But that girl who was running away, and the English hiker? No, I don't think Annie killed them.'

'Then who? How?' Laura asked.

Lex paused, took some deep breaths. 'Annie was a good shooter,' he said eventually. 'But not that good. To stand on that hill' – he pointed to the crest again – 'and shoot a running target over three hundred metres away? Only one person who could do that.' Light was now streaking down the valleys in rivers of gold.

'Over three hundred metres with a 30-30 and open sights.' Lex shook his head. 'The shooter would have had to aim higher than the target – it's a slow bullet with that gun – and he'd have had to calculate the drop. It was just one shot each, wasn't it, that killed them.' Lex wasn't asking for confirmation. 'That could only be Bill.'

Laura stared up at the low hill. 'So, *he* killed Tom.'

'And Brooke,' Sally added.

'I think so, yeah,' Lex said, defeated.

'But why?' Jim asked.

'Maybe . . .' Lex rubbed his leg, his voice fading. 'Maybe because Annie asked him to.'

The idea was preposterous, and yet . . .

Bill had been at the campsite. He'd been on or near the Razor track; he may have heard the gunshots, same as Jim did. He'd have seen Russell, his face smashed in. He'd have found Lyn dead in her tent. Kate must have been alive long enough to throw her pocketknife at him. Was that how it happened?

Sally pictured the scene: Annie pleading with her brother to shoot Brooke as she fled, knowing she could never make that shot.

And Bill hesitating, then kneeling and taking sight. Seeing Tom there too, having to shoot him as well. Did he spot Laura as she scrambled off the path? Did he see, maybe, a flicker of someone else crouching down in the valley?

Bill had been younger than Neil, but still old enough to have known better when his big brother was tormenting and abusing their sisters. So why not do this one thing for her? Everyone would blame him anyway.

And then, he'd turned the gun on himself.

Annie, looking at her brother dead. Going back to the campsite, then running to where the bodies of Tom and Brooke lay, checking for any evidence or maybe looking for the sat phone. Laura said she'd waited, hiding, for about twenty minutes before she heard the person on the path above.

Was that how it went?

'I can't believe it.' Laura shook her head. 'You wouldn't *kill* someone just because a sibling asked you to. No one would.'

Lex didn't say a word.

The helicopter was closer now, the noise deafening, whipping the snow gums and the low grass. The group moved from the cleared area into the safety of the shrub, Jim and Sally helping to carry the wounded Lex. They all crouched low, instinctively covering their heads against the rush of air. Sally felt Jim above her, protective, and in response, she put her arm around Laura's shoulders, the three of them bowing down like worshippers to a god.

When the two medics jumped out and carried Lex to the waiting chopper, Sally was by his side.

Lex turned to her. 'Annie was a sweet girl once. Our little shepherdess, we called her.' He coughed, then winced in pain. 'Life wasn't fair to her.'

'Lex, will you write a statement for me? About the harassment?'

He was in the chopper now, the others lining up to climb in.

'Don't give up, do you?' Lex gave a weak smile. 'Even now. Like one of them dogs with a bone.'

'That's me. Your friendly shih tzu.'

'Not a shih tzu,' he said. 'Bloody kelpie, you are.'

'You'll write the statement?'

'I might.' He smiled again as she climbed in and sat beside him.

A memory flashed into her mind: the figure outside her tent earlier; the pegs being pulled out. 'It was Annie who used to scare campers, wasn't it? Her and Bill? I know that Annie liked to play tricks.'

'Bill took photos. But only to document trespassers. Annie . . . she was different,' he admitted. 'She liked to watch people, see what they did. But I never, ever would have imagined she'd have done something like this.'

Annie was The Creeper, not Bill. A creeper online and in real life too, hiding behind a username, behind trees, in car parks, beside you in a tent: watching.

CHAPTER 59

Three weeks later

She'd made the phone call a day ago, and what she'd asked for would soon be set in motion.

Feeding the last of her report into the shredder, Sally pulls out the photo of her stepfather, the one she keeps in the back of her phone case. It is of the two of them hiking in the Grampians.

After she was brought down from the mountain, in shock and in pain, Angelo had taken time off to come and stay. He'd cooked and cleaned for her, turned off his work phone completely. In two weeks, he was coming up again. Jim was taking them to see the moss beds and precious bogs of Forlorn Hope, where Lyn and Terry liked to go.

Angelo can be neglectful, Sally thinks, as she turns to the shredder and collects the long strips of paper, before screwing them up and throwing them in the bin, *but he has been a good dad, and a patient stepfather. He's committed to his job, sometimes too much.* She understands that now – it's okay. There is a lot of him in her.

And yet: she is still her father's daughter.

Biology, it sticks.

And because of that, and the phone call she made, Norma Kerns's beloved caravan will be a mangled shell, burnt to a crisp, by the time she gets home tonight. And shortly, Blake Melus will know what terror feels like when he walks up the long muddy drive to his house. They'll take him somewhere quiet, rough him up, show him what they can do.

Fact is: you can ask family for things you would never ask from anyone else.

She looks for a moment at the paper in the bin. Her report was never going anywhere. In the weeks after her ordeal up the mountain, Sally had compiled first a lengthy statement from Lex about the alleged police harassment, and then, after some consideration, from the wife of the third cop Lex had mentioned, Harry Pickett. Trudy didn't hold back on some of the things Norma had encouraged Harry to do: fabricating restraining orders against Bill; alleging he was stalking campers, not simply recording suspected trespassers. Harry may have been a bad farmer, but according to Trudy, he was a worse cop. 'Should have moved up north,' she said. 'Harry was always easily led by Stormin' Norma.'

Norma had sneered when Sally had gone round to confront her.

'Good cops go after the ones that hurt us – you should know that,' she'd said after hearing Sally's allegations: that the police mistreatment of the Durants had been at Norma's encouragement; that she'd pressured Kyle not to follow up on the old harassment charges; that she'd kicked Sally in the back, got Blake to almost run her over. A stoned Blake had even admitted it

335

to a friend after Sally had questioned him. Eager to be a law-abiding citizen, Shambles, the soon-to-be father, duly passed on the confession to Pat. And then, there were the poisonous notes to Jim . . .

The old cop had denied the notes, been defiant about the rest. 'You can't prove a thing,' she'd said, 'and there's absolutely nothing you can do.'

Isn't there? Sally thought.

'The worst cops' – Norma grinned without humour – 'are the ones that snitch on their own.'

'Bill didn't shoot you,' Sally had replied. 'Neither did Lex.'

'No, but people like that, they're all the same. You'll find that out. Criminals pass it on in their genes: biology, it sticks.'

Yeah, Sally thought, remembering Blake's thin white body, his nasty smile. *Yeah, it does.*

'I'll die before you smear my name and that of my boys in this town,' Norma warned as she left. 'Don't think that just because you're the daughter of the Assistant Commissioner, you'll get special treatment.'

Now, Sally looks out of the window. Norma may be an old bitch, but she is a wily ex-cop. It will be almost impossible to pin the decades-old harassment on her, or the assault in the alleyway of the pub.

There's no hard evidence; there's no energy for it; the town will pull rank. What good would a lengthy internal investigation do? By the time the inevitably interminable review is complete, Norma will be half dead, and Sally will have no friends left in the force. Save for Angelo, of course.

Sally knows all of that, she does.

Hence the shredder. Hence the phone call.

She looks at her watch, almost time to go. Jim will be picking her up, they're going to look at a little house on the river. It's weird, but after what happened on the mountain, things like that, like moving in together, seem more pressing. It's only for the mountain that time is slow.

A shadow falls across the yard.

She watches as it thickens, spreads out like a grasping hand. Time to go.

She moves back to her desk, but not before she sees the school teacher, Glen, walk past the station. He stops and waves at her, and she waves back.

That's the second time he's walked past, she thinks vaguely. Unwittingly, her eyes turn to the poster he'd handed her, the one about the school fete.

She takes it down from the noticeboard and goes to screw it up, when she sees something that makes her frown. She holds it close to her eyes.

Sally notes the looping 'f', and the way Glen dots his 'i's with a circle. There's a dark unfurling in her chest. She's seen that writing before:

Your girlfriend is cheating on you.
Your girlfriend fucks Disco.

Heart thumping, Sally moves again to the window, where she can see the back of him, walking slowly, so slowly up the street.

She leans against the wall, trying to take it all in.

It could be a coincidence. She's just rattled from the events on the mountain.

Or . . . did Glen want Jim to break up with her so that he could swoop in, was that it?

No.

337

Glen? The beloved school teacher known as Gandhi for his glasses and gentle ways?

Glen?

But – perhaps.

Glen walks past the station every day, and it's not on his way home at all. The thought gives her pause. And didn't he turn up at the coffee shop at the same time she did yesterday? He's done that a few times, turn up to places where she is. Sally frowns, deep in thought. Glen standing close at the fete; Glen's frequent visits to the station; Glen's note on the fete poster: *Come, it'll be fun!*

All this time, she thinks.

She's not sure what to do. Not sure at all.

The station phone rings, jolting her from her thoughts. It's 9 am; it'll be Angelo's call. He said he'd ring at this time. She moves away from the window to answer it, and at the same time, her mobile rings. She sees the number, gives a brief laugh of disbelief. Barwon Prison. It'll be Eddie, calling to see how she is. Her two fathers! The phones ring on. What to do? The sound is maddening.

She runs a hand over her scalp and fixes her glasses firmly on her nose.

Trust your instinct, she thinks, as she hangs up one call, and answers the other.

Trust your family.

EPILOGUE

He could take her out right now.

She's there, right there in his sights, less than eighty metres away. He doesn't move. He barely breathes.

Wait.

All day, he's stalked along a game trail, stopping to glass, taking his time. He's seen a lyrebird, shot at wild dogs, passed hikers on his way.

There are too many people on the mountain.

At the Ladies Baths, he'd taken pictures of a group close to his boundaries. Good to have a record, although lately he doesn't know why he bothers.

He checks the range again, the wind and his scope. All is good. His finger rests on the trigger. He could take her out right now.

So, why doesn't he?

On the Razor, in the last few weeks, time has slowed. He's aware that for him now, it's less about the kill and more about time spent on the mountain. The endless valleys, the gnarled trees, the rounded peaks of the mountains like old men's heads. He'll miss it.

Three to six months. Bill sniffs, then spits hard on the dirt. Good enough. He's had a life.

His finger on the trigger tightens. He hesitates before he gives up and puts the gun down. Content to just watch, as the old deer eats and then pisses on the grass. Bill grins through his brown teeth: *that's* a life, he thinks.

A gunshot.

One.

Two.

The old hunter grabs his lens and glasses the area it's coming from. The Precipice campsite, not a five-minute jog away.

Probably kids, shooting in the air.

Another shot, and Bill is up, running along the faint path around the back of the campsite. He nears it just as he hears the first scream and another shot.

The sun's gone down, but there are streaks of light in the sky, and he can see the campsite. There's a sobbing, as though the bush itself is crying. Two dead, more shots, another scream. *Christ!*

His 30-06 beside him, Bill crouches, running low to where a woman is sitting by a tree, blood coming out of her mouth. He moves towards her, a terrible feeling inside him, his heart thumping as it hasn't done in years.

'You okay, lady?' he asks.

She's trying to speak, and he leans in, closer. She was at the Ladies Baths, he realises, and he's seen her before, walking on the mountain.

She reaches for something from her pocket and, just as he registers what's happening, there's pain. She's thrown a knife. It's pierced his knee.

A sudden call for help from the crest above.

The bloodied woman's a goner, he can see that. He pulls the knife out of his leg and throws it aside as he runs up the hill, knee burning.

'Bill!'

And before him, it's Annie. His little sister. She's holding their father's 30-30 out towards him and screaming, 'I need your help!'

A figure is running along the track down below.

'What are you doing?' he yells back.

'Shoot her!' Annie points now to the woman growing small in the dimming light. 'I can't take her out from here.'

'What? Why?' he asks, refusing to take the gun. 'Annie, no.'

His sister's face is wild, contorted. 'You owe me this one thing, Bill. I never asked for anything, you know that. You *have* to do it for me.'

And in a flash, it comes back to him. What Neil did to Annie and Faith. And Bill not helping her, not standing up to him.

'If she gets away, I'll go to prison. I'll never get out, Bill. I'll die in jail like Dad.'

The figure is now over two hundred metres away, and Annie is growing desperate. *'Please, Billy!'*

He'd let Neil do what he wanted with the girls while he'd walked outside, hidden himself in the bush.

But now, there was something he could do.

'Shoot!' she's screaming. *'Now!'*

He takes the 30-30, kneels, finds his moving target, and fires once. Sees another figure, and without thinking shoots that one too.

His breath is coming hard. He suddenly feels sicker than he ever has in his life.

'Give me the gun now, Billy,' Annie says, and her voice is suddenly calm. 'It's over.'

And Bill sees how it will go. No matter what happens here, he's the guilty one. He'll always be the one the cops blame. They've spent decades lying about his family, lying about him, and now it's all come home to roost.

But what does it matter anyway? Three to six months he's got left. Better to make it count.

Annie looks at him. He stares back at her. *She's crazy*, he thinks. *But she's my sister.*

He takes the gun and aims it at himself.

Family. In the end, that's all there is.

ACKNOWLEDGEMENTS

Many experienced people were generous with their knowledge for this book. The Reverend Mark Mickelburough, Kane Howell and Jack Bussell offered invaluable advice on hunting, the clever science teachers from my school considered various DNA scenarios, and seasoned bushwalkers provided crucial feedback. I was inspired by Tyrone Thomas, a well-known bushwalking author. His descriptions of walking in Australia often read like adventure fiction. Read his work if you want to set out walking!

As in the case with my earlier novels, I'm indebted to Beverley Cousins, Kalhari Jayaweera, Hannah Ludbrook, Adelaide Jensen, Tanaya Lowden, Claire Gatzen, Meaghan Amor and all the team at Penguin Random House Australia. They really are a powerhouse of professionalism and warmth.

Thank you always to Bernie for his support and to my sons who I dearly love, even though they never read my books.

AUTHOR'S NOTE

This book was written on the lands of the Waywurru and Dhudhuroa peoples, whom I would like to acknowledge as the Traditional Custodians and Storytellers of their country. I pay my respects to their Elders past and present, and celebrate all the histories, traditions and living cultures of Aboriginal and Torres Strait Islander people.

Margaret Hickey is an award-winning author and playwright from North East Victoria. She has a PhD in Creative Writing and is deeply interested in rural lives and communities. She is also the author of *Cutters End, Stone Town* and *Broken Bay*. *Cutters End* was awarded the BAD Crime Sydney Festival's Danger Prize, and was also shortlisted for the Ned Kelly Award for First Fiction.

Powered by Penguin

Looking for more great reads, exclusive content and book giveaways?

Subscribe to our weekly newsletter.

Scan the QR code or visit penguin.com.au/signup